THE

The Ovaro was ~~...~~ ed his hand on the stallio~~...~~ as they eased closer to the deadfall on the side of the trail. A few dry leaves rustled as someone inside moved, but Fargo held his powder until he heard it: the faint, but distinctive, stretching sound made by a buffalo-sinew bowstring being drawn back.

Fargo had no intention of waiting until a murdering ambusher formally announced his presence. In an explosive, deafening burst of firepower, he suddenly emptied his Colt's cylinder into the deadfall. Fargo heard a surprised grunt, then a crashing and crackling of dry brush as a dead Comanche warrior tumbled out, landing in a lifeless heap. . . .

DFT

SEP 0 7 2013

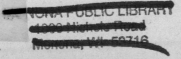

THE TRAILSMAN

#289

RENEGADE RAIDERS

by

Jon Sharpe

Ⓞ

A SIGNET BOOK

SIGNET
Published by New American Library, a division of
Penguin Group (USA) Inc., 375 Hudson Street,
New York, New York 10014, USA
Penguin Group (Canada), 90 Eglinton Avenue East, Suite 700, Toronto,
Ontario M4P 2Y3, Canada (a division of Pearson Penguin Canada Inc.)
Penguin Books Ltd., 80 Strand, London WC2R 0RL, England
Penguin Ireland, 25 St. Stephen's Green, Dublin 2,
Ireland (a division of Penguin Books Ltd.)
Penguin Group (Australia), 250 Camberwell Road, Camberwell, Victoria 3124,
Australia (a division of Pearson Australia Group Pty. Ltd.)
Penguin Books India Pvt. Ltd., 11 Community Centre, Panchsheel Park,
New Delhi - 110 017, India
Penguin Group (NZ), cnr Airborne and Rosedale Roads, Albany,
Auckland 1310, New Zealand (a division of Pearson New Zealand Ltd.)
Penguin Books (South Africa) (Pty.) Ltd., 24 Sturdee Avenue,
Rosebank, Johannesburg 2196, South Africa

Penguin Books Ltd., Registered Offices:
80 Strand, London WC2R 0RL, England

First published by Signet, an imprint of New American Library,
a division of Penguin Group (USA) Inc.

First Printing, November 2005
10 9 8 7 6 5 4 3 2 1

The first chapter of this book previously appeared in *Gila River Dry-Gulchers*,
the two hundred eighty-eighth volume in this series.

Copyright © Penguin Group (USA) Inc., 2005
All rights reserved

 REGISTERED TRADEMARK—MARCA REGISTRADA

The Trailsman

Beginnings . . . they bend the tree and they mark the man. Skye Fargo was born when he was eighteen. Terror was his midwife, vengeance his first cry. Killing spawned Skye Fargo, ruthless, cold-blooded murder. Out of the acrid smoke of gunpowder still hanging in the air, he rose, cried out a promise never forgotten.

The Trailsman they began to call him all across the West: searcher, scout, hunter, the man who could see where others only looked, his skills for hire but not his soul, the man who lived each day to the fullest, yet trailed each tomorrow. Skye Fargo, the Trailsman, the seeker who could take the wildness of a land and the wanting of a woman and make them his own.

Indian Territory, 1859–
where the War of the Plains is
about to erupt, and, for Fargo,
all the omens point to death.

1

Skye Fargo's idle thoughts were suddenly scattered by a spine-tingling scream from the mounted column behind him. The desperate trill raised the fine hairs on the back of his neck. Only the worst agony in the world could cause a cry like that.

His head swiveled around just in time to watch a swollen-faced cavalry trooper slide out of his saddle and land in a heap beside the dusty trail. The fallen man's body spasmed violently for a moment, then went limp in death.

"Dismount and take cover!" roared the young shavetail lieutenant in charge. "Hold your fire until you have confirmed targets!"

His men obeyed instantly, swinging down and leading their mounts into the screening timber. But neither the crop-bearded, buckskin-clad Fargo nor his fellow scout, a grizzled old explorer named Yellowstone Jack, bothered to take cover.

"This ain't the main attack," Jack said scornfully as they wheeled their mounts and rode back toward the dead man. "It's meant to get us in pursuit so's these red sons can ambush us when they choose."

Fargo nodded. "But there's still a few watching us now."

He was closely studying the cottonwood trees and thick patch of hawthorn bushes covering the slope to their right. The army unit had been following a timber-rich backwater of the river red men called *Akenzea,* and white men Arkansas. This spot was almost smack in the middle of The Nations—the vast Indian Territory, established not long after the War of 1812 as a permanent Indian home south of Kansas and immediately beyond the western borders of Missouri and Arkansas.

"There's one," Fargo said quietly, spotting an oval face painted green, yellow, and red. "A Kiowa intruder. I warned the kid to put flankers out."

"And the bone breastplate I spotted," Jack said, "was Staked Plain Comanches. Here to stir up the shit. Kiowas and Comanches . . . them two tribes don't never get together 'cept to kill and plunder."

By this time both riders, rifles to hand, had reached the fallen trooper. They could hear a few unshod ponies escaping toward the river and the scant-grown hills beyond. Fargo knew pursuing them was folly. A typical day's progress for a cavalry unit was about twenty-five miles; a fleeing Indian could cover as much as seventy.

"Hold in place, men!" the freckle-faced kid in charge of the soldiers shouted in a voice made reedy with nervousness. "They may mount a follow-on assault."

Fargo and Yellowstone Jack exchanged grins as they swung down. Jack was a head shorter than Fargo, but burly. He wore a slouched beaver hat and moccasins with hard soles of buffalo hide. His grizzled beard showed more salt than pepper.

" 'Follow-on assault.' " Jack sputtered with mirth. "Jimmy's a good lad, but he's fresh off ma's milk."

"No, he's fresh off the horseshit taught at West Point," Fargo said. "Takes a while to flush that rule book stuff out—"

Fargo suddenly fell silent as he got a better look at the dead soldier.

Yellowstone Jack, too, had just spotted what had riveted Fargo's attention. "Jesus Christ with a wooden leg!"

Both men knelt and stared at a gray-green face now swollen twice its normal size. A small, fletched dart protruded from his neck.

"Recognize that dart?" Fargo asked grimly, brass-framed Henry balanced across his thighs.

"You see any green on my antlers?" Jack demanded. He dug at a tick in his grizzled beard. "It's Cheraws."

He used the old mountain man name for Cherokees. No one knew for sure just what plant or plants provided the deadly poison used so effectively by Cherokees, but there

2

was no denying they were experts with their long-rifled blowguns. The virulent poison was both agonizing and fast-acting.

"It makes me ireful, Skye, it truly does," Jack muttered. "That Cheraw pizen is a hard way to give up the ghost. Mebbe that army report Jimmy showed us is right, after all, 'bout a Cheraw uprising in The Nations."

Fargo's shrewd, sun-crinkled, lake-blue eyes gazed all around them speculatively.

"Your calves are gone to grass, you old fool," he said. "Sure, a renegade Cherokee or two might be in the mix. But since when do peaceful Cherokees make common cause with Kiowas and Comanches?"

"Ahh, don't peddle that sweet-lavender 'peaceful Cherokee' sheep dip to *this* hoss. In the Cheraw nation, a young buck ain't got no status a-tall 'lessen he kills an enemy or takes a prisoner in battle. The boys are taught how they're dishonored forever if they don't avenge an insult. Hell, a Cheraw buck can't even look at a woman, happens he ain't took a scalp yet. *You'd* be spoiling for war, too, happens it was the only way to get you a little slap 'n' tickle."

Fargo had to concede Jack's main point. Because Cherokees had a written language and formal government, much like the whites, they were called a civilized tribe, not wild Indians. But they had always shown a fiercely warlike nature—to the point, even, of keeping their laws against murder deliberately weak so as not to discourage the killing instinct.

"Their warpath days," Fargo insisted to his trail companion, "were back when they lived east of the Mississippi. Hell, they been peaceful and law-abiding farmers and shepherds since they was forced out here."

"Pipe down, you jay! This child was makin' his beaver while you was still shittin' yellow. The Cheraws have greased for war, count on it."

"It only looks that way," Fargo insisted.

By now Lieutenant Jimmy Briscoe, looking a little sheepish, emerged cautiously from the screening timber behind Fargo. The young officer was so new to the West that he still sunburned easily.

"Sorry, Mr. Fargo," he apologized. "I should've sent out flankers like you advised."

3

Fargo nodded toward the corpse. "Hell, I'm still sassy, soldier blue. Apologize to him and his kin."

The shavetail flushed to his earlobes. "My orders are clear. Proceed immediately to Sweetwater Creek and rendezvous with Colonel Oglethorpe's group. I was ordered to avoid dividing my force."

The force in question was emerging from cover, their .56 caliber carbines at the ready. It was a small expedition: thirty sharpshooters, two scouts, two Osage Indian interpreters, two mule-drawn supply wagons. One wagon was filled with rations, water, ammunition, and medical supplies. The second hauled forage for the animals.

"Sending out flankers," Fargo advised the green officer, "ain't the same as dividing your force. I recommend it anytime the terrain closes in on you."

For a few moments Fargo was distracted as he watched Yellowstone Jack prepare to mount. The crusty old flint refused to ride a good-natured horse, on the reasoning that politeness was a sign of weakness. So Fargo bit back a grin as Jack stepped into a stirrup. His feisty ginger crowhopped just as Jack stuck his foot into leather. The old explorer went flat on his sitter, cussing like a stable sergeant.

"Skye," Jack muttered moments later, pointing with his chin toward a break in the trees. Puffs of dark signal smoke drifted against the deep blue morning sky.

"They're warning other braves that we're coming," Fargo said as he grabbed a fistful of the Ovaro's mane and swung up into the saddle. "It's still twenty miles to Sweetwater Creek, and some good ambush country. Things're gonna get lively, count on it."

Fargo rode out ahead, sending Yellowstone Jack back to guard their backtrail. Small but frequent canyons and ravines, as well as steep hills, made the terrain difficult for horse and rider. Expanses of deep, loose sand had to be avoided or the wagons would bog down.

Fargo marked a trail for the rest, ever alert to his surroundings, not forgetting that signal smoke earlier. But he also gave some thought to Colonel Lansford Oglethorpe, hero of the Mexican War and outspoken admirer of American Indians. Oglethorpe was convinced that recent grievances, among the many tribes in the Indian Territory, could be settled without warfare.

Thus, riding under a white truce flag, he and several military aides had gone on ahead to meet with tribal representatives at Sweetwater Creek. Fargo was all for the peace road, but considered the plan a fool's play. Colonel Oglethorpe was a popular hero, and if he was killed by Indians, the national wrath would get ugly—and turn against all Indians.

Fargo never stacked his conclusions higher than his evidence. So he still wasn't convinced that a genuine Indian uprising—especially one led by Cherokees—was even taking place in The Nations. But he did know that the reservation system itself was part of the problem because it was so damned illogical.

Most Indians were, by nature, restless people and confinement only increased that restlessness. Too, not all that long ago this area (the barren buffalo plains beyond the ninety-eighth meridian) was part of vast New Spain, worthless "desert" no one wanted. Now it was arbitrarily declared a homeland for dozens of tribes, many of whom were natural enemies.

The Trailsman's black-and-white stallion picked his way carefully over a hogback, or rocky spine, and now a good view opened up. The terrain out ahead was mostly low hills with scattered pine growth and some steep razorbacks well to the north of the river. In places near the Arkansas, the grass grew high as the knuckles of a full-grown buffalo. Fargo studied all of it a long time, looking for danger.

"Let's head back, old campaigner," he finally said to the Ovaro. "I draw my pay next week, and this nursemaid job is over."

Just as Fargo started to tighten the reins, he heard a distant, mournful howl that made his scalp tighten and tingle. He knew, being a lifelong drifter and trailsman, that it was only the sound of wind whistling through the nearby trees.

But memory brought back the old legends about the Hell Hounds—spectral hounds said to hunt in the wildest part of the woods. If one heard the baying of these hounds, the old legend said, it spelled death to the hearer within a year.

"Sounds mighty close to Sweetwater Creek," Fargo muttered as he reined the Ovaro around, thinking of Colonel Oglethorpe.

Fargo rejoined the main column, which had delayed only long enough to bury poison-dart victim Private Robinson in a humble grave beside the trail.

"Clear trail ahead?" Lieutenant Jimmy Briscoe asked, his voice tense.

Fargo grunted affirmation.

"But the country's not so open around Sweetwater Creek," Fargo added. "In fact, it's perfect ambush country."

"Colonel Oglethorpe rode in under a truce flag," Briscoe said. "And he's a friend to the Indian."

"*The* Indian don't exist," Fargo assured him. "Just many Indians, all with different ideas. Ain't that right, Ten Bears?"

This last question was directed to one of the two Osage interpreters riding beside Jimmy. Between them, Ten Bears and Standing Feather spoke ten Indian languages as well as good English. Yet they could go for days without speaking unless spoken to.

"Red men hate each other more than they hate whites," Ten Bears said, ignoring the question. Like his companion, he wore buckskin leg bands trimmed with dyed porcupine quills. "Make war on each other always instead of on whites. This is why we have lost our hunting grounds."

"Hell," Fargo said good-naturedly. "I see you speak good English. When you gonna learn to *listen* to it?"

Whooping hoarsely, Yellowstone Jack came galloping up from the rear of the formation.

"Eyes right!" he shouted to the rest. "Eyes right! God-in-whirlwinds! You'll call me a liar, Skye, happens I just *tell* you!"

The Arkansas, spilling over its low banks, formed a wide, shallow waterway just below them, a complex series of interconnecting pools and backwaters.

Fargo spotted a lone Cherokee expertly paddling a light, flat-bottomed bateau across a wide pool. The craft's tapered ends and shallow draw let it skim the mudbanks and allowed steady progress with easy paddling.

"I don't credit my own eyes!" Jack added. He began swearing with evident pleasure, a string of foul and creative

6

epithets that made even the Ovaro blush. "It's more of that goddamn petticoat gov'ment, is what it is. This is what comes from them damn Cheraws allowing women at war councils."

The Cherokee paddling the bateau was a female, and a true beauty at that.

"She's a Ghighau," Fargo told a staring Jimmy. "Means 'Beloved Women.' You'll also hear 'em called War Women. Besides fighting in battles, their job is to prepare the secret Black Drink that's taken before battle."

"Fighting in battle? A woman that easy to look at?" the young officer remarked. "Man! She's beautiful, and almost . . . regal. Somebody should paint her."

Fargo had to agree as he continued to watch the War Woman. She spotted the men up above and back-paddled a stroke to halt the bateau's easy glide, glancing up toward the trail.

The young woman's long jet hair was combed close to her head and held in back with a silver clasp. Fargo took in the huge, almond-shaped eyes, the fine Roman nose, the full lips that made him think of berries heavy with juice. His eyes cut to the tanned, exposed skin between her short jacket and skirt—it looked taut as a drumhead.

"*Paint* her?" Yellowstone Jack repeated, scorn coloring his tone. "*Plant* her, you mean. Look closer into that bateau, Lieutenant."

Fargo had already spotted what Jack meant: one of the huge Cherokee bows that could hurl an arrow four hundred yards, and one of the deadly rifled blowguns used to fire poison darts like the one that killed Private Robinson.

"Beautiful Death Bringer," Fargo remarked.

"The hell you babbling?" Jack demanded.

"That's what her Cherokee name means in English," Fargo explained, "if that's the same woman I've heard spoken of at Fort Courage and Fort Smith. Her English name is Sarah something or other. And she's an official Indian princess by right of birth."

Yellowstone Jack snorted. "Save your breath to cool your porridge," he scoffed. "I know 'B' from a bull's foot, and them ain't 'royal trappings' your princess is hauling. Matter fact, that very blowgun coulda done for Robinson. Ah, t'hell with this chinwag."

7

Jack reached for the .38 caliber magazine pistol in his sash.

"Not a good idea," Fargo warned. "A War Woman is best left alone."

"Ahh, purty little thing, she won't want to muss her hair. I'll just put a hole in her boat, under the waterline," Jack said. "Force her to nose in."

However, he never got his shot off. Moving with catlike speed, she pulled a quartz-tipped arrow from a quiver of soft fox skin. With deft fingers she notched it on her sinew-string bow and sent the arrow fwiping.

"Great jumpin' Judas!" Yellowstone Jack roared out as his beaver hat seemed to leap off his head.

Fargo, sporting an admiring grin, watched the arrow thwack into a nearby tree. It quivered for a few seconds with the force of its suddenly interrupted energy.

"That's one petticoat you best leave alone, hoss," Fargo advised him. "And don't snatch up that rifle, *you* started the trouble by dropping a bead on her. This is her home, not ours."

Fargo turned toward Jimmy Briscoe, who, like his men, was still staring in amazement at the receding Cherokee princess.

"Sweetwater Creek is about ten miles farther," Fargo said. "I got a hunch somebody hopes to make it there before we do. Since the trail is wide, I recommend advancing in columns of four to discourage ambush."

"Yessir," the kid said obediently, for Skye Fargo was the most celebrated contract scout the army ever hired.

Fargo seldom got bossy with young officers, not wanting to weaken their authority with the men. But lives were possibly on the line now, and this well-intended kid was brand-new to a command position.

"Place every man under orders of strict silence as we advance the last few miles," Fargo added. "Remove your saber, Jimmy, so it doesn't rattle. Any man who needs to cough or sneeze must cover his head in a blanket first."

Jimmy left to convey these orders. Yellowstone Jack turned toward the tree behind him to remove the arrow and his hat.

"Shit, piss, and corruption!" the crotchety old explorer exclaimed, staring at the gnarled bark of the tree. "Fargo, come glom this and *then* tell me the Cheraws ain't struck the war trail."

Fargo did look. Just below the embedded arrow, three fresh notches had been carved into the tree—a message from some Indian courier. But it had been a long time since Fargo had seen this distinctive pattern: three parallel lines slanting from right to left.

His face suddenly felt cold. "Jesus," he almost whispered, recalling that death omen from earlier. "Looks like the Cherokee Keetoowah is back."

"A-huh. The secret Nighthawk Society," Jack affirmed. "The bloodiest bunch of killers ever got up by any band of red devils. A Nighthawk knows fifty ways to kill a man before breakfast. And we might soon be riding right into their midst. Happens a man wants to get his life over quick, he only needs to throw in with Skye Fargo."

2

Finding a few scratches on a tree did not convince Fargo that the dreaded Cherokee Nighthawk Society had been revived here in the West. But he quickly began to suspect, as the mounted force rode the last few miles to Sweetwater Creek, that Colonel Oglethorpe and his party had ridden into a trap.

It appeared that someone also had plans to make sure Lieutenant Briscoe's cavalry patrol didn't arrive too soon.

"Whack the cork," Fargo snapped when he saw Yellowstone Jack wrapping a lip around a bottle of cheap forty-rod. "Get drunk later. We could be up against it any second now."

"So what?" Jack roared back, bouncing in the saddle. "Put a bounty on it, I'll scalp it."

"Stow that damn bottle, I said. The troopers will see you. Maybe you can fight drunk, you old grizz, but they can't."

"*Drunk*? Hell, this is medicine, turd. For the circulation and joints."

Yellowstone Jack scowled as he corked the bottle, cursing like a bullwhacker on a muddy road. "Fargo, a necklace made from your teeth will earn credit at any trading post, remember that."

"The fact's not easy to forget," Fargo assured him.

They were passing through sandy, hilly terrain that rapidly gave way to pines and granite cliffs as they neared the bluffs above the creek.

Jimmy Briscoe, making sure Fargo heard him do it, sent out flankers as the terrain closed in, numerous tangled coverts affording ambush spots.

"Think the colonel's had any luck restoring peace among

10

the Indians, Mr. Fargo?" the shavetail asked. "For a white man, he's well liked in the Indian Territory."

"I like him, too," Fargo replied. "Man's got guts, and a good think piece on his shoulders. But now and then he puts good will above good sense. I'm a mite suspicious of this meeting place. Seems too remote."

"You mean . . . it could be a trap?"

"Distinct possibility," Fargo replied, his slitted gaze always in motion. "We've had several harassment raids intended to slow us down and nothing else. Indians don't raid just for the practice—they've got some good reason for slowing us, and the best reason I can think of is Colonel Oglethorpe."

"You think they'd *kill* him?" the young officer asked, his sunburned, smooth-shaven face aghast.

Yellowstone Jack shook with phlegmy laughter. "Well, Christ sakes, colt, they're savages! You think they mean to powder his butt and tuck him in?"

Jimmy Briscoe's sunburn deepened as he flushed. "But . . . I mean, these tribes located in the Indian Territory are all signatories to the 1851 Laramie Treaty."

"A treaty ain't worth a busted tug chain," Fargo assured him. "And not all the tribes signed the Laramie Treaty anyway. Some of the heap big chiefs, like Yellow Hair of the Comanches, never agreed to the terms. Others only signed to get the presents."

Yellowstone Jack lowered his voice so only Fargo could hear. His tone became more serious.

"Speaking of the Comanches . . . why in blue blazes would Staked Plain Comanches be pointin' their bridles up here toward The Nations? I'd rather face devils from hell than that murderin' lot."

The flat Llano Estacado, or Staked Plain, covered much of the Texas Panhandle just west of Sweetwater Creek. It was the favorite hunting ground of the Comanches. Fargo, like Jack, was deeply curious: What would lure Comanches out there when those they most hated—Texans—were well to the south?

"And Kiowas with them," Fargo said. "The official Kiowa-Comanche reservation set aside for them here has got only a fraction of the two tribes, mostly the elderly and sick. They like making war too much to ever surrender their horses and weapons so they can start answering roll calls."

"Kiowas and Comanches, hell, that's trouble enough," Yellowstone Jack put in. "But happens the Cherokee Nighthawks are active again, this area is going to run red with blood."

Fargo didn't reply, his thoughts scattering like chaff in the wind. He definitely did not like the way that hen pheasant had suddenly whirred out from a stand of pine trees above the trail.

"Signal 'report' to the flank riders," he told Jimmy.

Lieutenant Briscoe ordered his bugler to sound report— the standard signal that an outrider should report immediately by firing two shots in response.

From the left, two shots immediately rang out. But from the right, no sound. All was eerily silent except for the wind in the pines, creaking leather and snuffling horses. The same when Briscoe ordered his bugler to try again.

"Christ," Fargo swore, his lips forming a grim slit through his short beard. "Likely, that slope's lousy with red sons, greased for war, and I'd wager they've killed your flank rider."

Despite the gray in his beard, Yellowstone Jack still had the vision of a hawk. He frowned as he studied the ridge above them.

"I don't see nary one, Skye. Happens they mean to get a good bead on us, there'd have to be some visible. The cover up there ain't that good."

"You say they *have* to be visible?" Fargo shot back. "What about that time out in Texas when they jumped us in Palo Duro Canyon?"

Yellowstone Jack frowned at the effort of memory, scanning back over the scores of scrapes he'd survived. Suddenly he turned an ashen pallor.

"God's trousers, that's right!" he exclaimed. "The arrow drop. And it was terrain just like this, wunnit?"

The two Osage interpreters, too, had guessed what was coming. Fargo saw Standing Feather and Ten Bears leap to the ground and grab their ponies by the horsehair bridles, leading them into some dogwood thickets to the left of the trail.

"Jimmy!" Fargo snapped. "The attackers aren't on this

side of the ridge—they're out of sight just behind it. They're going to shoot arrows almost straight up into the sky, drop them down on us without ever showing themselves. And they're *good* at it. Men and horses should be under some kind of shelter, and quick."

Jimmy was green, but gutsy. Never once flinching, so as not to panic the younger troops, he stood boldly in the open, directing the others to take cover.

One trooper paused to stare fearfully up into the china blue sky. Yellowstone Jack shook with laughter.

"The *last* damn thing you oughta be doing right now, turd," he called out, "is staring up into the sky. You won't see 'em arrahs coming till your eye pops out."

As things turned out, Fargo had spotted that fleeing pheasant just in the nick of time. Most of the men and horses made it to at least partial cover before a shrill, yipping cry broke from behind the ridge.

"Here it comes!" Fargo roared in a voice strong enough to fill a canyon. "Keep your faces down, and *don't move*!"

Fargo, too, pressed behind a fallen log and braced himself. He heard the sudden, fluttering, fwipping noise of scores of bowstrings releasing at once. Most braves could hold up to ten arrows in their hand and fire them almost nonstop. Arrows rained in, stripping leaves, snapping branches, thwacking into supply wagons, thudding hard into the ground. Not one brave showed himself.

A howl of human pain was followed by the even more unnerving bray of a mortally wounded mule. When the flood of arrows ceased, a few of the Indian attackers crawled up to the spine of the ridge and opened fire with rifles.

"Return fire!" Jimmy shouted, and the shooting battle was underway.

The Indians' cheaper, smaller-caliber trade rifles made a sharp crack in contrast to the heavier, more solid report of army carbines. But the skirmish was over in mere moments—the Indians quickly retreated, and Fargo knew they feared counterattack. It was not the Indian style to "fort up" for a battle.

"See it?" a grim-faced Fargo said to Yellowstone Jack. "They never intended to draw us off, like we figured earlier. All they're doing is delaying us from reaching

Sweetwater Creek. Likely, they're buying time so their comrades can get away before the news gets out."

"What news?" Jack demanded.

But Fargo was already stepping into leather. He saw a cursing trooper being loaded into a supply wagon, an arrow poking out of his left buttock. A jenny pierced in the neck was being unbuckled from the harness so it could be shot. The men looked unnerved, but Fargo knew they would have fared much worse on the open trail.

"You stay with the main column," Fargo told Jack. "I'm going on ahead to Sweetwater."

Fargo palmed the cylinder of his Colt to check the loads, then loosened the Henry in its saddle boot before kicking the Ovaro up to a fast lope.

Well before he reached the creek, Fargo spotted tatters of dark smoke hovering in the sky. Not signal smoke, either.

The trail was too rocky and sandy to risk a run or a gallop. But the Ovaro had the longest stride of any horse Fargo had ridden, turning even his lope into an impressive pace. The Ovaro laid his ears back flat, and Fargo could feel the powerful muscles coiling and releasing like well-oiled springs.

He needed that speed now because Fargo knew hidden eyes followed his progress. Confirming his instincts, an arrow whipped past his right ear, so close the fletching nicked his lobe. Fargo forged ahead, refusing to be stopped or lured off, moving too fast to be an easy target.

The meeting place, where Oglethorpe and four aides were to palaver with several tribal representatives, was a grassy meadow beside Sweetwater Creek. Fargo edged out of the tree cover cautiously, his Henry held high.

When he heard the frenzied buzzing of bluebottle flies, Fargo knew it was too late.

At first, all the smoke still wreathing the area made it difficult to make out details. But as the scene became clear, Fargo felt his stomach churn in the first stages of nausea.

"Christ Almighty," he said almost in a whisper. "Just what I was afraid of. Well, Colonel, I reckon you meant well. But you *and* the red nation are now in a world of hurt."

Lansford Oglethorpe and his four aides were all dead—in the case of one poor wretch, dead in all but animal reflex. Two of the aides had been stripped, tied to a tree, and stoned to death—a custom of warring Cherokees. Every inch of their skin was a pulpy bruise, and many of their bones were broken, even exposed.

Nor had the other two aides fared any better, having been beheaded and their brains scooped out. But the basest savagery of all, which Fargo recognized as the favorite torture among Kiowas and Comanches, had been reserved for Oglethorpe. Even Fargo, long hardened to shocking sights, could look only a few seconds before averting his eyes.

Just then he heard the rataplan of shod hoofs as Jimmy and the rest arrived, weapons drawn. The Trailsman knew what was coming—many of the troops had never seen the results of Indian torture, and their first glance doubled them up, retching. It was a hard lesson, but Fargo figured it shocked them into being better soldiers. Only the best fighters would prevail against Indians.

Jimmy, white as new snowcap, stared in revulsion at Oglethorpe, recognizable only by his rank insignia.

"Mr. Fargo," Jimmy finally managed to stammer, "shouldn't we cut him down quick? See how his upper body keeps—"

"He's long dead," Fargo assured the kid.

"But look, he keeps jerking—"

"Listen, Jimmy," Fargo said patiently. "See that small circle of rocks beneath him, all blackened from a long fire? Now, see how the Colonel was hung upside down over it? The heat causes the victim to keep twitching upward, an uncontrollable jackknifing that goes on for hours while the person's brain slowly roasts. Takes hours for death to set in. Even after death, the body goes on nerve-twitching, like his is doing now."

"You said . . . the brain *roasts*?" Jimmy repeated.

"Hell, whiff the air, tadpole," Yellowstone Jack scoffed. "That ain't Ma's Sunday roast you smell."

Jimmy did smell the air, then turned away, leaning forward to retch. Steeling himself, Fargo took a closer look to make sure the still twitching Oglethorpe was beyond all help. A bullet to the spine ended the ghoulish dance of the nerve-twitching corpse.

"Skye?"

Yellowstone Jack had a cast-iron stomach and bragged he could eat anything the flies found too disgusting. Unmoved by the scene of slaughter, he pointed toward a reed lance that lay on the ground nearby.

"That's Cheraw," Jack said. "So is that war hatchet a-layin' close to the crick. Now, *no* Indian warrior is likely to leave a weapon behind. But have you ever knowed any tribe that punishes its braves harsher'n the Cheraw for leaving weapons?"

"Never have," Fargo agreed. "And it wasn't Cherokees who chose Oglethorpe's method of torture. It was Kiowas and Comanches. I'd wager it was those two tribes who did this, with a few other renegades along—maybe even a Cherokee or two. It was deliberately meant to frame the entire Cherokee nation."

" 'Cept that 'framing' ain't no Injin trick," Yellowstone Jack pointed out. "An Injin's mind don't work that way. That's paleface style."

"And speaking of that, this region has become a haven for white outlaws," Fargo pointed out. "By law, no Indian courts can prosecute whites, and whites refuse to indict fellow whites for crimes they commit in the Indian Territory."

Jack grunted. "Makes it a damn owlhoot paradise."

Fargo nodded. "So it's prob'ly whites bribing Indians to frame other Indians. I smell a land grab. The Cherokees have a long history of proving up land only to have it stolen from under them. Even since they were marched out here, they've been forced off their original land. The day's been coming when it has to begin—nothing given to the Indians by the U.S. government is permanent."

The late Colonel Oglethorpe himself had admitted it in a widely read letter in *Harper's Weekly:* the various Indian tribes were stuck out here only because nobody figured the land was valuable. But already the railroad plutocrats, among others, had their eye on this huge nation of Indians, saying it was too much land to give to savages.

"My God, Mr. Fargo," Jimmy Briscoe finally recovered enough to gasp out. "I was sent here to rendezvous with the colonel, not to bring his body back. Some first mission! For me, it's the Quartermaster Corps for sure—after I get out of the stockade."

"You're a bigger fool than God made you," Fargo assured the gold-bar lieutenant, "if you haul *any* of these bodies back."

The kid tugged at the point of his freckled chin, uncertain. "Well, the aides could be buried here, I s'pose. They're just junior officers. But Colonel Oglethorpe is—was—important. He lectured in Paris and—"

"Jimmy, forget Paris. This skull's been cooked until you can hear the brains bubbling—*still* bubbling. The face, too, is literally roasted. You send that mess back to the States, and the sensational story *will* get out. The anti-Indian backlash will only make matters worse for you soldiers. Besides, if you was his kin, would you want such remains stretched out on chairs in the parlor?"

"Course not." Jimmy wiped his forehead, weary with the weight of command. "The field manual says the commanding officer of a patrol has the discretion to return bodies or bury them in place. We'll bury these."

"Stout lad. But don't bury 'em in marked graves," Fargo advised. "We don't want Oglethorpe's kin sending someone to bring him home. Nobody needs to see this atrocity except us—the ones who are going to settle accounts."

The usual custom, when soldiers buried a fellow soldier along the trail, was for each man to sign his name on a small piece of paper. The paper was then rolled up tight and inserted into a spent cartridge, which was then pounded into a simple wooden cross. This burial detail, however, simply placed all five men in a mass, unmarked grave. Gunpowder was burned over it, then rocks piled on, to discourage predators.

Fargo nodded to Jimmy's request for a rifle salute to honor Oglethorpe. One of the troopers was a preacher in civilian life, and he delivered a stirring oration and prayer.

"I just can't believe this," Jimmy opined to Fargo and Yellowstone Jack after the brief service. "The Cherokees, of all tribes, killing the one man who could help them the most. Cripes, this will set the tribe back fifty years. And they'd been model citizens out West until lately. I even read their reservation newspaper—it's a good one."

"Never get tripped up," Fargo advised, "between what things look like and the truth."

"You don't think Cherokees did this?"

"Oh, maybe one or two rode along," Fargo said. "But the signs don't point to a Cherokee war party. Besides, warpath Indians ain't the only culprits. The Indian Territory is infested with white outlaws on the dodge because lawmen don't like to come in."

Fargo knew it would be easier for a man to write his name on water than to make sense of the Cherokees. Some said that, with time, the tribe would zealously take to white man's civilization. After all, they were a clever, industrious, and ambitious people. Most could even cipher. But at this moment in history, war was still strong in their collective memory. The great plundering of the Cherokees by Spaniards under the brutal de Soto could be thanked for that.

Yellowstone Jack squatted and placed three fingers on the ground.

"One rider coming in," he announced. "Shod hoofs."

A few minutes later, a soldier thick with trail dust rode cautiously into the clearing, his face a mask of nervous fear.

"Courier from Fort Gibson, sir," he reported to Jimmy, saluting. "Urgent message for Mr. Skye Fargo."

Fort Gibson was located in the eastern Indian Territory. The courier walked his trail-weary cavalry sorrel farther into the grassy clearing, the thirsty animal heading toward the creek on its own.

"Got here in two days," the young private boasted, handing Fargo a note. "I slept in the saddle and ate while I rode, Mr. Fargo. It's urgent, the post commander told me."

Fargo broke the wax seal and unfolded the sheet. It was from Talcott Mumford, agent for the vast sector of the Indian Territory that included the Cherokees.

"The hell's it say?" demanded Yellowstone Jack, who was illiterate.

"Most of it's left out," Fargo replied, eyes sweeping over the brief note. "Practically begs me to report to the agency office as soon as possible. He's even got authority to break my contract so I can work for the Indian Bureau at higher pay."

"If you do go back alone, sir," the private interjected, "take care. I saw pissed-off Indians the whole way here."

"Hell, Talcott Mumford is a perfumed schoolman," Yellowstone Jack scoffed. "Talks like a book, and he ain't got the stones for controlling savages the proper way. Why throw in with him?"

"He's a mite bookish," Fargo agreed. "And maybe he's got some queer notions about the red man. But he's a rare thing for an Indian agent—he's honest."

Fargo checked the time by the slant of the sun. Then he whistled to the Ovaro.

"Still time to make good progress today," he said. "Jack, you'll stay on as scout. I'll ride back and meet with Mumford."

"Damn stupid idea," Jack warned, "with Cherokee Nighthawks out there. They'll lift your dander in your sleep."

"No," Fargo corrected him as he swung up onto the hurricane deck, "*those* mean bastards will wake me up before they scalp me."

3

The renegade named Wolf Sleeve belonged to the Quohada, or Antelope Eaters, band of Staked Plain Comanches. Like most men of his tribe he was short and homely, and severely bowlegged from so much time spent on horseback. The long, thin Russian knife protruding from one of his knee-length moccasins was cast iron and had deep blood gutters carved into the blade to facilitate rapid bleeding.

Comanches, like their battle cousins the Kiowas, spoke several languages well, including Spanish and English.

"Two sleeps ago," Wolf Sleeve told his white visitor, "up north at Sweetwater Creek, the bluecoat colonel was killed. And already, Menard, you see the results."

Wolf Sleeve pointed to a pair of supply wagons parked in front of a nearby pole corral.

"The soldiers are nervous, confused. Some of our braves seized this shipment earlier with no resistance," he boasted. "Indeed, the guards fled without firing a shot. These goods were meant for the soldier town called Fort Adobe, in Texas. Grain, flour, jerked meat, sugar, tea, black powder, pig lead for making bullets."

Baptiste Menard, a former sutler at Fort Gibson, had said little since arriving at this renegade hideout in the southeastern Indian Territory. The surrounding mountains were called Ouachita by the Quapaws, a Sioux tribe. The renegades, about thirty strong and mostly free-ranging Kiowas and Comanches, did not live in The Nations—Menard had lured them here with all the right promises. They had temporarily taken over a shanty-and-sod village deserted by white fur trappers.

But, at Menard's insistence, this hideout was only one of

several in the Indian Territory. He believed the mouse that has but one hole is quickly taken.

"You did fine work up at Sweetwater, Wolf Sleeve," Menard said, his French accent quite noticeable. "You and Iron Mountain both," he added.

He turned to look at the Kiowa battle leader who had raided beside Wolf Sleeve for years. Iron Mountain was a giant of a man, towering a full head above Menard, himself a tall man. Heavy copper brassards protected the Kiowa's upper arms, for he preferred close-in fighting.

"*Both* you bucks," Menard emphasized, "stand to gain much by nailing your colors to my mast."

Iron Mountain had less English than did his Comanche comrade and did not understand how one could possibly "nail colors." Wolf Sleeve, however, smiled slyly at the Frenchman.

"And you, Baptiste, will gain most of all when your sawmill is built," he pointed out.

A gross understatement, Menard knew. There was already a thriving overland commerce between this area and the Texas trading post at Nacogdoches. But the great demand lately was for lumber. Trees were practically everywhere, but without sawmills boards remained scarce—and valuable. The best supply of various trees, and running water for a millrace, was in the heart of the Cherokee sector.

"Of course I'll profit nicely, but a rising tide lifts *all* the boats," he assured Wolf Sleeve. "Look here at your fat supply wagon—enough rations to get you and your men through the cold moons. But with the arrival of Skye Fargo, we all have a new problem."

Hearing the name, Wolf Sleeve nodded and Iron Mountain frowned. The latter made a fist, then sent it curving toward the ground—sign talk for "kill."

Wolf Sleeve said, "Fargo is a warrior who stands behind no man in skill and valor. Still, perhaps he will soon ride through—he is not one to settle long in one area."

"He'll stick, curse his bones," Menard said, his eyes suddenly gloomy. "I know the bastard. *Mon Dieu!* He has a knack for being wherever he's least wanted."

As if foreshadowing the fight he expected, his right hand touched the Colt Navy with walnut grips riding on his right hip. "My spies tell me the Indian agent, Talcott Mumford, has sent for him. This situation is perfect for a crusading meddler like Fargo."

"Talcott Mumford." Iron Mountain spat with contempt. "He is a squaw man, this agent, and he would make *us* squaws."

"Mumford," the Frenchman said with a mysterious little smile, "will soon be . . . celestial. Forget him, the Trailsman is the rock we'll split on."

"Fargo," Wolf Sleeve assured Menard, "is a good man, but *only* a man. I have sent one of the best killers among the Quohadas, a brave named Coyote Who Hunts Grinning, to find and kill him. We have more serious trouble, I fear, from this she-bitch princess, Sarah Blackburn. She has the rank, and warrior status, to ` organize a Cherokee resistance."

Baptiste Menard nodded. "I still say that killing her wouldn't be wise. She's been written up in Eastern newspapers and was even a guest of the Royal Court in London. But framing her for the death of a popular hero like Oglethorpe will change all that and solve our problem nicely. Initial reports have already blamed the atrocity on Cherokees. Nice work."

Menard glanced around them in the late-morning sunshine, eyeing the renegades lounging about in the small camp clearing—they mistrusted these crude white man's buildings and would not spend much time inside, especially after dark.

Menard saw they carried mostly older firearms. Wolf Sleeve's sidearm, tucked into his scarlet sash, was a .38 caliber flintlock pistol with over-and-under barrels. And most of the long guns he could see were breech-loading muskets. He even saw one old British Ferguson gun, a Colonial-era flintlock.

Wolf Sleeve read the thoughts in Menard's face.

"*Those* weapons," the Comanche said, "are mostly for noise. In battle we rely on our osage-wood bows, the strongest of all. And our stone skull crackers. Ask the Texans if our weapons kill—but hurry, for we have nearly wiped them out."

"Oh, I know your two tribes well," Menard assured him. "That's why I chose you to work with. It's just . .˙. I do *nothing* by halves. I mean to win the horse or lose the saddle. Trouble is, Fargo has the same attitude."

"By the time of the first frost," Wolf Sleeve promised, "your sawmill will be in place and *you* will control Cherokee lands. And Fargo will be worm fodder."

The small detonation of primer powder was followed, an eyeblink later, by a louder explosion as the main charge ignited.

The honed reflexes of a bobcat sent Fargo rolling out of the saddle even before the sound of the shot quit echoing through the wooded hills surrounding him.

The shot was not intended for him, Fargo quickly realized. He snatched his Henry from its boot and began working his way through the dense growth of a bottom woods near the Arkansas River. Even though Fargo was not a superstitious man, the memory of that death omen, two days ago near this very river, had been picking at him like a burr. When that primer had popped just now, he couldn't help wondering: were the Hell Hounds after him again?

After the initial shot, Fargo had heard nothing. He crept forward silently, walking on his heels to minimize ground noise. He parted a curtain of vines, then stared in dumb astonishment at the incredible sight before him.

Sarah Blackburn, the Cherokee princess, was calmly drying her magnificent, copper-tinted body, fresh from bathing in a secluded backwater of the river. Fargo took in the firm, high-riding breasts capped by cocoa nipples; a gently curving stomach set like polished topaz between flaring hips; a dark thatch of mons wool; and when she turned around to grab her quilled doeskin dress from a tree branch, Fargo admired a high-split derriere, as tempting as a Georgia peach.

"Girl, you're right out of the top drawer," he muttered, reaching down to adjust himself.

Hard to believe, Fargo thought, that this alluring woman was calmly drying off as if a dead man—freshly killed, at that, and still oozing blood—were not lying close enough to spit on. He might as well have been a natural part of the landscape, for all she cared. A German musketoon, a musket with a half-sized barrel, leaned against a tree, still smoking.

Fargo watched as the Cherokee set her dress aside. Still naked, she picked up her elk-skin moccasins and stuffed dry grass into them to ease the discomfort of much walking. So she was on foot, Fargo thought, which explained her missing bateau.

He stepped out into plain view, his Henry trained on the woman. For all he knew, a murder had just been committed.

He forgot, however, that he was confronting a Cherokee War Woman. Fear was not her response, nor hesitancy. The moment she saw him, her hand flew back to seize the small knife she carried in a net over her nape.

"Bridge the gap, hair-face!" she called out defiantly, her big, jet-black eyes blazing with challenge. "*Try* to rape me! You will have to kill me, or I will kill you as I did *this* stag-in-rut."

Now she did indeed spit on the corpse.

"Pull in your claws, lady," Fargo said, glancing down at the body of the dead white man. "At least let this one grow cold before you kill the next one."

She appreciated his joke and smiled briefly. A moment later, however, her defiance was back.

"I will kill *any* man who tries to rape me."

"Yeah, I see that. But rape ain't my style. Why should a man take by force that which is given freely—and often?"

Again his wry humor cracked her stern mask. "A tall man like you, with broad shoulders, eyes blue as Sacred Lake, and a smile that makes women melt in their secret places—no, you are not a rapist."

Fargo glanced again at the dead man. His drawn weapon, a Volcanic revolver, was still clutched in his dead fingers, and his trousers were partially drawn, supporting her story. He rolled the corpse over with his foot and recognized the vanquished ravisher as an owlhoot named Cody Davis, an outlaw who rode with Mike Winkler's gang. Winkler and his bunch, all wanted men on the dodge, favored the Indian Territory as a region virtually free of starmen. They had raped several Indian women without reprisal—until now.

Fargo looked up at the Cherokee woman. "This two-legged vermin has required killing for some time. But I saw you two days ago, armed for battle. Anybody else you're planning to send under?"

"Do you reveal your plans to anyone who asks?"

"Nope," he admitted. "Do you know anything about what happened at Sweetwater Creek two days ago?"

"I know it happened," she said evasively. "And I was sorry to learn of it, for it will be blamed on my people. Also, though a soldier, the one who is gone was a fine man."

Fargo knew she was afraid, despite her obvious education, to say Colonel Oglethorpe's name. Many Indians believed the recently departed might answer if they heard their names spoken.

"All right, Your Highness," Fargo said, sparking a little glint of surprise in her eyes. He lowered his rifle. "I believed you from the start. You just did the world a favor by crushing that cockroach."

Sarah Blackburn may have been fierce in protecting her virtue, but Fargo noticed she wasn't at all "modest" about standing before him naked. Nor offended that he was enjoying great, tantalizing eyefuls.

"You must be the one they call the Trailsman," she decided out loud. "The drums announced you were here. I trust no white man. But many of my people say you are a fair man toward the red nations."

"The white man's stick floats one way," Fargo replied, "and the red man's another. The two peoples aren't meant to live as close neighbors. But I hope you can at least see me as a friend."

"My *friend*? You are indeed pleasing to look upon, Trailsman, but you are a whiteskin. Your people—for campfires they light our lodges! East of Big Muddy, they drove us from our fine homes at gunpoint, then force-marched us thousands of miles to this alien place. Our dead litter the trail."

Some whites were offended by the widespread Cherokee habit of looking away from the person with whom they were speaking. Many saw it as disrespect, but Fargo had traveled too widely and seen too many various customs. The princess was doing it now, and he found it downright charming.

"You have filled your eyes with sight of me," she told him. "Will I be in your thoughts now? Your . . . night thoughts?"

"Night *and* day," he assured her, still looking.

"Good. As you will be in mine."

"You just got done telling me," Fargo reminded her, "that we can never be friends."

Sarah laughed with a silvery little tinkle sound. "A man like you can be very useful to a woman without being her friend. I can tell," she added, glancing down at the pup tent in his buckskin trousers, "that you like what you see. Will *I* be allowed a turn to look?"

Fargo shook his head in welcome amazement at this saucy little wench. He knew there was a serious shortage of "eligible" men in the Nations, but he didn't realize things had gotten so bad that a beautiful princess like this could be so desperately horny. Well, hell, any service he could render . . .

"I have killed men in battle," she said, reading his thoughts. "I am a War Woman. Indian men want women who will cook for them and sew them new moccasins. Women who will suffer a beating in silence. Yes, the men enjoy looking at me, but I frighten them. They—"

She fell silent as Fargo's trousers dropped to his knees and he lifted his shirt out of the way.

"You requested a peek," he reminded her.

"Is that a tree limb?" she blurted out, mouth dropping open and eyes widening. Each heartbeat made his aroused shaft leap like it was feeding time.

"At the moment," Fargo replied, "it *is* a limb, thanks to you."

Fargo could see, in her strikingly pretty face, that Sarah was rethinking her idea about being in each other's thoughts only. He turned sideways to give her a better view of what she was passing up.

"Why don't we move away from here a little distance?" she suggested, glancing at the body of Cody Davis. "Just past the backwater where I bathed is a grassy glade."

"Sure, why don't we?" Fargo agreed, tying his trousers and throwing his Henry over a shoulder.

Still naked but holding her dress in front of her, the princess led the way. Fargo was so busy admiring those long, supple legs and that shapely ass that he conked himself on the noggin against a low-hanging limb. But he felt better in a hurry when he reached the little glade and found her already on her back waiting for him.

"This is the place you have not seen, Fargo," she said boldly.

She bent her legs at the knees, then spread them wide to open and expose the rose-colored petals and folds of her sex. When Fargo saw how she was glistening, and smelled the damp-earth odor of female arousal, he realized how much their conversation had excited her, too, not just him.

"Girl, it's been too long for you," he said as he placed his Henry to hand and unbuckled his heavy leather gun belt. When his trousers came down, she started whimpering with pent-up need, urging him to *please* hurry and put it inside her.

Fargo shimmied into his favorite saddle and reached down to find the perfect angle for his member. When just the purple-swollen dome was nudged inside her, he flexed his buttocks and parted the slippery, elastic walls of her belly mouth.

"Fargo, you fill my *body*!" she marveled on a long moan of pleasure. "It's not just big—you employ it like the violin bow. Oh, *oh . . . ahh . . .* deeper, Fargo, faster!"

The Trailsman had always been more than happy to take orders from naked and demanding females. As he drove repeatedly into her, the force of his thrusts was sliding them across the grass. Sarah, screeching with erotic delight, was whipped about by a string of explosive climaxes. Fargo showed her no mercy, switching his hungry mouth from left breast to right, licking and kissing the chewy-gumdrop nipples until they were hard and throbbing.

"Fargo!" she gasped as soon as she'd recovered from her latest climax. "Most men finish in mere moments. How can you hold off so long?"

"To me, it ain't holding off. It's just building up."

Fargo proceeded to prove his point by winding into the strong finish. He slid both hands under those gorgeous copper half-globes of her butt, lifting her up and spreading her open even wider. Harder, faster, he pistoned his length into her, so athletically that she was keening now as a continuous climax kept her shuddering powerfully.

Fargo shuddered, too, as he spent himself in a series of strong, conclusive thrusts, and slipped into the deep, drifting, thought-free daze that always followed sex with an exciting partner.

Her musical voice nudged him back to the present.

"*You* I trust, Trailsman. The pleasure you just gave me was the gift of an extraordinary man. But your chiefs in Washington City," she added as she squirmed into her dress, "speak from both sides of their mouths."

Fargo shrugged, enjoying the "jiggle" as she squirmed.

"So what?" he replied, getting dressed himself. "Hell, all governments lie most of the time. They lie to white men, too. And plenty of red leaders lie to their people. You Cherokees, though, were honorable in your dealings with whites, and all it got you was the crappy end of the stick."

A smile flitted across her lips.

"At least *you* know the truth," she said. "And so does Talcott Mumford. But for every white man like you two, a thousand more choose ignorance and hatred. The troubles are far from over for the Indians. Your government plans to cage all of us."

She wasn't just being melodramatic, Fargo knew. The U.S. government did indeed plan to eventually cage all Indians in two controlled areas: here, south of Kansas in the Indian Territory, and north of Nebraska in the yet-to-be-approved Great Sioux Reservation.

"And even once we are caged," she added bitterly, "we are not safe. South of us, the Red River does not protect us from Texans and their new herds of cattle. Right now this cattle enterprise is new. But some of them are already pressing for a new 'trade route' to the railroad towns they envision building up north in Kansas. A trade route across Indian land."

"All that's true enough," Fargo told her. "But you've got troubles more pressing than that. Troubles right here in the Cherokee Nation, troubles so bad you've gone on the secret warpath to stop them, right?"

"*Toeuhah,*" she confirmed in Cherokee, her face suddenly pensive. "It is true."

"You're from the Middle Towns," Fargo guessed from her dialect.

Impressed, Sarah looked him directly in the eye and nodded. "No white man has ever guessed that about me. So it is not just legend—you *do* know about Indians."

There had been sixty-four towns in the former Cherokee Nation back east. The Lower Towns were those clustered around the head branches of the Savannah River. Moving farther and farther west, travelers encountered the Middle Towns and, finally, the Overhill Towns.

"I admire your fighting spirit," Fargo told her. "But whatever's going on around here, somebody obviously means to pin it on the Cherokees. The very fact you've taken up arms might be used as so-called proof you're guilty."

She nodded. "Straight words. And the reason I am fighting alone. If someone does not fight for my people, they will surely be punished—probably by removal to less desirable land than we now occupy."

"All right, but why should that fighter be you?" Fargo demanded. "Sure, the War Women are fine warriors. But the Cherokee men should take up this battle."

"*You* are a fine one to talk, Fargo," she said with a warm smile. "When do you ever wait for someone else to die in your place?"

She had a point, and Fargo knew he was caught upon it.

"Besides, my mother was the ceremonial queen of our people," she said proudly. "And my British father was a warlord. When they died, the sacred wampum belt that relates the history of our tribe from its beginnings passed into my hands. I am obligated to my people."

"Fair enough. But I might be joining the fight."

Fargo explained that he was headed toward the Indian Agent's office in the Cherokee sector, answering a summons from Talcott Mumford.

"He is a well-intended man," Sarah said. "But a man steeped in books and poetry, an Indian agent who avoids weapons and fighting, is like a farmer who avoids soil. The harvest will never come."

Fargo untied the Ovaro, still watching her. "I see you're on foot instead of in your bateau. Where you headed?"

Her face closed up. "I have told you enough already. Go now and talk to Mumford. I hope you will join the fight, Trailsman, because then it will become a fight that can be won. But for now ask me no more questions. Just know that your enemies are all around you, and dreaming of tying *you* to a tree near Sweetwater Creek."

4

The sun had begun westering by the time Fargo drew near the agency office at Dragging Canoe Springs.

Thanks to his daylight dalliance with the princess, he had forgotten to fill his canteens. When a dogleg bend in the Arkansas suddenly placed him next to the river, he dismounted and tossed the reins forward to hold the Ovaro in place. Then Fargo used a flat stone to dig a shallow hole in the mud near the river.

It quickly filled with ground-filtered water that was much less muddy than the river water at this point. Fargo flopped onto his belly and drank his fill. Then, after filling his canteens, he threw the Ovaro's bridle and let him tank up.

Fargo was about to hit leather when he heard it again: that distant, mournful howling of wind racing through the wooded hills. The legendary Hell Hounds, some insisted, warning Fargo that Death had his name near the top of his list.

Ignorant folkways, Fargo knew. But his stallion, not one to go puny easily, resisted Fargo and tried to wheel away from the direction of the sound.

"Nerve up, old warhorse," Fargo scoffed, barely winning the fight to swing the Ovaro's head back around. "It's just spooky wind. I hope."

The trail next took Fargo past a Cherokee clan cluster— a group of a few dozen split-log cabins, the notched logs chinked with clay and wooden wedges. New corn grew knee-high to Fargo. It wasn't planted in fields, nor even rows, but grew in wild profusion in the yards, like weeds.

Fargo felt eyes watching him, but spotted no one.

"Ain't like the Cherokees," he remarked to his stallion.

"Only time they start hiding is when they're preparing for war."

For some time the Ovaro had been lifting his head to track a scent he couldn't seem to pinpoint. A chance-met scent, Fargo figured, that would soon be passed and forgotten—but this scent was staying with them, and had been for hours. Now, it seemed to have moved ahead of them. Fargo knew the familiar pattern.

"Pile on the agony," he muttered, shucking out his Colt and sending a puff of air through the works to clear out the blow sand.

Fargo had learned to think like the killers whom he confronted. When he saw a "saddle" up ahead—a point where adjacent bluffs were divided by a narrow expanse of passable growth—he knew it was a perfect death trap. There was no other way around the saddle without doubling back and losing hours.

Since there was no middle course of action, Fargo smiled grimly and kneed the Ovaro forward. The Henry lay across Fargo's thighs, the Colt filled his right fist. He had already knocked the riding thong off the hammer and thumb-cocked the revolver.

Soon they entered the narrow, tree-dense saddle. The light grew dimmer, and excellent hiding places, for a marksman bent on murder, were abundant. But years of frontier survival, for Fargo, had not been the result of blind luck. Rather, he had learned to always be ready for the vital clues nature often provided.

Just then he heard the warning cries of larkspurs and river swallows, angry at someone's intrusion—someone besides him.

Someone, Fargo guessed, hidden in that tangled deadfall about fifty feet ahead.

The Ovaro was moving at an easy trot. Fargo placed his left hand on the stallion's neck to steady him, kept his right curled around the Colt. They eased closer to the deadfall, which was almost even with the Ovaro's forelegs.

A few dry leaves rustled as someone inside moved, perhaps preparing to strike. But Fargo held his powder until he heard it: the faint, but distinctive, stretching sound made by a buffalo-sinew bowstring being drawn back.

Fargo had no intention of waiting until a murdering ambusher formally announced his presence. In an explosive, deafening burst of firepower, he emptied the Colt's cylinder into the deadfall.

Fargo heard a surprised grunt, then a crashing and crackling of mostly dry brush as a dead Comanche warrior tumbled out, landing in a lifeless heap. But the deadly game wasn't quite over: Just before he fell, his arrow, notched in the bow, released with a twanging *fwip*.

"Damn!"

Fargo felt the arrow punch into his saddle fender, missing his thigh only by inches. When the Ovaro suddenly whickered and chinned the moon, almost tossing Fargo into the undergrowth, the Trailsman feared his mount must have been seriously wounded. But a quick check showed the arrow point had only scratched the pinto. Fargo swabbed the small cut with whiskey, then smeared gall salve on it.

"Quartz-tipped arrow," Fargo remarked, puzzling things out aloud. "That's Cherokee. Comanches use flaked flint."

Fargo rolled the hide-clad body over with one foot. The war hatchet in the Comanche's sash was also of Cherokee design.

"C'mon, boy," Fargo said, stepping into leather. "We'll let the scavengers bury *this* red son. We best dust our hocks toward the Cherokee agency. I'm beginning to see why Mumford sent for us—looks like a blood bath is in the works."

A late-afternoon sun was still hot on his shoulders when Fargo hitched the Ovaro to the tie-rail out front of the Indian Bureau office. Even here, the split-log walls of the building were loopholed for rifles.

Fargo lifted the rawhide thong that served as a latchstring and nudged open the door. Talcott Mumford, agent for the vast sector of the Indian Territory that included the Cherokee Nation, was seated at a large oak desk, blotting a letter with sand. The man wore a monocle on a fine gold chain, and when he heard the door open, he placed it in his right eye.

"Skye Fargo!" he exclaimed. "Am I ever relieved to see you."

"Uh-oh," Fargo said, but with a smile. "Seems every time I hear those words, I end up picking lead out of my sitter."

"I know, Skye, I know. You've seen more scrapes than a barber's razor. But while there's no shortage of thieves and killers out here, reliable, honest men are few and far between. And the torture-murder of Colonel Lansford Oglethorpe, two days ago, has already created a full-blown crisis here."

Talcott Mumford, whom Fargo knew slightly, was somewhat of a dandy. He wore a spotless linsey shirt, with trousers of twilled fustian tucked into high, glossy boots. Fargo knew the man's parents were among the privileged "silk cravats" back in Boston. But their son had a strong sense of social justice that drew him west to help the American Indians.

Fargo felt his ideals were too lofty, yet admired the man for having them. A city boy like Mumford faced real danger out here in rugged buffalo country—perfumed hair or not, he was no coward, and that rated aces high in Fargo's book.

"So word about Oglethorpe has leaked out already?" Fargo asked as he straddled a chair.

"Leaked? Hell, it's *gushing* out. And burying the bodies at Sweetwater Creek rather than returning them to the families might have been absolutely necessary, based on the report I read. But that's got the ink slingers champing at the bit to learn the gory details. This situation with Oglethorpe is going to explode out of control, Skye, and once again the Cherokees will be the scapegoats. Along with me, the 'Indian lover.'"

Mumford's Osage assistant, an old squaw in a buckskin dress, was boiling coffee beans on a Franklin stove. She brought both men a cup, flirting shamelessly with the famous Trailsman.

"I seem to recall," Fargo told the agent, "that you got into six sorts of trouble a while back for letting your Indians go on a hunt?"

Mumford grimaced, then nodded. "Yes, even I unwittingly contributed to the tension around here. The 'best-laid plans' and all that. You know about the quarterly food allotments that reservation Indians are owed by law?"

Fargo nodded. "Coffee, sugar, flour, bacon, and such."

"Exactly. And as I'm sure you know, ration deliveries out here are erratic at best. When they do arrive, we often find maggoty meat, or flat stones substituted for sides of bacon. The government is good at making lavish promises, but Congress doesn't seem all that eager to fund them."

Fargo grinned and pointed his chin toward a sign glued to the front of the agent's desk:

IF THE OPPOSITE OF "PRO" IS "CON," THEN THE OPPOSITE OF PROGRESS IS CONGRESS!

"Pretty much says it all, Mr. Mumford."

"That sign *used* to be funny, Skye—before I came out here. The high hats in Congress don't have to look these hungry Indians in the eye and explain why the rations are moldy and weevilly, or missing completely. Which is why I got in trouble with the Bureau. Last time my people came in to draw their rations, I had nothing for them."

Mumford, agitated by the memory, sprang out of his chair and began pacing before a large wall map of the Indian Territory.

"If some of the women hadn't managed to gather up acorns and grind and cook them, their tribes would have starved. Eventually they *did* begin to starve, and I decided, to blazes with the paper-collar regulations. I issued some of the braves a few antiquated weapons so they could hunt buffalo. Which they did, with great success."

"Let me guess," Fargo took over when Mumford fell silent. "You dodged a flood only to step into a stampede?"

"Well put. A few reservation bucks fell under the sway of a young hothead named Wolf Sleeve, a Staked Plains Comanche. They attacked a surveying party in the Ouachita Mountains."

"I heard about it," Fargo said. "Killed three men and destroyed all their equipment. The attack has seriously jeopardized an army contract to build a line of new forts between the Red River and the Cimarron."

"Ah, so word of my disgrace has spread wide, I see. Well, I'd do it again," the agent spat out defiantly. "That hunt saved them. Skye, I'm no starry-eyed optimist. But I'm convinced the Indians need to be self-reliant, not wards of the government. Even a fool can put on his own clothes better than a wise man can do it for him."

That one coaxed a grin from the Trailsman. "Now *that's*

34

well put. But all this hunt business is smoke behind us. I'm figuring you called me in here about the massacre of Oglethorpe's party?"

Mumford nodded, slacking into his chair again. "Among other reasons. It's huge, Skye, and growing bigger. I'm also the area telegrapher, so it's easy to 'spy.' An investigator from the War Department was at Fort Gibson when it happened. He's already made a preliminary report and concluded the culprits were Cherokees. Now he's looking for a ringleader to swing from the gallows."

Fargo had a sudden and unpleasant hunch. "And he's leaning toward Sarah Blackburn?"

Surprised, Mumford again placed his monocle in his eye to study this tall, buckskin-clad man. "You know her?"

"Met her," Fargo said, leaving it there.

"At any rate, the problem is far more than just the Oglethorpe incident," Mumford conceded. "Just last night the driver of a Butterfield mail coach was killed near Broken Arrow and fifteen bags of mail torched. Texans living directly below their border with the Indian Territory are being attacked savagely and often. There are also plenty of furious farmers in the Baxter Springs area of southeastern Kansas, likewise under siege."

"Tell me straight out," Fargo said. "Are your reservation Indians behind the attacks?"

"Not as leaders. A *few* are participating, yes. Younger braves, especially some Delawares and Kickapoos, have been jumping the rez periodically to raid up in Kansas. And I suspect a few may even have joined Wolf Sleeve's Staked Plains Comanches in bloody raids on farmers and ranchers in the Salt Creek Prairie."

Mumford finished taking a pinch of snuff and snapped his silver snuffbox shut. "Man proposes, but God disposes," he said on a sigh.

Then, his bookish features firming with determination, the agent looked at Fargo again.

"But by no means is it all the tribes, nor even most. The Cherokees who relocated from eastern Tennessee are model citizens, as are the Mississippi Choctaws. Most of the Seminoles, Delawares, Shawnees, Miamis, Kickapoos have caused little or no trouble. Nor have the Senecas up here"—with his snuffbox he tapped the northeastern sector of the wall map behind him—"near the Neosho River. Nor the Creeks at Honey Springs. It's just those proverbial few bad apples, Skye. Including some *white* apples."

Fargo nodded. "I figured that out when I realized the Cherokees are being deliberately framed. Indians don't think that way. Got any particular white apple in mind?"

"Have you heard of a Frenchman named Baptiste Menard? A former sutler at Fort Gibson?"

Fargo had been tilting back on the hind legs of his chair. At mention of Menard's name, the front legs came crashing down hard to the floor.

"Menard?" he repeated. "That vulture is back in this area?"

"Thought to be. I see you know his reputation?"

"They won't let him in hell, he's so wicked," Fargo said, his lake-blue eyes clouding. "He'd take over and put Satan on the payroll."

"You know him, all right. The man's very name has become gall and wormwood to me. I *know* he's up to something, something which requires stirring up the tribes and framing the Cherokees. But I can't *prove* it." Mumford sighed, glanced at the wall map, then looked at Fargo. "I was hoping you would agree to immediately terminate your contract with the army and do some emergency investigating for the Indian Bureau."

"Investigating? I'm not a Pinkerton man."

Mumford looked scared now, truly scared. "Skye, a hundred Pinkertons couldn't handle this. Never mind the word 'investigating'—may I emphasize 'emergency'? If this damned mess blows up, hundreds could die, red and white. I think that's what Menard wants, with the Cherokees declared guilty."

Fargo pulled at the point of his bearded chin. For a moment he again saw that dead Comanche tumbling out of the deadfall, his arrow barely missing Fargo. And Colonel Lansford Oglethorpe, once a great man but turned into a grotesque monstrosity.

"Well, it's a job worth doing, all right," he agreed. "But I surely do hate to break a contract. Never done it before. Got anybody else to help you?"

"Gabe Johnson, the U.S. marshal for this territory, just turned fifty and can't sit a saddle because of his lumbago. Since the Oglethorpe atrocity, your Lieutenant Jimmy

Briscoe and his men are ordered to remain on constant mounted patrol. Jimmy is a good kid, but this is a huge area, bigger than most states back east."

Fargo nodded at the frustrating truth of all this.

"As for breaking that contract," Mumford added, "consider it broken the moment you nod your head. The Indian Bureau has priority over the War Department in reservation matters. As for 'deserting' Jimmy Briscoe and his men—since they'll be patrolling constantly, you'll likely be working with them at some point."

"All right," Fargo gave in. "But on one condition: I want a scout named Yellowstone Jack McQuady siding me."

Mumford started. "That old reprobate? I'd figure him for Menard's side, not ours."

Fargo grinned. "Oh, sure, a man better not leave Jack alone with his wife or daughter—or with the old gray mare, for that matter. And he'll steal what ain't nailed down, and he smells like a bear's den. His cussing can raise blisters on new leather."

Fargo nodded toward the wall map. "But Jack knows the Indian Territory better than most men know their wives' geography. He was one of the first buffalo hunters into this region, and he's been scouting and tracking in this area since before the Mexican War. He also knows Indians, and even better, how to fight Indians *like* an Indian."

Mumford, visibly impressed by this defense, raised both hands in surrender. "If you vouch for him, Skye, then the matter's closed. Can you get started right away?"

"Actually, I've already started," Fargo assured him. "And I've got a question to ask you."

There was one important subject about which Talcott Mumford—a leading expert on American Indians—had been suspiciously quiet. Fargo leaned forward over the desk, picked up the steel nib Mumford had been writing with, and dipped it in the ink pot. Using a scrap of paper, Fargo drew three diagonal lines slanting downward from right to left.

"Mean anything to you?" he asked the agent. "Found one just like it carved into a tree."

Mumford poked in his monocle, looked at the drawing, then paled noticeably. This confirmed Fargo's suspicion as to why Mumford had looked so scared a few minutes ago.

"The Keetoowah," Mumford almost whispered, for he

had immediately recognized the symbol of the highly feared Cherokee secret order. "The Nighthawk Society, as white men call them."

Fargo nodded. "Sioux, Cheyenne, Kiowa, Comanche, even the Apache—*no* Indian warriors can match them in killing skills. Once they drink the Black Drink, they're sworn to victory or death. Were you by any chance aware the Nighthawks might be active out here?"

Mumford looked like he'd been caught palming a card. "Sorry, Skye. I was afraid to tell you unless I knew for sure. No white man with an ounce of good sense would take on the Keetoowah—*if* they are indeed active again."

"If they are active, do you think Sarah Blackburn is a Nighthawk? After all, only the War Women know the secret formula for the Black Drink."

Mumford looked miserable. "God, I *hope* not. The Keetoowah has been outlawed by the U.S. government. Anyone participating now would face a long prison term just for belonging."

Fargo said, "On the subject of framing Cherokees—why would Menard pick Princess Sarah to frame as the renegade ringleader? Sure, she's a War Woman. But she's pretty as four aces and even a little famous. It would be easier to pin it on a brave."

"True enough," Mumford said. "But, you see, Menard once succeeded in raping Sarah by doing it while his men held guns to her family. Now he regrets that foolish mistake, and he'll do anything to get her killed or locked up before she splits his skull open."

"So that's the way of it," Fargo mused, nodding slowly. That explained the determination in her voice when she assured him no man would rape her.

He stood up and clapped his hat on his head. "I don't know if the Nighthawk Society has revived or not. Personally, I'd rather tangle with a sore-tailed grizzly. But I'll run my traps, see what we catch. I got a hunch we'll find Baptiste Menard is the wheelhorse, not the Cherokees."

"Be careful anyway. Menard is no less dangerous than the Keetoowah," Mumford warned.

"I know," Fargo said over his shoulder as he lifted the latchstring. "But he'd be a greater pleasure to kill."

5

Even before the dawn mist had burned off, Fargo was awake and ready to break camp.

He had spread his blankets in a grassy meadow of the vast Ozark Plateau, a hilly, elevated region that included the northeast section of the Indian Territory. Even though it was still late summer, he had to place his firearms between the folds of his blankets to protect them from early morning dew.

He shook his boots out before putting them on, just in case some poisonous guest had crawled in for the night. Then he watered the Ovaro from a little rill nearby.

Since it was still almost dark, Fargo considered the idea of making a fire and cooking some bacon. It had been a long time since he'd gotten outside of some solid grub. But when he led the Ovaro to drink, the stallion's ears pricked forward and he shied back.

"No fire this morning," Fargo muttered, his eyes studying the dark mass of dogwoods and cottonwoods that bordered the upland meadow.

Fargo gnawed on a heel of cold pone for breakfast, watching the new sun leave salmon-pink streaks on the horizon. He sat on a log, his Henry leaning beside him. He couldn't prove it, but he had a gut hunch there was an assassin hidden somewhere in that dark foliage surrounding him.

Why? Fargo knew Indians could be brutal, but they were direct and open about it. That attack on him yesterday by the Comanche—that was ordered, planned, not just random opportunism. The brave had stalked him for hours. And though Fargo still needed solid proof, Baptiste Menard was a perfect culprit. Stirring up Indians was his hallmark.

A fox suddenly darted out from cover and streaked across the meadow, so frightened it almost ran smack into Fargo. He fixed the exact spot where the fox had emerged, then snatched up his rifle and jacked a round into the chamber.

Fargo slapped the Henry's butt plate into his shoulder socket, dropped a bead on the spot where the fox emerged, and split the morning silence as he squeezed off a round.

The sound multiplied off through the wooded hills.

Thwack!

"Shit!" A completely surprised Fargo swore, his heart turning over, when a quartz-tipped arrow punched into the log about six inches from his left leg.

Even as he rolled behind the log for cover, Fargo was working the Henry's lever.

"All right, you white-livered son of a bitch!" he shouted toward his hidden nemesis. "Let's open the ball!"

B. Tyler Henry's repeating rifle did not have the knock-down power of some weapons, but Fargo carried it because of its superior feed-and-eject mechanism and magazine capacity. He put both to the test now as he peppered that forest wall with lead.

Over and over the wood stock slapped his cheek, and the ejector mechanism clicked flawlessly as more than a dozen spent cartridges rained into the grass. By the time Fargo's Henry fell silent, an acrid blue haze hovered over his position.

But, in the distance, he heard it: the sounds of a panicked retreat on horseback.

That's twice now in two days, Fargo reminded himself as he began rigging his pinto, that some bushwhacking redskin had tried to free him from his soul. The Trailsman was one to rile cool. But as he hit leather and swung up into the saddle, his weather-tanned face was grim with deadly purpose.

Fargo already knew, from Talcott Mumford, where Lieutenant Jimmy Briscoe and his men were camped in pine bluffs overlooking the Arkansas River. Fargo had meant to join them, but had to settle for camping nearby when darkness and rain overtook him.

The next morning he was nearing camp when the rapid bugle notes of "Boots and Saddles" startled the Ovaro. Soon came the creaking, clinking sounds of horses being rigged for another day on the trail. A trooper at a picket outpost recognized Fargo and waved him through.

Conditions in this sector, Fargo thought, were not so bad, as army life in the field went. Drift cottonwood supplied the squad cooking fires, and fresh fish and game were plentiful. Fargo could remember expeditions into the Arizona and Utah Territories so grueling that soldiers had died without ever seeing battle.

"Skye Fargo, you're a born widow-maker!"

It was the gravel-pan voice of Yellowstone Jack greeting him across the misty camp clearing. The old explorer sat on an upended ammunition crate, scrubbing what remained of his teeth with a hog-bristle brush.

"Heard all the shootin'," Jack added. "Knowed the Henry by its sound. Plug the son of a bitch?"

"Nope, just made him rabbit," Fargo replied as he swung down and tethered the Ovaro in lush grass.

"Cheraw?" Yellowstone Jack demanded.

Fargo loosened the girth, but left the saddle in place. He'd be riding out soon.

"The arrow was Cherokee," he replied. "But I didn't see my attacker. Could have been any tribe or even a white man."

Jack made a farting noise with his lips. "There you commence again, Fargo! That was a Cheraw pizen dart in Trooper Robinson's neck, not a bee stinger. It's just blame stupid, this mollycoddling of the Cheraws."

"You'd just kill 'em all, that it?"

"A-course not, you muttonhead. I was Bible-raised, and I don't favor easy-go killing. But with Injins, you give an inch, you lose an ell. These ones that call theirselves renegades just require a good boot up their sitters, is all. Not mollycoddling."

Nearby, Jimmy Briscoe, up and dressed before most of his men, was standing between the supply wagons performing the morning inventory. Packs, panniers, saddles, hobbles, sidelines, picket pins, carbines, pistols, bridles, ordnance, stores, forage—everything had to be carefully measured and recorded.

"Morning, Lieutenant," Fargo greeted him, strolling over. "I see you weren't busted to latrine duty over the Oglethorpe massacre."

Jimmy, startled back to the present, began to salute Fargo, then checked himself, flushing. With a bigger-than-life man like the Trailsman around, it was hard to remember *who* was in charge.

"I sure wasn't busted, Mr. Fargo," the kid replied. "All because of your report. You told headquarters I did an outstanding job on my first mission."

"So what? You did."

"But, all due respect, I didn't! Look how I messed up by not sending out flankers before we were ambushed four days ago. Got us attacked and a man killed."

Fargo waved this off. "Every officer loses men. Main thing is, you learned from it. Jimmy, you just need some time in the saddle. Far as that glowing report of mine—when the God-almighty 'public opinion' is outraged, the army usually sacrifices a buck lieutenant. And I'm damned if I'm letting some rule book ranger blame *you* for Oglethorpe's death."

"Damn straight, Jimmy," Yellowstone Jack chimed in, joining them as he hitched up his red long-handles. "Hell, you're my favorite turd."

By now the squad fires were going, and the main body of men had divided into their separate messes. Fargo, accepting a cup of coffee from an enlisted man, explained to Jimmy and Jack that he now worked for the Indian Bureau, as did Jack.

"But we'll all be working close together on this," Fargo assured the officer. "The trouble seems to cover the entire Indian Territory and even spills over into Kansas and Texas. By staying on constant patrol, especially if you avoid set routes and times, your mounted unit makes it harder for any renegades to raid freely. That also frees me and Jack to look for the nest—and Baptiste Menard."

Yellowstone Jack scowled and threw down his toothbrush. "Menard, huh? And by any goddamn stinking happenchance would this *nest* be in the Ouachitas?"

Fargo finally lost the effort not to grin. "Distinct possibility."

Jack looked like a man trying to swallow without chewing. "God's garters, boy! First it's 'em damn Cheraw Nighthawks you go pokin' with a stick. Now it's time to ride hell-bent into the teeth of a Comanche and Kiowa snake den, too?"

"You plan to live forever?" Fargo roweled the old flint.

Yellowstone Jack always spoke loud when he was ireful, and several troopers heard some of his last remark. Fargo watched one edge closer to eavesdrop, nor could he blame him—even the greenest recruits knew what it meant to face Kiowas and Comanches. But the preliminary signs, and logic, pointed toward the Ouachita Mountains. Fargo knew it as a dangerous hellhole, best avoided by whites. But enter it he would.

"This is easy work I got now," Jack groused, "and you want me to give it up for a shit detail."

"Yeah, I forgot how your calves have gone to grass, old fossil," Fargo replied. "You can retire to the liar's bench, and I'll scratch your name off the pay voucher."

Jack thumbed back his slouch hat and gave the younger man his fiercest hoodoo eye. "Fossil? Fargo, you *had* teeth when you got here."

"Mr. Fargo," Jimmy said, "headquarters has sent urgent word to all surrounding posts that an Indian uprising is taking place in The Nations. You agree?"

Fargo shook his head, noticing that a sentry at port arms, across the way, was guarding someone Fargo couldn't make out because of a tree.

"I doubt there's any full-bore uprising, Jimmy," Fargo replied. "To me it looks like most of the violent, murderous raids are carried out by Staked Plains Comanches and their Kiowa allies. Outsiders stirring up trouble. And, with orders from Menard, the worst crimes are pinned on the Cherokees."

"Fargo, teach your grandmother to suck eggs," Yellowstone Jack cut in. "Outsiders, my lily-white ass! Sure, there's Comanches and Kiowas involved, but Cheraws are *deep* in the mix. Hell, you 'n' Jimmy was both standing there when a Cheraw done this."

He took off his beaver hat and pointed out the hole where Sarah Blackburn had sent an arrow through it.

"She only took aim at you," Fargo reminded his friend, "after you started drawing a bead on her boat."

"If it's Menard behind the trouble," Jimmy asked Fargo, "what's he up to?"

This time the Trailsman paused longer, tasting bitter acid spurt into his throat. Jimmy's question went to the heart of what was destroying the pristine frontier.

The details might differ case by case. But it was a sickeningly familiar pattern, by now, to Fargo. Time and again the explorers and Indian fighters had opened new tracts of wilderness farther west, only to be driven out. Driven out by those who turned the explorers' own trace into a road to overrun them with taxes and lawyers, with shady land speculators—in short, those who relaxed in their feather beds and grew rich off someone else's labor and risks.

"A land grab seems most likely, to me," Fargo finally answered the kid. "How big a parcel is hard to say right now."

"Land grabbed for what?" Jimmy asked. "Is there gold around here?"

"Menard could want it for his own purposes, or maybe he's acting for railroad men. From what I've seen over the years, the usual U.S. government punishment, when a reservation tribe becomes too much trouble, is to strip them of their land and put them in prison camps. And the Cherokees have some of the best land in The Nations."

"Aww, boohoo, the poor damn Cheraws," Yellowstone Jack barbed. "What about all 'em damn Cheraw lances, hatchets, and arrahs? They been popping up around here like worms after a hard rain."

"Yeah, think about that, you old windbag," Fargo fired back. "Takes weeks to fashion a good war hatchet, no brave would leave one behind like a spent shell casing. Hell, those weapons're being planted."

Jack believed that, too, but was too contrary to admit it. "Ahh . . . how 'bout that damn 'Beautiful Death Bringer' of yours—how's come she's running around with the same kind of blowgun that kilt Oglethorpe's aide? And a-course, Private Robinson."

"Oglethorpe," Jimmy repeated nervously. "Man, now *that's* getting messy, Mr. Fargo. Looks like the word is get-

44

ting out fast. There's already talk of vengeance raids on peaceful Indian villages."

"See, and that's how's come," Yellowstone Jack said, sly eyes watching Fargo, "the order went out from Fort Gibson: *any* member of the Keetoowah is to be arrested under martial law."

Arrested . . . Fargo glanced again toward the guard and his hidden prisoner. Then Jimmy's voice distracted him.

"I'm worried about the morale of my men, Mr. Fargo. They know the army has a crisis on its hands, and they're scared they'll be massacred in a massive uprising."

"No uprising," Fargo insisted. "I've seen them before and hope I never do again."

"I believe you, Mr. Fargo, but the men don't. First they saw Trooper Robinson die hard, then yesterday we found Dave Helzer, our missing flank rider, beheaded."

"Your men'll soldier just fine," Fargo predicted confidently. "They're mostly green recruits, and now they've seen two men killed. When the fear passes, pride sets in. They'll nerve up."

Two more men . . . Fargo wasn't one for slopping over. Besides, soldiers sometimes died, that was duty, but warfare was not cold-blooded murder, and those two men were murdered at someone's order. That same someone *would* answer for their souls.

"I'll be taking Jack with me," Fargo told the officer. "But you still got Standing Feather and Ten Bears to handle the scouting and tracking. Just oil them up with a jolt of whiskey—they've got lazy since they was promoted to interpreters."

Fargo's eyes swept the camp. Because the unit was on standby, waiting for new orders from a courier, the men were on "commander's time"—free recreation—once they finished breakfast. Some played at whist or horseshoes, others were boiling their clothes in a battered vat, killing the vermin. A few troopers with a taste for gambling were pitting red ants against black ants in a fierce war. Anything to break up the frontier monotony that was nearly as bad as terror.

"Do you know a Comanche renegade called Wolf Sleeve?" he asked Yellowstone Jack.

"Know of him, is all. I hear tell that red son is meaner than Satan with a sunburn. In battle, him and some big Kiowa named Iron Mountain are joined at the hip."

Fargo was about to ask another question when a musical female voice, tense now with anger and exhaustion but still familiar, struck him silent.

"Well, noble Skye Fargo, so *this* is how you befriend the Cherokee?"

He glanced toward the sentry, who had changed positions to light his pipe, and spotted an empty fox-skin quiver folded on the ground. Then, as she eased around the tree to taunt him again, Fargo stared into the fierce dark eyes of the Cherokee prisoner.

"Fargo," she spat with contempt, "you are a pig's afterbirth!"

Yellowstone Jack sputtered with laughter.

"Toldja, Jimmy!" he shouted. "Fargo topped her, all right, that horndog!"

Fargo was forced to wait, in embarrassed silence, while the bored troops who overheard this howled with mirth.

"Honest, Mr. Fargo!" Jimmy hastened to explain. "This wasn't my idea. But Yellowstone Jack, he kept reminding me how my new orders say all hostile Indians are to be arrested and held for interrogation. And we found her not far from Cody Davis's body—armed to the teeth."

The kid handed Fargo an old scent-bottle type Forsyth pistol. "Had this in a parfleche on her hip," he added. "Recently fired."

Actually, Fargo recalled, she had killed Davis with a musketoon, a sawed-off musket. But the bullet hole would look the same either way.

"Musta shot the poor bastard whilst he was takin' a crap, too," Yellowstone Jack opined as the three men approached the princess. "His pants was half down."

"Heroic Fargo!" the Cherokee woman taunted. "Friend of the Cherokee. Only moments after . . . talking with me yesterday, you reported me to your comrades as a murderer! You are no man, just a cowardly liar."

Her hands were lashed behind her, her ankles bound.

"*Now* she talks, with Fargo in camp," Yellowstone Jack told Jimmy. "He poked her, all right."

"Launder your speech," Fargo said mildly. "This here's a princess."

"Princess? Hookey Walker!" Jack exclaimed. "By God, this is America, not England. Rank otter be based on achievement, not birth."

Jack stared down at the defiant prisoner. "Hey, *Princess*! I hear you War Women're death to the devil. Hear how some of yous even sear off your right dug so's you can toss spears and hatchets farther. That true?"

She stared at him with murderous contempt, saying nothing.

"You got a fish bone caught in your throat?" he goaded. Jack's eyes cut to her snug, short jacket.

"*Looks* like you got a full set," he remarked. "Hell, let's have a quick peek anyhow. It's evidence."

"Yellowstone," Jimmy protested, "I don't—"

"Stand down, hoss," Fargo said, stopping the old flint with a hand on his shoulder. The eagle-talon grip told Jack that Fargo wouldn't bother saying it again.

Fargo looked at the young officer. "Jimmy, you have a suspicion that this woman is a hostile—but hostile to who? Hell, killing a roach like Cody Davis, if she did, puts her on our side."

"That makes sense," Jimmy agreed, obviously eager to let Sarah go if he possibly could.

"Besides," Fargo added, "Davis had a reputation for raping Indian women. Sarah is a beauty, his pants were half down . . . it's the custom, in the West, to assume a woman's innocence when there's no evidence to dispute it."

"That damn blowgun of hers was 'evidence,'" Yellowstone Jack protested. "A pizen dart was used in the massacre at Sweetwater Creek."

"Coincidence alone is no grounds for arresting someone," Fargo insisted. "If you can't directly link her to Oglethorpe, Robinson, or some other crime, you have to let her go."

"That's what I tried to tell Yellowstone yesterday," the kid said.

"God's galoshes, Fargo!" Jack exploded. "You sound like some kiss-my-ass Philadelphia lawyer. T'hell with that legal swamp gas. That damned Cheraw wench is loaded for bear even when she's been disarmed—look-a-here what she done to me yestiddy."

The old explorer pushed up his doeskin shirt, but Fargo barely glanced at the deep red claw marks on the old goat's hairy white belly.

"You know, Jack," Fargo said, winking at Sarah and Jimmy, "it's the damndest thing."

Yellowstone Jack, who was just getting into a creative string of curses, suddenly fell silent, curious. "What is, Skye?"

"Why, you and Sarah. I noticed right off how, when it comes to temperament, you and her are two peas in a pod."

Jack squinted. "Hunh? Turd, did you smoke your peyote or eat it?"

However, as he studied the pretty princess, his stern features softened. He scratched his beard-scruffed chin. "Well . . . p'r'aps there *is* a sorter resemblance. I mean, she's good-lookin' and so'm I."

Fargo nearly choked on the effort not to laugh.

Yellowstone Jack turned to Jimmy. "Skye's right for wunst. That little slyboots is up to somethin', all right. But it ain't jake to haul her in just yet. She done for Cody Davis, straight enough, but that'll earn her jewels in paradise."

Sarah, finally realizing Fargo had not helped in her capture, sent him a grateful glance as Jimmy untied her. But the moment she'd gathered up her gear, she was gone.

"Fargo, you shameless horndog," Yellowstone Jack said as they watched her lithe form fade into the dense pines. "You *did* plant your carrot in her, dint'cha?"

"Never mind that, you dirty old goat. It's time we dusted our hocks south toward the Ouachitas."

Just hearing the name of that dangerous bastion of the lawless wiped the mirth from the older man's face. But as he pulled the .38 caliber magazine pistol from his sash to check the loads, Jack's nervous manner disappeared.

"Then what the hell we dillydallying for?" he demanded. "Let's make tracks."

6

Not very long after Fargo and Yellowstone Jack hit the trail south, bearing toward the remote and dangerous Ouachita Mountains, the first mirror flashes went up to warn Baptiste Menard and his minions.

On a sunny and clear day like today, mirror flashes could be seen up to fifty miles away. Thus, within no time the desperadoes holed up in the mountains had dependable knowledge of Fargo's current movements.

"Skye Fargo's evidently coming to visit us, gentlemen," Menard remarked around midmorning. "Knowing him like I do, that's not good news. *Ciel!*"

Menard and five hardcases, all armed like express riders, had met in one of the few remaining structures in the deserted buffalo-hiders camp. The split-log cabin had never been chinked and had only a rammed-earth floor.

"If it's not good news, then why in hell you smiling about it?" demanded Mike Winkler.

Winkler was one of dozens of white criminals who had fled to the Indian Territory when it evolved into an outlaw haven. He was a lean, hard man with a livid knife scar that ran from under his left ear to the corner of his mouth.

"I am smiling about it, Mike," Menard answered patiently, "because, as we say in my country, 'the pitcher can go once too often to the well.'"

Winkler glanced around at each of his men, sharing their disgust at this dandy Frenchman who bathed every damn blessed day and spoke in riddles. But the wages he paid made sense enough.

"Pitcher . . . well? Shit, that's too far north for us

chicken-plucking chawbacons, Baptiste, we're just ignut rubes. The hell's it mean?''

"It means *any* man's luck has to dry up. Especially when he keeps repeating a dangerous behavior such as riding into these renegade-and-outlaw badlands.''

There were no Indians present at this meeting—they were out "on field assignment,'' as Menard put it. He had learned to pit even his dirt workers against each other, to keep them separated, so they wouldn't unite against him.

"Gents,'' he said, his tone confident, "do not worry about Fargo. It's the *man* we're up against, not the reputation. You watch—if we do this right, we'll toss the net around that lanky bastard quicker than an Indian going to crap.''

"Talk's cheap,'' Winkler gainsaid. "A month ago, you bragged how the Cherokees would be off their land by now. This keeps up, the soldiers will flush all whites out of The Nations, then where are we? And there goes your big-money sawmill, too.''

" 'Sides that,'' tossed in Stone Jeffries, a killer Menard had recruited out in Cimarron, New Mexico Territory, "word's out how Fargo's already killed that Comanche buck Wolf Sleeve just sicced on him. This mother-ruttin' Trailsman is hell on two sticks.''

"And don't forget Cody,'' chimed in another man, meaning Cody Davis, who'd been a member of the Winkler gang.

"Cody,'' Menard spoke up quickly, "was *not* killed by Fargo. My spy in Briscoe's cavalry unit insists it was Sarah Blackburn who did him in.''

"Yeah,'' Winkler said, his scar furrowing when he scowled, "and now that highfalutin princess bitch is running free again. I ain't no Doctor Johnson, but that sure's hell don't seem like the authorities are cracking down on Cherokees.''

Menard, trim and neat in tailored buckskins and glossy, knee-length boots, waved all this off like a diner shooing flies.

"Boys,'' he said, "your impatience is understandable, but it's cockeyed. Oglethorpe's death made this a new game. Give it a few more days now to fester, and you *will* see our fortunes change.''

Menard had honed in on two goals from the beginning

of this latest campaign of crime: stir up trouble and make sure the Cherokees were blamed for it, relocating them from their timber-and-water rich land; and make sure *enough* trouble was fomented so that more forts would be quickly built in The Nations, army contracts for lumber being especially lucrative.

Menard glanced out the doorless frame into the rutted slough out front. A few dozen yards up the mountain slope, some motley-colored Indian scrubs were grazing the lush grass.

"Besides, Mike," he added confidently, "if it's government pressure on the Cherokees you want, when Wolf Sleeve and his braves are finished at Broken Bow Lake, it will live up to its name. And the official outrage against the Cherokees will be immediate and sharp."

"So . . . if you got all the blanket asses doing the main work, where do me and the boys fit in?" Winkler demanded.

"From the beginning," Menard explained in his nasal, accented voice, "I have wanted the newfound trouble in the Indian Territory to look widespread. But there haven't been enough Indians willing to take orders. So you and your boys, Mike, will add to the 'red menace.' "

Winkler grinned, baring stained and broken teeth. "Now, that's right up our road, Frenchie."

"You're going to launch a series of simultaneous attacks to spread panic and confusion. Stage stations, ranches, travelers, mail riders. Naturally, you'll use, and leave behind, a few Cherokee weapons."

"Since it's s'posed to be redskins," Winkler said, "it would have to be daylight raids, right? But, hell, I don't want to paint up and wear a damn wig to look Indian."

"No, strike only at night. You forget, Cherokees have few religious taboos and are one of the few tribes who like to war at night. And while you're at it, make sure you or one of your men drops *this* near a body—a white person's body, preferably a woman or child."

Menard was sitting on one edge of a crude deal table as he spoke. Now he slid off and poked a hand into the musette bag draped over one shoulder. The men stared in fascination at the unusual weapon he pulled out and showed to them.

"Good God a-gorry!" Winkler exclaimed. "The hell you got there, Baptiste? Damn my eyes if I ever seen its like! I see it's a gun, but it also looks like a musical instrument."

"Patented in Paris by a gunsmith named Jarre," Menard replied, pride evident in his tone. "Technically, it is a single barrel, horizontal sliding, multishot pinfire cartridge pistol. Better known as the harmonica pistol."

The "harmonica" part was a sliding breechblock, hinged for loading, with space for ten balls and primer caps.

"One of the first multishots," Menard explained. "Each time you fire, you simply push the harmonica bar one space to the right, and the next load is ready."

"Hunh. Damndest thing," Winkler said. "But what makes it so important?"

Menard handed it to him. "Read the inscription on the butt plate."

Winkler flipped it over. Carved in the soft brass were the words *Presented to Sarah Blackburn by the Royal Academy, London, 1853*.

"I took it from her house," Menard explained, "while she's been away making trouble. This pistol is famous—it's been written about in newspaper articles about the 'Cherokee royalty.' "

"Hell," Winkler objected, "framing one damn Cherokee woman won't get the whole passel of 'em removed. She's small potatoes."

"Don't believe it," Menard said. "Remember, Sarah Blackburn is beloved by many."

"Frenchie oughta know," Stone Jeffries muttered, and one of the men snickered.

"I missed that, Stone," Menard said, his eyes suddenly two chips of glittering ice. One finger of his right hand tickled the walnut grip of his revolver.

Suddenly, nobody perceived the Frenchman as a "poncy." This perfumed and frilled adventurer was a cold-blooded killer who could cut a man's throat as casually as buttering his bread. He had cut a bloody swath from the Great Lakes to Mexico City, those icy eyes reminded the others, and nobody was going to stop him now.

"Nothing, Mr. Menard," Stone finally muttered. "Sorry for interruptin'."

"Quite all right. Now, as I was saying: in some senses

Sarah Blackburn is the leader of her people. So it's crucial to pin the no-good label on her. And don't forget, her stunning beauty aside, the woman *is* an elite warrior who could rally the Cherokees to a deadly defense."

This made sense to Winkler and his gun-throwers, even though they knew about Menard's longtime infatuation with the Cherokee beauty. In truth, Menard wasn't lying in what he'd just said.

But he had another motive for involving her. Ever since raping the Cherokee woman several years ago, Menard couldn't get the beauty out of his mind. He burned for her, even knowing he would have to force himself on her again. What he planned—what he hoped—was to make Sarah *his* prisoner soon after that gun was planted. She'd be forced to stay with him, her only safe haven from fearsome American authority.

All that, however, was personal. Menard's chief goal was always the same, and he reminded the others of it now.

"Boys, honest toil is for idiots, not intelligent men. A man can pull and burn stumps all day long and earn perhaps a dollar. Or—he can pay a few laborers to saw down free trees into boards and soon be rolling in it."

"You're gettin' ahead of the roundup, Baptiste," Winkler reminded him. "You forgettin' that Fargo and that hard twist Yellowstone Jack have lit a shuck toward this place?"

"No, they won't come right *here,*" Menard said. "Not yet. This spot is in the western Ouachitas. But Wolf Sleeve and his band will leave a trail straight toward Broken Bow Lake in the eastern Ouachitas. And believe me, the sights Fargo will encounter there will take the heart out of him—and the stomach."

"Yeah, but Fargo ain't delicate," Winkler said bluntly. "He'll just shake it off quick, and when he does, he'll not only come after us, he'll bring hell with him. He's the crusader type."

"All the better," Menard insisted. "Crusaders have died by the canyon load. Remember, the savages are making things lively for him right about now. As I told you: the pitcher can go once too often to the well. I've noticed that Skye Fargo's buckskins look ragged these days. He's long overdue for a new suit—the kind with no back in it."

* * *

53

"Well, I'm clemmed!" exclaimed Yellowstone Jack, twisting around in the saddle and pointing into the heavens. "Look at that, Skye!"

It was full daylight now and the Arkansas River military encampment was several miles behind them. Fargo followed Jack's stubby finger, then felt his jaw drop at the rare and astonishing sight: the sun and the moon both in the sky at the same time, both full and tinted blood red from a dusty haze.

"I don't need no shaman," Jack muttered, "to tell me that's a mighty consequential omen."

"T'hell with omens," Fargo said, thinking of the Hell Hounds. "I've had my belly full of 'em lately."

"Everybody knows that's a consequential omen," Jack insisted as they kneed their mounts forward again. "You're spoze to heed it."

"Tell you what I heed, Methuselah," Fargo said, his lake-water eyes always in motion as he spoke. "I heed mirror signals like the ones that've been flashed south almost since we left."

"I seen 'em, too," Yellowstone Jack growled. "Fargo, you was still at the tit when *this* child learned his lore. Come to think on it, you're always at the tit, you randy stallion."

Fargo listened to Jack, but missed nothing around them. "Could be renegades or owlhoots, or both, making those flashes. Ambush will be our biggest problem."

"Fresh off ma's milk," Jack muttered. "A-course ambush is our biggest problem, you damned clod-pole! Hell, you're the most famous target west of Omaha, and I'm just so *damn* lucky to side you."

Fargo's eyes swept the familiar landscape, with its sandy washes and numerous stands of dogwood, scrub oak, and cottonwoods. Pretty terrain maybe, but also deadly. Fargo thought like his enemies, and he spotted countless hiding places for a shooter.

As for the terrain farther south, over the years both Fargo and Yellowstone Jack had scouted most sections of the Indian Territory. It would be a two-day ride with a stretch of thick, wild forest they would skirt to the west.

"Look-a-here. We're comin' to *your woman's* people," Jack said from a smirk.

"Keep it up, old man, you'll be gumming your supper."

"Balls! I'll kick your skinny ass so hard, colt, you'll have to take off your hat to crap."

Just ahead, tucked into a stream-fed, tree-protected clearing, was one of several Cherokee clan clusters in the area. At least this time, Fargo noted, everyone had not fled as whites rode near. Perhaps a dozen men and older boys remained among the corn and beans scattered randomly about.

"Buncha damn totem poles, ain't they?" Jack muttered, for no one seemed to be moving an inch—only standing in place and staring at the two horsebackers.

However, both white men knew that, among themselves, Cherokees were quite animated and gesticulated frequently, laughing at their own jokes. But by firm custom they remained stoic and deadpan around outsiders.

"Look yonder," Fargo said without pointing. "The buck watching us from the doorway of that cabin with chickens out front."

The man Fargo meant was, at first glance, a typical Cherokee male: tall with straight black hair and prominent cheekbones. But his red turban and a collar made of wampum beads designated him as a chief.

"*You* reckon he's a Cheraw king, uh?" Yellowstone Jack roweled Fargo. "Likely, he's your princess's sire. And me, I'm the goldang Queen of England after I shave."

Fargo ignored these barbs, thinking out loud. "If the Cherokees are supposed to be in an uprising, who in the hell is tending their crops and animals? Look at those stove-lengths piled up in the woodbin—freshly cut."

"You're full of sheep dip," Jack insisted as the rustic settlement receded behind them. "Any one of them bucks back there could be a Nighthawk. Measurin' both of us for coffins."

Fargo grinned and slapped the reins against his Ovaro's neck, opening the pinto out to a lope.

"Coffin?" he repeated with a scornful laugh. "If the Keetoowah get hold of us, won't be much left to stick in any coffin. They'll just bury us with a rake."

Two hours south of the Arkansas River, Fargo and Yellowstone Jack reined in at a spring bubbling up from a clutch of rocks. Both riders threw the bridles and let their horses drink, meanwhile studying the hill country around them from sun-slitted eyes.

"Them red sons is watching us," Jack stated with flat conviction. "And they want to kill us, sure as cats fighting."

Fargo nodded agreement. "And this has been excellent dry-gulch country, yet they've made no play. Curious, ain't it?"

Jack grunted. "It ain't so curious, happens they got other mischief planned."

Fargo took the point. He and Jack both believed the main body of renegades—mostly Kiowa and Comanche— was holed up in the Ouachitas. Those who were farther north, raising holy hell, might be spread thin right now, unable to provide an adequate force to trap and bring down the Trailsman. Like it or not, Fargo knew his bigger than life reputation had spread to the Indians, too. Indeed, some of them told even bigger stretchers about him than did the newspapers back in the States.

"Other mischief," Fargo repeated as he threw his hat aside and plunged his head into the bracing water. "Like what, I wonder?"

Jack shook his shaggy head. "Tryin' to unnerstan' the mind of a redskin is sorter like tryin' to write your name on water. We'll know what they're up to, right enough, when we feel the first arrahs pokin' us in the sitter."

"Just a short distance to the east," Fargo mused aloud as he quickly inspected the Ovaro's hoofs for cracks or embedded stones, "is the Buffalo water trace."

The Buffalo Trace, beginning at Buffalo Lake to the north, was an interconnecting series of lakes, creeks, rivers, and extensive backwaters that eventually led into the western Ouachitas.

Yellowstone Jack bared his teeth in a wolf grin. "I see which way the wind sets. You're frettin' that mebbe your little sugar squaw headed south in her boat."

"She was bearing south when she left camp this morning. And she's got some axe to grind where Baptiste Menard is involved."

A grudge, Fargo told himself, perhaps related to her avowal that she would kill *any* man who tried to rape her.

"Sure she's headed south," Jack scoffed. "She's a War

Woman, ain't she? She's prob'ly one of the leaders of the uprising."

"You don't believe that, you contrary old fool. It just rankles in your craw that a woman that pretty could kill you easier than slicing a biscuit open."

"Kill *me*? Boy, she'll make cheese out of chalk first!"

Fargo seated the bridle again, the Ovaro taking the bit easily. He puffed the blow sand out of the Colt's chamber and barrel, again studying the vast, rolling landscape with its patchwork of sun and shadow.

Fargo had been hoping for a lighter moment, and one came now when Yellowstone Jack bent over to fill his canteen at the spring. His ginger gelding, as ill-mannered and ornery as its master, took the opportunity to suddenly nip the old codger a good one on the ass. He yelped and tumbled face first into the spring.

"Ouch! You spavined son of a bitch!" Jack roared at the devilish horse while Fargo sputtered with laughter. The string of vivid curses Jack spewed forth would have provoked blushes in hell.

"Your problem, hoss," Fargo suggested when he could speak again, "is how you're always contrary to things. Now, you take a wildcat. Clap your hands at one, it'll run for a mile. But no, you got to corner it and make it fight like a trapped Apache. See, you'd rather piss and moan all day long 'bout how dangerous wildcats are. That same contrary nature makes you pick a man-hating horse like this one so's you can cuss it out all day long."

"Cuss a cat's tail, Fargo, *this* child was makin' his beaver 'fore you was in long pants."

By now the two riders had resumed the trail, holding their mounts to a fast trot, an energy-saving gait most horses could keep up for hours.

"Lookit yonder," Yellowstone Jack said, inclining his head left toward the east.

Jack had superb vision. Fargo thumbed back his hat and, after a few moments of searching, noticed a column of agitated birds spiraling above the ground like a twister.

"Something or somebody has crowded them in their nesting grounds," he remarked. "Right next to the Buffalo Trace. It's a fair piece away from us, but why don't we ride over and take a squint?"

"Hell, why not? The Princess might need her butt wiped," Yellowstone Jack retorted sarcastically. But he, too, tugged rein and veered toward the east, muttering curses.

They rode in silence for perhaps twenty minutes. Then the peace was suddenly shattered when gunshots erupted, followed by savage, yipping cries.

"Grab your partner and do-si-do!" Jack roared out, tugging his Sharps from its leather boot. "Fargo, here's your next chance to get my life over quick."

Both men were still at least five minutes away from the fight, so it caught them by surprise when an arrow punched into Fargo's bedroll. Seconds later, the air turned deadly around them as more arrows were launched.

"There!" the hawkeyed Yellowstone Jack shouted as they quickly dismounted and led their mounts behind a pile of scree. "There's the lookout post. Looks like three of 'em up there."

Fargo, too, spotted it, a protective wall of rocks at the crest of a grassy hill. The battle, still out of sight from Fargo's location, raged behind the lookouts.

The two friends quickly hobbled their mounts.

"Skye," Jack said, "you can shoot the eyes out of a sparrow at two hunnert yards. See that Comanch with his face painted in hailstones?"

Fargo nodded as he jacked a round into the Henry's chamber.

"He's the linchpin up there. Plug him," Jack said, "and them other two will run like a river when the snow melts."

Fargo agreed they'd likely run, but not out of cowardice. Fighting from forted up positions was alien to Indians, even renegades, who preferred to stay in motion when fighting. They believed there was power in motion, as with the wind, while staying still tempted death, a likewise motionless thing.

More arrows clattered into the protective rocks even as the main battle raged. Fargo laid the Henry's muzzle across the rocks, then brought the front sight up in line with the exposed Comanche's chest. Fargo would go to great lengths to avoid killing any man. But once one opened fire on him, it was kill or be killed.

A flint-tipped arrow struck rock only inches from Fargo's

face, burning his face with sparks. He stoically ignored the danger and checked his aim.

"Welcome to the Land Beyond the Sun, red ghost," Yellowstone Jack muttered as Fargo began to squeeze the trigger back slow.

The Henry bucked, blue-white smoke belched from the barrel, and a scarlet rope of blood erupted from the brave's chest. He came tumbling down the hill, gathering speed and dust. His two companions stared after him in shock until Fargo, working the Henry's lever as if it were a pump handle, sent a hornet-buzzing mass of bullets into their position.

That sent the other two braves fleeing down the backside of the hill.

"Let's go," Fargo said, booting his Henry and stooping to untie the Ovaro's hobbles. "Lively battle raging straight ahead, let's see if we can't get a piece of it."

7

Princess Sarah Blackburn had always been reluctant to use her carefully honed warrior skills in battle.

After all, the Beloved Women had formally disbanded with the passage of time, and the Trail of Tears had relocated her people from their cherished homeland in the American South. They had once waged war along rivers, fighting from huge war dugouts. But this was the land of the horse warriors, and thus, the fighting spirit of the Cherokees had become little more than memories and old war stories.

Sarah had no problem with that. As a blooded warrior herself, and a cultured and educated woman, she welcomed peace. But these things happening daily in The Nations—clearly, that filthy jackal Baptiste Menard intended to once again get her people relocated, shipped to some desert waste or swamp-infested hellhole that no white men wanted. That way Menard could bid on the vacated government land at ten cents an acre.

She fumed silently as she paddled her tapered, flat-bottomed bateau through a narrow ditch that was part of the Buffalo Trace, a favorite Cherokee waterway. Overhead, great white sails of cloud raced across a magnificent sky, but Sarah kept her attention focused much closer to hand. The rough, round shapes poking out of the water were beaver houses. Any one of them, however, might conceal an enemy ready to grab her boat and flip it over.

It wasn't bad enough, she thought, that Menard raped her while his lick-spittles held guns on her family and made them watch. Cherokees were not used to such vile crimes.

The shame of it caused her father to kill himself, and her mother to wither and die half out of her mind.

But no, even all that wasn't enough for Menard. Because Sarah had spurned him—had in fact promised to kill him—he was going to do dirt on the entire Cherokee Nation this time.

Or so he thought. Two nights ago, Sarah had brewed and drunk the secret Black Drink.

Solemnly, she had chanted the ancient Cherokee song that always preceded a bloody campaign:

> *Where'er the earth's enlightened by sun,*
> *Moon shines by night, grass grows, or waters run,*
> *Be't known that we are going like men, afar,*
> *In hostile fields to wage destructive war.*

Now she was sworn to one of only two courses of action: victory or death. Since it was the *head* of a snake that carried the poison, that's what Sarah intended to lop off. She would kill Baptiste Menard once she tracked him down in his mountain hideout. She had avoided it too long, and *now* look at how her delay had cost her people.

As the afternoon sun began to fade toward the horizon, she was suddenly worried. For some time dust puffs had been rising from the sandy terrain bordering the water, terrain partially blocked from her view by a screen of pine and dogwood trees, by thick tangles of vines and brambles. Somebody was tracking her.

Sarah did not let fear paralyze her. She made sure the powder load in her scent-bottle pistol had not clumped, then laid it beside her on the thwart, the board seat. A light, but deadly, reed lance lay in the bottom of the boat alongside a war hatchet, her musketoon, and her blowgun. Her primary weapon, however, was her huge osage-wood bow and the fox-skin quiver stuffed double full with fire-hardened arrows. Every War Woman was an expert with one weapon, and Sarah had mastered the bow. The weapon was silent, deadly, and, after years of practice, she could fire up to fifteen arrows accurately in one minute.

Suddenly, a quail darted from cover right beside her. *"Yiii-eee-yah!"*

Sarah's heart leaped into her throat when a powerfully built renegade Kiowa, grinning with triumph, popped up from his well-hidden blind near the water's edge. Sarah recognized the object in his right hand as a toss net braided from horsehair.

He cocked back his arm to flip it over the pretty Cherokee. But War Women never panicked—and knowing their fate if captured, they never surrendered. A heartbeat later, the Kiowa shrieked like a hog under the blade when Sarah's spinning war hatchet sliced deep into the meat of his right thigh.

However, Sarah was far from safe. The renegade was down in the water and screaming, but close by, others were debouching from a narrow defile between two adjacent ridges and converging on her location.

She quickly back-paddled toward the opposite bank, ducking another toss net. The water was shallow, and another warrior, yipping hideously to unnerve her, leaped out to grab her boat. Sarah notched an arrow, and the huge bowstring *fwipped,* slapping hard against the leather band protecting her left wrist.

The arrow punched clear through the warrior's vitals and dropped out of his back, leaving him dead in the water. But Sarah felt her heart sink like a stone when she started to paddle furiously away, to the south: several braves stood in the water ahead, waiting for her with a net stretched between them.

And when she glanced quickly north, behind her, the same trap awaited her.

"All right, War Woman," she muttered to herself as she realized the grim facts. "It is victory or death, no middle way. Save the last bullet for yourself."

Oddly, though, given the terrible danger she faced, her last thoughts were not of her entire life flashing before her eyes. Rather, she thought of Skye Fargo and their stolen pleasure in the forest. And the disappointing realization that she'd never have that pleasure again.

"Damnation!" crusty old Yellowstone Jack was moved to exclaim. "That pretty little Cheraw gal is a reg'lar tiger in a whirlwind, ain't she? *Look* at that little hellcat dealin' misery to them Injins."

Fargo and Jack had left their mounts ground-hitched in screening timber and moved rapidly toward the water on foot, weapons at the ready. One renegade, a hatchet still embedded in his thigh, had crawled into the tall weeds to hide his shame at his screaming—Indian men were exhorted to endure pain in silence. Another brave floated facedown in the water, and several more had been wounded.

But Fargo saw that Sarah, too, was in trouble.

The "Beautiful Death Bringer" was living up to her name, all right, in all regards. The long jet hair in its silver clasp, the wine-red lips, the short jacket that exposed a flat stomach and outlined magnificent breasts—she was a stunning beauty. But she was also badly outnumbered, and these were the worst among Indian hardcases.

"Look at those damn nets," Fargo said as they sprinted forward to better positions. "Sure, she's a looker. But all this trouble *can't* just be to rape her. Indians don't risk death for that. So why is it so damn important to take her alive?"

"Ransom, mebbe? On account she's a boner-fee-day blue blood."

Fargo nodded. "Distinct possibility. And come to think on it, taking her alive may not be the renegades' idea, at that. Baptiste Menard is infamous for his taste in Indian females. One of the biggest squaw men in the West."

A moment later Fargo called out, "Shit! Up and on the line, Jack. They're charging her!"

There was no time to move closer—a ferocious charge by at least six braves had the gutsy Cherokee War Woman bent, but not quite broken. Though overwhelmed, she obviously intended to die fighting.

"Hell, I done that little gal wrong," Jack fretted as he opened fire. "She's fightin' the very same scum I accused her of leading. Right outta the top drawer, she is."

The racket took on an authoritative new sound as Fargo's Henry and Yellowstone Jack's pistol joined the battle. Before they had time to take cover, several braves went down like grain before the scythe.

"Don't let up!" Fargo said, dropping his empty Henry and shucking out his Colt. "We got the only repeating weapons—let's keep it lively for 'em!"

"Just hope we can get reloaded 'fore they swarm on us," Jack muttered as he squeezed off the single shot in his Sharps. "Elsewise, we're in some deep sheep dip."

"They won't charge," Fargo predicted. "Indians don't cotton at all to this many unexpected casualties on their side. Too many spirits died restless and are hovering nearby, looking for new bodies to take over. These braves'll ride off to get shut of the bad medicine hereabouts."

Fargo was right. One of the renegades blew a shrill eagle-bone whistle, and they immediately retreated into the nearby hills, taking their dead and wounded. Both men immediately reloaded.

"Where are you, Fargo?" Princess Sarah Blackburn called out through the blue haze of powder smoke drifting like fog over the water. "Only you could have routed them so quickly."

"Oh, he had some fine help with them skunk-bitten coyotes, Your Highness," Yellowstone Jack called out in his rusty bray as the two men stepped into the clear. Jack even managed a quick, awkward bow. "The boy tends to choke, happens I ain't around to nurse him."

Fargo shook his head at the contrary old fool. Just earlier today Jack was treating Sarah like an Indian criminal. Now he was ready to bow and scrape before royalty.

"*You* helped me, snowbeard?" Sarah said, incredulous.

"And would again, *mam'selle*. Pleasure to serve, Your Purple."

Sarah studied him from skeptical, bemused eyes. "You have insulted me terribly and even tried to undress me."

"Why, sure, Your Loftiness, but that was only so's I could look at—"

Flustered, Jack fell silent and blushed. Fargo had to chew on his lower lip to keep from howling in mirth at the old fool.

"But you were both my brave friends here today," Sarah added, "and I thank you. You saved my life, and I will not forget this thing."

She took up her paddle.

"As for you, Skye," she said as she began paddling south again, "please forgive me for the unkind things I said in the soldier camp this morning. Later, I realized I was wrong, you did not report me."

She was already past them and picking up speed.

"Hey!" Fargo shouted after her. "You're not *staying* on the trace, are you? After that battle just now?"

"Of course, thanks to you and the grumpy snowbeard."

"Hold up! You're not heading into the Ouachitas?" Fargo called.

But a final wave was her only response before she disappeared around a bend.

"God's garters!" Yellowstone Jack exclaimed. "*That* gal's got starch in her corset. Though, a-course, a corset would be wasted on her."

"There goes trouble," Fargo mused.

"Trouble?" Jack repeated, still watching the Cherokee from admiring eyes. "Absodamnlutely, but she'll dish out more than she takes. She's pure hellfire unleashed."

Jack squinted at Fargo. "Didja diddle her, you lucky sumbitch?"

"Mind your own halter," Fargo told him. "The hell do you care, anyhow? You're the man who believes the perfect knothole is waiting for him somewhere. C'mon, let's make sure those renegades ain't doubling back on us."

"They was all holler and no heart," Jack scoffed as they moved cautiously out from cover. "They showed the white feather without even seeing how many guns we was."

Fargo shook his head. "I'll gamble my horse that it wasn't lack of courage. It's because of the size of their force and the fact that they have other orders. What we fought here today was only a fraction of the braves under Wolf Sleeve and Iron Mountain."

"That shines," Yellowstone Jack conceded. "Which a-course leads a man to wunner—where the hell's the rest?"

By tacit accord both men, having reached the clearing beyond the trees, gazed toward the south.

And the Ouachita Mountains, toward which the Cherokee princess appeared to be headed.

"Could be you called it right, Skye," Yellowstone Jack said. "The 'chitas. Mountains that're wendigo to any normal savage. A goddamn bloody hellhole that even the Texas Rangers refuse to ride into, and *them* boys wasn't born in the woods to be scairt by an owl."

By now they could see distant dust puffs that were fading—their enemy had not doubled back.

"Before we ride out," Fargo said, "let's go back to the water."

The renegades had left no dead behind. But an elkskin parfleche had been dropped, and the air trapped inside had kept it partially afloat. Fargo waded out into the brackish water and scooped it up.

"There it is again," he said, holding out a bone-handle knife with an obsidian blade for Yellowstone Jack to see. "Recognize the work?"

"A-course I recognize the work—it's Cheraw."

Fargo nodded. "And I didn't see one Cherokee in the bunch."

"Nary one," Jack agreed.

"If it's Menard behind this, he ain't just framing the Cherokees. He's trying to create the impression a full-bore Indian uprising is brewing in The Nations."

"To chew it a little finer," Jack reminded him as the two men headed toward their hidden horses, "he might damn well cause a *real* uprisin', not just some 'impression.' Happens he pulls that off, gonna be plenty of fresh graves poppin' up like prairie dog holes."

Fargo knew his salty friend was not just exaggerating. Any threat of Indian "uprising" was worrisome. No one tribe, of course, could ever defeat the white settlers. But if the Indians—*all* of them—ever decided to stop warring among themselves, and joined forces to defeat their common enemy, the highly feared "War of the Plains" could drive white men back east of the Mississippi.

"It could get ugly," Fargo admitted as they swung up into leather and pointed their bridles south again. "I ciphered it out once. Amongst Indians, *every* male between fifteen and late thirties is deemed a warrior, am I right?"

Yellowstone Jack grunted affirmation.

"All right, so that means that one out of six members of any tribe is ready to go to glory at any moment. Whites can't even pretend to put that many soldiers in the field."

"Hear you tell it," Jack retorted, "we might's well rein in now and dig our own graves."

A moment later, however, the old explorer cast a wary glance into the afternoon sky.

"Earlier we seen the sun and the moon," he muttered, "both in the sky at the same time. Both blood red. And us two fools ridin' smack into mountains infested with red and white devils. Hell, ain't life grand?"

Just north of the Ouachita Mountains was a huge expanse of forest and, east of the forest, a smaller mountain range called the Winding Stair Mountains. The sun was westering when the Comanche renegade Wolf Sleeve, his long black hair held back by a leather thong, raised his streamered lance overhead to signal a halt in this nearly uninhabited country.

The main force of his band, faces painted fierce for battle, gathered around him and his Kiowa battle ally, Iron Mountain.

"Brothers, have ears for my words!" Wolf Sleeve shouted. "You know me! I am a Quohada, and we Antelope Eaters are the rulers of the Staked Plain. *Never* have I cowered in my wickiup while my brothers rode to war. *Never* have I shown my back to an enemy!"

Most Indians were impressed by a forceful speaker, and now Wolf Sleeve had their full attention. He pointed south, where the Ouachitas rose stark against the sky.

"This night, like Rawhead and Bloody Bones unleashed, we will strike. You must harden your hearts until there is no soft place left. From here, let your thoughts be bloody and nothing else!"

A rallying shout went up from the mostly Kiowa and Comanche warriors, none of whom actually lived in the Indian Territory.

"But we, too, have worthy enemies," Wolf Sleeve cautioned. "You saw the mirror signals. This day, the Cherokee she bitch has eluded the band I sent to capture her. And by now you all know that he who may not be mentioned is dead."

Wolf Sleeve meant Coyote Who Hunts Grinning. Many tribes would not name the departed, believing a dead man might answer if he heard his name pronounced.

"There was no better killer on the Plains. But the Trailsman killed him. Fargo is a warrior to be reckoned with. And, even as I speak, he and the old one with snow on his face are bearing toward us. And, count upon it, Fargo *will* find our trail. He can track an ant across granite."

Wolf Sleeve untied a stolen U.S. Army blanket from his sheepskin saddle.

"Fargo is still well behind us, but they can move fast. We need time to complete our raid and return to our camp. We cannot throw Fargo off the scent forever. But we can delay him with these blankets and a false trail. Just as we rode across rocks and confused the Rangers during our attack on the Texans at Red River. You know what to do."

Working quickly, using their razor-sharp knives, each brave cut his blanket into four pieces and tied one around each of his pony's hooves. The material would not hold up very long, between sharp hoof and hard rock, but would eliminate scratch marks on rock for a distance of a few thousand feet.

When his men were ready, Wolf Sleeve turned them due east across an expanse of almost bare rock. Ten braves, however, had not covered their ponies' hooves and were sent due west. This was the usual trail taken by anyone wanting to enter the western end of the Ouachitas, where most hardcases—red *and* white—holed up.

"Will Fargo take the bait?" Iron Mountain asked, breaking his usual silence.

"At first," Wolf Sleeve predicted. "But a cunning man like him will puzzle the false trail out. Remember, brother: we only need to delay him, not fool him utterly."

The big Kiowa shook his head at this. "Fool him? We had better *kill* him. He will ride upon the aftermath of what we will do this night. And when he discovers the slaughter, his wrath will be great."

"I said to respect him, not fear him," Wolf Sleeve said, his sun-bronzed face twisted into a determined frown. "Of course we will kill him, and his slow dying will make the recent deaths at Sweetwater Creek look merciful."

8

Hour after weary hour, Fargo and Yellowstone Jack pounded their saddles, heading south toward the mountain country. They had picked up a worrisome trail—also bearing south and about a day ahead of them were at least two-dozen Indians, moving rapidly.

"Looky here," Jack called out, reining in his rebellious ginger and swinging down to pick up an object from beside the trail.

The old man's eyes, Fargo marveled, were worth more than two extra men. He watched Jack hold up a discarded length of bark, covered with remnants of bright mineral paints.

"Indians only paint for battle or holy ceremonies," Fargo remarked.

"A-huh. And don't seem likely they're headed to a sun dance, huh?"

Fargo shook his head, the ruggedly handsome features troubled. "I've faced down Apaches making their last stand. Been trapped by Comanches on the Llano. Tortured by Mountain Utes, held captive by Cheyenne Dog Soldiers. But this bunch under Wolf Sleeve and Iron Mountain would gut their own mothers for a good belch."

"Tell the truth and shame the devil, boy. But why would they attack their own stronghold?" Jack wondered aloud. "Happens they hold this trail, they're on a plumb bead straight into the western part of the 'chitas. Ain't like Injins to shit where they eat."

"Seems loco," Fargo agreed. "But I've met damn few crazy Indians. They got no plans to foul their own nest. Remember, Menard is the big bushway, to them. At his orders, they mean to bring somebody the worst hurt in the world."

"But who?" Jack pestered. "Who's up there but worthless hardcases?"

"Best I know, there was some buffalo hiders squatting there a long time ago. But they were killed or driven off by Kiowas."

As the two men heeled their mounts into motion again, Fargo gazed around in frowning scrutiny.

"It's possible," he conceded, "that they've already struck somewhere else and are heading back."

"Possible," Yellowstone Jack agreed, his tone as skeptical as his walnut-wrinkled face.

Fargo shared his skepticism. Usually, Indian braves divided up after an attack, to leave confusing trails. This group was sticking together.

The two riders held a fast trot, conserving their horses' energy while also maintaining a steady pace mile after mile. A dry-weather sandstorm suddenly stirred up, stinging tears from their eyes; both men braved it. Their urgency spurred them on.

About an hour of sunlight remained when Fargo suddenly caught a scent of woodsmoke.

"Southern Cheyenne rez is just ahead," he said. "And they ain't so tolerant of whites as the Cherokees are. Be better if we could skirt it."

"Can't be did," Jack said bluntly. "This here's the driest stretch of the Territory—dry as a year-old cow chip. Our horses'll hafta tank up here at the creek. Happens it ain't dried up 'r pizened with dead animals."

Fargo reluctantly agreed. They broke free of the scant tree cover and saw the desolate Southern Cheyenne sector below them in the mellow glow of a dying sun. Seeing it, Fargo realized why most of the Cheyenne tribe, including the entire Northern branch, refused to report to the reservation.

"God's trousers," Jack muttered. "*This* old stag would druther be gutshot than live like that."

Fargo could only agree. In the glory days, a Cheyenne summer camp at the confluence of the Powder and Little Powder rivers was one of the great wonders of the West.

Here there was only a drab gravel slope rising up from the bed of nearly dry Crying Horse Creek. Rustic dwellings of mud-chinked logs were scattered among shriveled, leather-leafed cottonwoods. The women and children scattered about looked as listless as the trees.

"Crops all died in the fields," Fargo remarked. "No rain, and the creek got too low for irrigation. Though it's true most Plains Indians don't take to farming."

"Provin' even a savage has his points," Yellowstone Jack opined.

The moment the two horsebackers debouched from tree cover, they had been assaulted by a hot, dry, gravel-laden wind that seemed continuous.

"Those braves down by the pole corral," Fargo remarked as they kneed their mounts forward, "have already spotted us. Best give the sign."

Both men raised one hand high, palm forward, in the universal sign that a rider was approaching with no weapon in hand.

"Don't feel right," Yellowstone Jack said quietly as they drew nearer. "Agin' the law or no, them bucks got weapons somewheres. A Cheyenne is *born* on the warpath. 'Sides, an Injin what's got no weapons feels naked and won't meet a white man's eyes. These bucks is starin' at us like preachers at sinners."

Fargo feared his friend was right. "Eyes to all sides," he muttered. "Christ sakes, try not to insult one, Jack."

"Hunh! Might try not to *kill* one."

Fargo snorted. "That's a good idea, seein's how you work for the Indian Bureau now."

The old man's dour face brightened. "Hell, I forgot. I do, don't I? Well, they's a few soldiers I wouldn't mind pluggin'."

About a half-dozen braves had been breaking a mustang to the halter in the corral near the creek, but as the two whiteskins rode closer, the young men stopped and stared at them in hostile silence.

Fargo ran a quick eye over the group and selected the most likely hothead, a tall, fiery-eyed youth who wore scalps on his sash in defiance of Indian Bureau rules.

The moment the brave's hand went toward his parfleche,

Fargo brought his arm down. Quicker than eyesight, his Colt leaped into his fist and made an authoritative click as he thumbed back the hammer.

Indian warriors were often impressed by a demonstration of battle skill and were usually respectful of a superior warrior. Fargo picked a brave wearing a long crow feather with clan notchings. He fired three quick shots, and the feather was lopped off from eight inches to two.

Fargo did not insult the group by holding his weapon on them. He simply holstered it and kept riding on toward the pathetic trickle of the creek.

"You played it foxy, Skye," Yellowstone Jack murmured. "But there's prob'ly a hunnert warriors within a drum call of here. Might be, we should ride all night."

"Should, my ass," Fargo replied as he swung down and threw the Ovaro's bridle so he could drink. "We have to anyway. That way we can make the Ouachitas by sunrise or so. Trouble's headed that way, and it's coming with a bone in its teeth."

Only thirty minutes of sunlight remained when Fargo and Yellowstone Jack resumed the trail. They had just put the reservation behind them when Jack, whose ears were as good as his eyes, suddenly reined in.

"Hear that?" he said, one ear cocked toward a willow thicket beside the trail.

Fargo listened and detected monotonous chanting.

"Smell that?" he said. "Somebody's burning sweet grass."

Jack, who spoke more Indian tongues than did Fargo, listened a little longer. " 'Nothing lasts long, only the earth and the mountains.' Why, it's the Cheyenne death song."

Fargo swung down and threw the reins forward to hold the Ovaro in place. "Might be none of our mix. But let's take a squint."

With his palm resting on the butt of his Colt, Fargo threaded his way carefully through the thicket with its curtain of willow fronds. The chanting, though in a weak voice, grew louder.

He pushed into the interior clearing and saw a small fire burning within a circle of rocks. A funeral scaffold made from strong saplings filled much of the clearing. An emaciated old brave, wrapped in a moth-eaten buffalo robe swarming with vermin, seemed completely unsurprised by the sudden appearance of a curious white man.

"Fargo," he greeted the new arrival in English, his voice airy with weakness.

Yellowstone Jack pushed in beside Fargo. It took the Trailsman a few moments to recognize any features in the face stretched parchment thin over its skull.

"Silver Bear," he finally said, recognizing a former sub-chief from the Powder River country up north. "Why are you here alone?"

"My time has come," Silver Bear rasped, pointing a sticklike finger at the scaffold. "A warrior should die in solitude. But I am not alone, Fargo. Maiyun, the Good Supernatural, stands beside every brave Cheyenne to guide him to the Land Beyond the Sun."

Fargo and Jack exchanged a quick look. One glance made it clear that Silver Bear was indeed on the threshold of death. Even crusty old Jack's eyes were bright with sympathy and respect for the tough old brave.

"Tell me how you die," Jack whispered to Fargo, "and I'll tell you what you're worth."

"Fargo," Silver Bear said, "many visions come to a dying man. Some of them are false visions placed over his eyes by enemies. But I have seen you, in my fever dreams, riding into the Ouachita Mountains."

Fargo felt an uneasy stirring in his stomach. He was no huge believer in things supernatural. But Silver Bear had been a great shaman in his day—and how could a dying old man, holed up in a willow thicket, possibly know where Skye Fargo was headed?

The ghostly howling of the Hell Hounds . . . seeing the sun and the moon in the sky at the same time . . . was this yet another death omen?

"See anything else, grandfather?" he coaxed, using the Indian term of respect for older men.

"Sadly, very little. Just blood. So much blood that my vision ran red."

Fargo knelt to stir up the fire. The day was still warm, but the suffering Cheyenne was wracked by chills.

"Blood," Fargo repeated, confused and uncertain. But whose?

"Don't make sense a-tall," Yellowstone Jack whispered,

reading Fargo's troubled face. " 'Sides white owlhoots and renegade Injins, ain't nobody in them mountains. The buff hiders what use to squat there was put to rout by Kiowas years ago."

Silver Bear somehow overheard this.

"You are wrong, salt beard," he said. "There is a clan of Creek Indians, perhaps two dozen of them, living in the Ouachitas. No warriors. Only farmers with squaws and young ones. They have defied the boundaries of their lowland reservation—the water is more plentiful in the mountains. So far the bluecoats and the Indian Bureau have ignored them."

It was nearly pitch dark now, and Silver Bear's face seemed to float, ghostlike, in the burnt-orange glow of the fire.

"Western end of the Ouachitas, right?" Fargo asked.

The old chief shook his head. "They live at Broken Bow Lake."

Fargo and Yellowstone Jack exchanged a puzzled look.

"That lake is due east from here—damn near over in Arkansas," Jack said.

"While the war trail definitely leads to the *western* Ouachitas," Fargo added.

"It's a pisser," Jack agreed. He lowered his voice and added: "But we hafta believe a fresh trail over an old man's dyin' visions."

"Unless this bunch is just *returning* from a raid," Fargo reminded him.

Old Silver Bear, who they thought could not hear them whispering, again surprised them by speaking up.

"The braves who rode by here earlier were not merely returning, Fargo. They were painted for battle and singing the strong-heart songs sung *before* battle."

"So you actually saw them?"

The old man nodded. "Perhaps twenty warriors, Kiowas and Comanches under Wolf Sleeve and Iron Mountain. Some of their renegades were missing."

Worried now, Fargo nodded. "The missing bunch were sent to the Buffalo Trace to capture a Cherokee."

A Cherokee . . . something else occurred to Fargo. He looked at Jack, who knew plenty about the formerly eastern tribes.

"Don't the Cherokees and the Creeks have an old blood feud going?" he asked.

Jack grunted affirmation. "Feud is the very word, boy. They come to blows over river damming in the Black Mountains of Tennessee. Started even afore Dan'l Boone opened his Wilderness Trail."

The old timer paused, watching Fargo's bearded face in the flickering light. "I take your drift. Bein's how there's so much framin' of Cheraws lately, you're thinkin' mebbe the renegades mean to attack the Creeks and blame it on the Cheraws."

"It makes sense," Fargo said, "except for the trail. It's real, it's fresh. And, so far, it leads straight into the western Ouachitas. We're damn fools if we ignore a fresh trail for a hunch. C'mon, let's raise dust."

The last daylight bled from the sky, and a pale wafer of full moon took over. Fargo left the old man some strips of jerked buffalo and his extra blanket; Yellowstone Jack left a cup of whiskey and a plug of tobacco.

"Ipewa," the old chief said with a parting nod. "Good. I will not have to die without one last taste of earthly pleasures. May the high holy ones ride with both of you. Perhaps we will meet as friends in the Land of Ghosts."

Perhaps, Fargo thought as he stirruped and swung up onto the hurricane deck. But when he gazed into the dark maw of the night, so like a giant cave, he hoped he and Silver Bear wouldn't meet *too* damn soon.

Orienting by the polestar and the major constellations, the two frontiersmen continued riding through the night.

Only a truly dire situation could induce Fargo to ride after sunset. A horse was a wondrously designed creature except for its one weakness—the area from the fetlock, just behind the hoof, to the cannon bone of the lower leg. The chances of laming a horse on a rock, or in a gopher hole, were alarmingly high at night. In hostile country, a man whose horse foundered was marked for carrion bait.

Several hours after leaving the dying Cheyenne, the two friends stopped at Red Oak Creek to spell and water the horses. A quick meal of tack and beans was Fargo's first nourishment of the long day.

"Good clay here," Yellowstone Jack remarked, scooping a handful out of the creek bed.

Fargo took his meaning. White facial skin reflected moonlight and made riders easier targets. When Jack started to smear his cheeks and forehead, Fargo stayed his hand.

"Do that when we ride out," he said. "Right now we're going to prepare our eyes for night riding."

"Cost us time."

"True. But considering who we're up against, we'll need every advantage."

"That rings right," Jack agreed.

So both men freed their blankets from the cantle straps and wrapped them tightly around their heads. For the next half hour, while the horses rested and grazed the lush bunch grass, they let their eyes adjust to absolute, total darkness.

When he finally unwrapped his head, Fargo marveled at his increased night vision. Night was now more like dawn. He could see farther into the darkness, and make out far more details.

"Hear that?" Jack remarked as the two riders hit the trail again, bearing west to skirt the huge forest that told them the Ouachitas were only hours away.

Fargo nodded. The yipping bark of a "coyote" had just sounded—answered by another bark. There were indeed coyotes in this area. But their long, drawn-out howl was cleverly imitated by various Plains Indians.

"Harassment's coming," Fargo guessed aloud. "I'd wager Wolf Sleeve has left a couple braves back to slow us down. Prob'ly watching us right now."

"Piss on you mother-ruttin' blanket asses!" Yellowstone Jack roared out in a rusty bray that silenced the insects. Recalling a battle rhyme from his early Indian-fighting days in the Blackfeet Wars, he also roared out at the night:

> I and the gun,
> With Brother Ball;
> In whatever fight,
> We equal *all*!

76

This filled Jack with such bravado that he began pounding his chest. But the very instant he fell silent, an arrow sliced through the night. It missed the old explorer by inches as it thwacked into his cantle roll.

Scared witless, Jack nearly leaped off his horse. Then he fired off a stream of vivid curses to mask his shame at being spooked like a raw pilgrim. Despite the danger they both faced, Fargo couldn't help sputtering with laughter.

"You contrary old blowhard," he was finally able to remark. "All those white hairs, yet you don't know better than to taunt Indians? Hell, talk about poking fire with a sword."

"Did it a-purpose," Jack lied, "to flush 'em out."

"Yeah? Well, now they're flushed, go bag 'em."

"Bag a cat's tail!"

The two men were traversing open grassland now, the terrain mostly low hills and the huge, dark mass of forest on their left. The outline of the Ouachita Mountains was visible straight ahead, blocking out thousands of fiery stars.

Fargo peered through his hands to cut reflection from his face. But even with his increased night vision, he couldn't see anything that didn't belong to the place.

"Our 'coyote' friends are still out there somewhere," he remarked, reaching down to knock the riding thong off the hammer of his Colt. "Wonder what they got planned for us next?"

"Nothin' *I* can't skin," Yellowstone Jack bragged. "Back in the shining times, *this* hoss prac'ly sent entire goldang tribes to glory by hisself. Ain't a red son alive can—*by the twin balls of Christ!*"

Real fear charged Jack's voice, and a second later Fargo saw why. A large, bright orange flame was streaking like a meteor through the grass toward them! It did not appear like any "natural phenomenon" Fargo had ever seen— more like some demon that had just broken loose from Hades, bringing hellfire with it.

Fargo hoped to turn the Ovaro away before he spotted it, but he was too late. The black-and-white pinto, driven to instant panic by fire, damn near dumped Fargo when he reared straight up, chinning the moon.

Jack's gelding, too, went wild with fear, quickly bucking

its stupefied rider, then tearing off into the night. Fargo managed to control the Ovaro just long enough to leap safely off.

"Suffering Moses! It's African juju!" screamed Jack as he came to his knees, unable to move farther.

Fargo wasn't ready to go that far. But it *still* reminded him of something loosed from hell as the plume of fire continued racing straight toward them.

"Good heart of God, Skye! Shoot the son of a bitch! It's after us, boy!"

Fargo, unsure exactly how to shoot a demon, aimed for a point just ahead of the flames. The red-belching Colt leaped several times as he fired. Relief washed over Fargo when the flames abruptly stopped moving forward.

"The *hell*?" Yellowstone Jack fumed as he stood up, slapping at dirt.

"Think I just figured it out," Fargo said as the two men moved cautiously toward the flames, still sawing in the wind.

Fargo's hunch was right: he had just shot a coyote whose tail had been oiled and set ablaze.

"Saw it done once years ago in the Mormon country," Fargo said, stamping out the small grass fire. "Utes harassing freighters along the California Trail."

He glanced carefully around them as he thumbed reloads into his Colt. "We'll have to track down our horses before those braves kill them. Keep a weather eye out, old son."

"Never mind the horses," Jack told him, pointing ahead of them. "Yonder comes another burnin' pup!"

Both men filled their hands, waiting until the terrified animal was within range. Now that they knew what they faced, there was no danger to them from the coyote. But unless they killed it, it could ignite a horrific grass fire.

"Hold your powder another few seconds," he told Jack.

At first, when a firearm detonated close by, Fargo thought Jack had fired early. But when the old scout whirled around, cursing like a Bowery pimp, Fargo felt a ball of ice replace his stomach. This second coyote was only a feint so the renegades could attack from behind.

Fargo, too, whirled and dropped to one knee. The full moon, and star-shot sky, revealed a harrowing sight: two Comanches, stripped and painted for battle, rushing them

with a kill cry on their lips. Fargo thanked God the renegades didn't have repeaters—they had already fired their
old cap-and-ball pistols, missed, and switched to bows and
arrows.

But their deadly skill left the issue in doubt. Neither
Fargo nor Yellowstone Jack could get a good bead while
wildly ducking to save their hides. Arrows *fwipped* through
the tall grass, so many the air fairly hissed. Fargo felt a
sharp tug, and a hot tickle of fletching, as one passed
through the folds of his buckskin shirt.

"I and the gun!" Jack roared out, and Fargo heard the
loud, repeated explosions of his magazine pistol peppering
the two Comanches.

But, incredibly, even a fusillade of six bullets whistling
past their ears did not delay the headlong charge. And now
they were close enough for Fargo to guess why: they were
in a battle trance induced by long hours of dancing and
chanting. Both white men knew what that state meant—
their attackers had become numb to fear.

"It's come down to the nut-cuttin'!" Fargo told Jack.
"We break the charge *now* or we're gone beavers!"

He regretted that the Ovaro had absconded with his
Henry. Fargo rose boldly into view, sighted on the right-
hand Comanche, and squeezed off three rounds. At least
one tagged the brave in the chest, and he collapsed in a
rolling tumble.

Fargo swerved his aim toward the second renegade, but
before he could fire the Comanche had bolted off. Fargo
heard his dying comrade groaning in the grass, but ignored
it. He gave no help to any man who tried to murder him.

"Don't make sense a-tall," Yellowstone Jack repeated as
the two men set off to track down their mounts. "Lookit
all the trouble Menard has took to keep us from catchin'
them redskins afore they get to the 'chitas. Yet, there ain't
nothin' *in* them damn mountains worth a kiss-my-ass. It
just don't cipher."

"Nothing in *this* end, you mean," Fargo reminded him.

"The trail leads this-a-way, don't it? You been a trailsman since you went to long britches. Now, alla sudden, you
gonna follow *visions* and just ignore hoofprints?"

"Pains me to say it, but you're right," Fargo said. "All
we can do is read the sign and wait."

"Well, God's garters!" Jack exclaimed. He had turned around to glance back toward the dying Comanche. Fargo looked, too. Silver-white moonlight limned everything in a ghostly light.

The second Comanche had sneaked back to his fallen comrade. With his arms he embraced the dying brave. Then, flapping his arms, he imitated an eagle's call. When he started chanting in Comanche, Jack translated: "Father in heaven, this, our brother, is coming."

"Be *two* of yous this trip," Jack muttered, jerking his pistol from his sash.

Fargo stayed his hand.

"H'ar now!" Jack protested. "You a damn Quaker now? That red varmint just tried to lift our dander!"

"He was armed, that was battle. He's praying now. Let him do his rituals."

"Hell, ain't *you* sweet lavender?" Jack spat out. "Since when do you believe in that religious claptrap, Skye?"

"I don't, but they do. And I respect a man's beliefs."

Jack spat again, his contempt clear in his voice. "Looks like you been palaverin' with that Indian lover, Talcott Mumford."

"Put a sock in it," Fargo whispered. "I see my pinto, and your ginger is grazing nearby."

" 'I respect a man's beliefs,' " Jack repeated. "Son of a bitch tried to kill us."

"So what?" Fargo shot back, stealing closer to the horses. "You got plans to cheat the Reaper?"

9

The fifth day after the shocking massacre of Colonel Oglethorpe dawned overcast and chilly. Riding all night, Fargo and Yellowstone Jack had skirted the large expanse of forest that included the Winding Stair Mountains. Now they were in the foothills of the Ouachitas, following the fresh war trail and staying close to the murky shadows under the trees.

A deep, almost unnatural silence hung like a heavy cape over these ancient mountains, first named by the Sioux. Thickly treed slopes, shelving rock overhead, and huge tumbles of scree made the Ouachitas an ambusher's paradise.

"Would you goldang mind tellin' me," Jack groused, extra scratchy from lack of sleep, " 'zacly *why* we rode up into these god-forgotten mountains, anyhow? Besides your itch to bull that Cheraw beauty."

"Why, to get your life over quick, old man," Fargo replied affably, lake-blue eyes prowling the slopes above them. "And because the trail leads here."

"Serve it on toast, Fargo! You was headed here *before* we picked up that trail."

"Sure. Scuttlebutt has it that Menard's got his headquarters in these mountains."

Yellowstone Jack farted with his lips. "Menard? Huh! That slick bastard's always got many holes to his burrow."

"Pipe down, you doddering old pus bag," Fargo snapped. "Sound carries in these mountains."

They not only had Menard and his paid gun-throwers to watch for—these mountains were crawling with renegades, at least some of whom were clearly working for Menard.

Fargo trusted Sarah Blackburn's skills as a warrior, especially after watching her in action. But coming into this evil bastion, all alone, a beautiful woman—she had better pray for death over capture.

"The hell they headed?" Jack speculated aloud, watching Fargo study the churned-up earth in front of them.

"Damned if I know," Fargo admitted. "But I just realized something now that it's light enough to see better. We're following fewer riders now than before. Matter fact, looks like the main body has peeled off."

Fargo gazed at the trail in frowning scrutiny.

"Shit!" he swore, irritated at being fooled. "They knew we wouldn't be able to get an accurate count of riders by moonlight. Wolf Sleeve sent about ten riders on up here, enough to keep us riding drag on the decoy."

Yellowstone Jack nodded, for it was typical Indian cunning.

"So where the hell *are* them red devils?" he wondered, glancing around them. Pockets of mist lay like mattresses in the hollows.

"Only way to find out," Fargo replied, reining the Ovaro around, "is to head down our backtrail and see where they veered off."

It proved to be a slow, painstaking, back-wrenching effort. Yellowstone Jack kept his eagle eye out for trouble while Fargo, the superior tracker, climbed in and out of the saddle searching for a side trail.

An hour ticked by, then two, the September sun growing warmer and heavier on Fargo's shoulders as the clouds blew away.

"Hell's bells, Skye!" Jack finally carped, mopping at his forehead with a bandanna. "A passel of Injins can't just turn into vapor! Use to was, Skye Fargo could track a tiptoeing flea through a herd of buffalo. Now you—"

"Stow the chinwag, Methuselah," Fargo cut him short, swinging down from the saddle. "Look there."

By now they were nearly down on the level plain again. Fargo pointed east, toward a long slope of ridged and ribbed rock.

"Right here," he told Jack, "is where the number of riders on the original trail gets smaller. The main body split off here, most likely across that rock."

"Happens that's so," the older man reminded him, "the rock will be scratched. Even unshod hooves make scratches."

"Should," Fargo agreed, though secretly he never underestimated the wily, resourceful mind of a free-ranging Indian.

They left their horses standing, bridles down, behind a motte of pines. More time went wasting as Fargo walked slowly along the rock slope, spotting nothing to indicate a fresh trail.

"Fargo," Yellowstone Jack grumped, "mebbe you best move east and open you a barbershop. Your damn trail skills . . ."

Jack fell silent as he watched Fargo spot something on the ground. He bent down and picked up a minute fiber the color of a U.S. Army blanket. Both men understood its meaning immediately.

Their eyes met.

"Headed due east," Fargo said.

"Shit! They mean to make it hot for them Creek Injins squattin' at Broken Bow Lake," Jack replied. "Wolf Sleeve led us down a false trail."

Fargo broke into a run, returning to his horse.

"They've got a good jump on us," he called out. "Matter fact, prob'ly already attacked. But maybe not. All we can do now is eat their dust and hope we're on time to stop the butchering."

The Comanches had earned the name "Red Raiders of the Plains" because of their unmatched ability to use nature for their deadly surprise attacks. Most terrifying was their unsurpassed skill at striking out of a rising, bursting sun, then fading back into the landscape—exactly the way Wolf Sleeve led the sunrise raid on the Creek clan at Broken Bow Lake.

The terrified residents, most still in their beds, were awakened by a thunder of galloping hooves and yipping kill cries. Those brave enough to glance outside saw a circling blur of pintos, mostly piebalds and skewbalds.

This close to the Texas longhorn country, lost cattle often strayed into the southern Indian Territory. The Creek clan at Broken Bow had a few bulls, along with a cow, a calf, and several yearlings, in a hillside pen. All the livestock was killed, along with the plow horses, the pigs, and the chickens.

A few of the frightened Creeks attempted to flee into the hills. They were chased down and scalped alive while their loved ones watched; then their bellies were slit open, their entrails pulled out and fed to the ravenous dogs while the horrified, screaming victims watched their own guts being devoured.

All of this rapid death and destruction required only minutes. Then the marauding renegades ransacked the dwellings before setting them ablaze.

Those who ran outside—men, women, children, the elderly—to escape the searing heat were immediately slaughtered. A few chose the flames and died amidst agonizing screams.

The raid was over in less than ten minutes, nothing left of the settlement except scattered, mutilated bodies and flaming ruins. Wolf Sleeve raised his lance overhead, and moments later the blood-lusting raiders disappeared back into the bloodred sun.

"Smell that?" Yellowstone Jack asked around midday.

Fargo had been noticing it for some time. This region was planted with sweet-smelling clover and alfalfa. Mixed in with the nose-tickling tang was the acrid stench of fire.

"I smell it," he replied, his tired face grim as he guessed the meaning of that smell.

The two friends were following a narrow, stone-walled, upland trail, still dogging the tracks of the war party. Finally they broke out onto a grassy meadow near Broken Bow Lake. Fargo watched cloud shadows, dark blue against the waving grass, move with the wind.

The mournful shriek of that wind made Fargo's skin crawl against his shirt. With all the death omens lately, at least one of them had to be right.

"Damnit," he said quietly, "no need for caution now."

Yellowstone Jack took his drift, nodding. Those lazy wisps of smoke, curling black against the china-blue sky, probably meant they were too damned late.

Fargo loosed the reins, letting the Ovaro break into a full gallop up the gentle slope. Despite the ominous signs that the attackers had struck and fled, he snatched his Henry from its leather boot and levered a round into the chamber.

As he rounded the wooded end of the lake and crested a ridge, he spotted the smoking ruins, then the scattered bodies. Fargo reined in, feeling his stomach pinch. Yellowstone Jack eased up beside him.

"Damnit," Fargo cursed with quiet bitterness. "Why did I have to fall for that blanket-around-the-hooves trick? Fell for it like a New York greenhorn. Now look what my bone-headed stupidity has caused."

"Hush that female caterwaulin'," Jack said gruffly, though the sight shocked him sick and silly, too. "We know who done this, and it sure's hell wasn't Skye Fargo."

Both horses, sniffing death, shied back and had to be coaxed when they were heeled forward at a walk.

"Damnation," Jack said when they had edged closer. "Ain't been but a few hours, judgin' by them still smokin' fires. Yet, them bodies already been chewed by vultures and coyotes. *Every*thing's double rough up here in the 'chitas.''

The debris was everywhere: bone grubbing hoes, stone hammers, weaving looms, dogskins, antelope and elk hides, tom-toms, pottery dishes—all of it scattered as if by some giant, angry hand.

"Lookit there," Jack said, pointing to an adult Creek male with a double-bitted axe buried in him to the helve— a Cherokee axe, Fargo noted, conveniently left behind.

Jack shook his hoary head at the savagery. "By the prophet's beard! Even Old Churnbrain don't make the blanket asses *this* mean."

The sight of wicker baskets lying everywhere caused Fargo's throat to shut hard, for he knew Indians used them as infants' cradles. The actual slain children he could not even gaze upon—the sight stirred up old memories he usually kept buried.

When the two men had steeled themselves, they quickly checked the bodies. One, a pregnant young woman, was somehow still alive despite having been shot in the abdomen, scalped, and viciously hacked with an axe or hatchet.

She was unconscious and bloody, bubbling froth coated her lips. Fargo glanced at Jack, who nodded once. Both men knew full well that pink froth meant a punctured lung. Out here, with no doctor or medicine, and with all her other serious injuries, she stood no chance at all.

Fargo, hating the responsibility but unwilling to let the doomed woman suffer in agony for hours in a hopeless cause, stepped behind her and drew his Colt. When it was over he turned quickly away, hot anger washing over him.

"This won't stand," he told Jack in a quiet, dangerous voice. "What they did to Oglethorpe was bad enough. But at least he was a soldier and knew the risks. These folks up here were peaceful, unarmed farmers."

Jack knew Fargo's tones, and he knew this quiet one now was the voice of implacable wrath and determination. A voice that said: *Skye Fargo is coming after you, killers, and all the devils in hell won't stop him.*

"We both seen some soul-rackin' sights in our day, Skye," Jack said, gazing around. "Thissen caps the climax."

The fires were nearly out, but when Fargo knelt near a pile of smoldering ruins, the heat was still so intense he could feel it drying the surfaces of his eyeballs.

"They most likely struck at sunrise," Fargo remarked, standing back up and feeling suddenly old. "Wolf Sleeve and most of the renegades are Comanches, and they favor sunrise attacks."

"That shines. Which means we mighta been in time, happens we hadn't been bamboozled by a false trail."

"I don't require the reminder," Fargo snapped, feeling guilty enough.

Fargo had learned to identify an attacking tribe by the ritual mutilations at the massacre scene, which differed according to tribe. The Cheyennes slashed legs so the dead could not pursue them; the Sioux battered skulls and faces to a pulp with stone clubs.

But many of the dead here had been beheaded: a ritual mutilation formerly practiced by Cherokees in their warring days.

"Them chopped-off heads ain't the half of it," Yellowstone Jack said, watching Fargo. "Lookit here."

He used the toe of his boot to roll a plumed war helmet. "That's Cheraw. So's this here."

He picked up a reed lance and pointed out the Cherokee clan marking.

"A brave with his ass on fire," Jack said, "*might* leave a lance behind—they can be made quick. But a helmet like that, made from hammered silver? A warrior would die afore he'd leave it behind."

"All this obvious framing of the Cherokees is hog stupid," Fargo said. "This was a mounted raid. But the Cherokees ain't even a horse tribe. Everybody knows they were once river warriors who fought from dugout canoes."

"Hell yes it's hog stupid," Jack retorted. "And that's ig-*zac*ly why the army will believe it."

"That, and the gold cartwheels Menard likes to spread around like manure. Even a military officer is poorly paid, let alone a common soldier."

Circling vultures reminded Fargo that the two men had a tall order on their hands: nearly two dozen bodies, and various unattached body parts, required some kind of burial.

There was no alternative—they spent a good part of the afternoon digging a common grave on a slope behind the massacre site. Using blankets, they moved the dead into their final home.

Yellowstone Jack, who occasionally professed to be a believer, mangled the Lord's Prayer. Even Fargo, ever the honest pagan, said a heartfelt "amen" and knuckled moisture from his eyes before shoveling in dirt to cover those anguished faces.

"What now?" Jack demanded. "Long as we're in the 'chitas, I say we track down that nose-talkin' bastard Menard and castrate the son of a bitch."

Fargo whistled to the grazing Ovaro, who came trotting toward him.

"Nothing I'd love better," Fargo said. "But it'll have to wait. First, you and me got to find a covert somewhere and get some sleep. The horses are near done in, too. Then we're gonna ride to the military outpost close by at Clayton. There's a telegrapher there."

"So what?" Jack demanded. "There's a wart on my ass, too. The hell we need a telegrapher for?"

"We have to notify Talcott Mumford about the massacre."

Jack goggled. "Turd, have you been grazin' loco weed? Notify Mumford? Why, Jesus Katy Christ on a crutch! Oh, he ain't so bad, for a white-livered schoolman. But wunst we tell him, *he* has to notify them dough-bellied snuff-takers in the gum'ment."

Fargo nodded, not liking it any more than did his angry friend. A massacre report now could very easily trigger a fearsome official response that included martial law and even lockdowns of reservation Indians. Such a response *would* cause an uprising—a real one.

"We can't be drawing Indian Bureau pay," Fargo explained as he tacked the Ovaro, "and not report this. Matter fact, keeping it quiet would be a crime. That gives Menard and his bought-off soldiers an excuse to lock us in the stockade."

"Menard," Yellowstone Jack said in a low, ominous tone as he sneaked up on his ginger gelding so it couldn't nip him in the ass, "is gonna die just as hard as the folks done here today. And then I mean to piss on his bones. I ain't no Injin lover, Skye, but the red man was made by the same God what made white men. You was right—this won't stand."

"Yeah, but before we get to Menard," Fargo said as the two men rode out, bearing northwest toward Clayton, "we'll have to face off with Wolf Sleeve and Iron Mountain. And dozens of renegades."

The first grin all day parted Jack's cracked and parched lips.

"So what, Fargo?" he mocked, quoting the Trailsman's own words from earlier. "You got plans to cheat the Reaper?"

10

Even as Fargo and Yellowstone Jack were burying the dead in the eastern Ouachitas, Cherokee War Woman Sarah Blackburn was courting death in the western section.

She was on foot now, her bateau well hidden in reeds down on the flats near Clayton Lake. The craft was easy to paddle and maneuver; nonetheless, she had been long at it, and her arms and shoulders were hot with pain.

Now, after an eternity spent inching upslope through knee-high grass, she was finally hidden close enough to see and hear the white outlaws hanging around the former buffalo hiders' camp.

Menard's outlaws, at the moment.

They were heavily armed and kept a sharp eye out, as if expecting trouble. Even the one renegade Comanche left behind as herd guard wore his bone breastplate.

Two of Menard's men stood so close to her, smoking and talking, that she could have reached out and spun their spur wheels. She recognized the lout with the long, angry red knife scar as Mike Winkler. The other was Stone Jeffries, close friend to the rapist Sarah recently killed.

"All set for tonight, Stone?" Winkler asked his man.

"I'll be hittin' the trail for Van Buren in about an hour," Jeffries replied. "I'm taking Lorenzo with me."

Sarah, through the protective screen of grass, saw Winkler's jagged slash of smile. "Good choice. Lorenzo *does* enjoy a brutal killing."

"Enjoys a good scalping, too, which I don't. Makes me damn near puke, the noise the scalp makes when it rips free. Sounds like a buncha damn bubbles popping."

"That's the sound of money, boy. The sound of money."

Cold fear and hot rage warred within Sarah. No doubt more slaughter of innocents was planned, and more framing of the Cherokees.

Winkler said, "Me and Seth will be handling the strike near Camp Roberts. We pull foot in just a few minutes. As for the mail rider, Tom will handle that all by himself. He left this morning."

"Gives a nice spread to the attacks," Jeffries approved. "One killing, all alone, don't even get ink. But if them newspaper calamity howlers get wind of several in one night, spread all over, now they got a 'rebellion' to gin up sales."

"That's what Menard wants," Winkler said, and Sarah alerted like a hound on point—this was the first mention of that stone-hearted monster.

"Say . . . where the hell *is* Frenchie?" Jeffries asked. "Ain't seen hide nor hair of him."

"You won't, neither. He'll stay on the move now, always does once the bloodletting starts."

"I hear he's got a hideout in the Winding Stair Mountains," Jeffries said.

"Hell, with that cunning bastard, who knows?" Winkler replied. "I've heard that about the Winding Stairs, too. But even if it's true, he's got more hideouts than that. Ol' Baptiste has made plenty of enemies. Plus, he don't trust even his own men. He'll stay on the move now."

"Let him move to the moon, long as we get paid first."

The two men strolled away, still talking, while Sarah felt her heart sink. Menard not here! Evidently no one knew for sure where he was. At least she had one clue and was familiar with the Winding Stairs, along with a good waterway to reach them from the west. If only she could find Menard there, kill him, and stop this madness.

Afternoon shadows were growing longer. Inch by careful inch, she slithered backward down the slope. Mixed with her disappointment was shame. Both of her parents had died as a direct result of what Baptiste Menard did in disgracing her for the first and only time in her life. She had delayed too long in killing him, not wanting to face the stern military authorities or jeopardize her fellow Cherokees just for vengeance.

Somehow, the horror of it all had forced her to "forget,"

to keep the images of that awful night under a tight lid. Menard's recent return to the Indian Territory had made her memories come rushing back like blood to a dead limb.

And now, imbibing the Black Drink had resolved the matter. For vengeance *and* her people, she was ready to face Death, the King of Terrors.

"There's Clayton Station," Yellowstone Jack announced just before sunset, exhaustion apparent in his tone. " 'Bout damn time. I gave Silver Bear the last of my cheerwater."

Fargo, sagging in the saddle and light-headed from lack of sleep, glanced through an opening in the trees and spotted a tight cluster of log buildings—one of the half dozen civilian trading posts authorized by the Indian Bureau. About a hundred yards beyond it was a baked-mud barracks, for this was also a small military outpost manned by a dozen, mostly forgotten soldiers.

Jack, too, gazed at the barracks as they drew nearer.

"Wunner how the shavetail's doin'?" he remarked.

"Jimmy's a good kid," Fargo said. "But Ten Bears and Standing Feather will play him like a piano. He's too damned good-natured."

Fargo watched a rider on a cinnamon gelding emerge from the trees ahead, bearing right for them.

"Be damn," said eagle-eyed Jack. "It's Gabe Johnson."

Fargo cursed quietly. He had forgotten that U.S. Marshal Gabe Johnson had his cubbyhole office and jail at Clayton. The man was middling honest, but highly incompetent, especially now that lumbago kept him in bed more than in the saddle.

"Well, we got no choice but to report the massacre to him," Fargo decided. "I was hoping to at least get first word to Talcott Mumford before it spreads like grass fire."

"Sainted backsides," Jack muttered when the marshal was in plain view. "Happens he looked any lower, he'd be ridin' on his bottom lip."

"They say he's taken to the Bible heavy lately," Fargo recalled. "With a preference for Revelation."

"That'll gloomify any man," Jack agreed.

Something had sure changed Gabe, Fargo decided. The big, neatly shorn Swede looked older than his fifty years. Big pouches sagged under his eyes. He nodded to the two new arrivals, reining in his horse. A red corduroy pillow eased the ride for his bad back.

"Skye . . . Yellowstone," he greeted them. "Hear you two are working for Mumford?"

Fargo nodded. "Speaking of which . . . we ran across a massacre earlier today at Broken Bow Lake."

Johnson flinched, then his face paled. "The Creeks?"

Fargo nodded, suddenly thinking of that woman he was forced to shoot. Anger quickened his pulse. "Wiped out."

"Lucifer's in it," Johnson muttered. "The Foul Tyrant himself. Those Indians were nothing but harmless farmers."

Jack and Fargo exchanged quick glances at the "Foul Tyrant" reference. Plenty of human devils, that look said.

"Well, there *sure's* hell harmless now," Jack put in.

"I'm pure sorry to hear it," Johnson told them sincerely. "I rode up there several times to evict them for Mumford. But they were so kind to me, I didn't have the heart. Wish I had, now. Still . . . there's no point in reporting it to me."

He opened his long black duster to show them the bare spot over his left breast.

"I just resigned," Johnson said, his tone that of a man at the end of his tether. "And I don't give a hoot *who* blames me."

"I sure don't," Fargo said honestly. "Thirty dollars a month, and beans, ain't much incentive to paint a target on your ass."

"It's not *just* the money, Skye. Jiminy! In the four years I been totin' a badge out here, I never had more than two part-time deputies for the entire Indian Territory. Why, there's dozens of *countries* ain't as big as this jurisdiction. Besides renegades, we've had scores of white owlhoots gunning for us. I've buried two good men and picked plenty of lead outta my hide. I'm shut of it."

Johnson fell silent, watching the other two men closely in the fading light of day. Fargo could see this next point was important to Johnson.

"Even all that, Skye, I was willing to face—I'm a little crazy anyway. But this trouble coming to a head now, especially since Oglethorpe was killed . . . what you found today in the mountains only proves it *will* explode like unstable nitro. Already is."

"No gainsaying that," Fargo agreed.

"And when it does, any white man foolish enough to get caught in The Nations will discover 'hell' ain't just a word. I got no shame in admitting it: I'm too damn old and too damn scared. You boys cover your ampersands, hear?"

With a curt nod, the former lawman clucked to his horse. Fargo watched a tired old man head off to an uncertain future.

"I'll be damned," Jack mused as they heeled their mounts forward. "Gabe never was no two-gun hero nor nothin'. But I never knowed him to get chicken guts."

"It ain't chicken guts," Fargo suggested, "if it's fear that comes from facing the facts for four years."

The two riders reined in before the main building that housed a trading post with a rustic saloon in the rear, connected by a dogtrot, or covered breezeway. There was still plenty of light to see the loafers whittling sticks out front, seated on empty powder kegs and hardtack boxes. They watched the new arrivals from caged eyes.

"Ever dang one is wearin' a tie-down gun," Jack muttered as the two men tied off their horses close to a stone watering trough. "Outlaw trash. Best get set to kick asses and take names."

"No, but do take your rifle," Fargo said, pulling his Henry from its boot, "or they will."

"I *hope* they try to boost that hell nag of mine, too," Jack said, chuckling. "That'll drive 'em to religion with Gabe."

"We'll send the telegram to Mumford," Fargo decided, "then have a drink, lay in some jerky and bread, and clear out. We're going to have to meet with Mumford and Jimmy, anyway, so we can all work out one strategy. We'll camp near here for a night to rest up, then head north."

Out front, where the last of the day's hot sun was fading rapidly to a copper glow, animal pelts were stretched drumhead tight on wooden frames. They had been heated by the sun all day in readiness for salting, scraping, softening, and finally, tanning.

Fargo reached for the latchstring to open the door, then stopped, staring at the wall beside it.

"Damnit, Fargo," Jack carped, trying to push around him. "Boy, you're a-courtin' hellacious death when you keep *this* child from his dram."

Fargo stayed him with a hand on the shoulder. "Damn

93

your dram. You'll wet your beak soon enough. Look at this."

"Consarn it, Skye, you know damn well I can't read nor cipher."

"You can look at simple pictures, can't you?" Fargo said.

The wall was covered with various notices, wanted dodgers, requests about missing persons, and the like. The picture Fargo meant was a crudely drawn map of the Indian Territory. Shown most prominently on the foolscap map were the major rivers, from north to south: the Cimarron, North Canadian, Canadian, Washita, and Red Rivers.

"Any problem ciphering *these* out?" Fargo demanded, pointing to a crudely drawn cannon beside each river.

"Why, they's forts," Yellowstone Jack said, puzzled. " 'Cept there *ain't* no forts at them places."

"Nope. But you know how it is. If the government suddenly feels pushed to build forts, especially in a puffing hurry, it's going to mean a bonanza in public money—especially to whoever supplies the lumber."

Jack suddenly caught on. "Menard!"

Fargo nodded. "Most likely he put this up to spread the idea and get support for it. He got rich years ago with a sawmill in the Sierras, so why not try again?"

"Rings right to me. Hell, the Cheraws are sittin' on some of the best timber ridges in The Nations."

The two men stepped inside the trading post, boot heels thumping on the rough-hewn, split-slab floor. The place smelled of leather and the strong musk smeared on beaver traps as a lure. Beaver, fox, and other pelts were stacked everywhere, pressed into tight packs for shipping back east.

The place was surprisingly crowded with loafers. Just like with the men outside, Fargo quickly realized, these were mostly frontier desperadoes. They barely looked at the two new arrivals—a sure sign that trouble would soon erupt.

The telegraph apparatus was located within plain view—and plain hearing—of anyone who cared to listen. At least the telegrapher, Fargo noticed, was a soldier, albeit a pimple-faced kid.

"Don't read this back to me, soldier blue," Fargo muttered as he slid the message form across the crude deal counter, placing a quarter-eagle gold piece on it. "Official government business."

At first the kid did as instructed, tapping out the message in Morse code, but when he reached the signature, he gaped in astonishment at his customer.

"*You're* Skye Fargo, the Trailsman?" he blurted out loud, and Fargo cringed when every head in the room swiveled toward him.

So much for secrecy, he realized. That message would be leaked before he finished a drink. Fargo knew he wouldn't get out of this watering hole without gunplay.

"Let's toss one back and then dust our hocks outta here," Fargo muttered to Yellowstone Jack, and both men headed toward the dogtrot and the saloon in back. Fargo felt every eye in the room tempted by his back.

A hardcase with a big dragoon pistol in his belt was nursing a bottle at the crude plank bar. He looked vaguely familiar to Fargo.

"One of Mike Winkler's dirt workers," Jack muttered, seeing Fargo watch the man. "Don't ride with the gang no more on account of a stove-up leg. Now the sneaky little barn rat spies for Winkler."

Fargo gazed warily about the room as they edged up to the bar. He counted eight men, all of them heeled and none of them a scholar. Fargo's glance took in the mud chimney rising from a large flagstone hearth, now being swept by a Kickapoo Indian.

"Whiskey," Yellowstone Jack barked to the baldheaded barkeep. "And slop it over the brim!"

"No need to blow like an old buffalo, gramps," complained a young tough at the far end of the bar. "Was quiet in here until *you* creaked in. Smelled a mite better, too."

While it was Fargo's way to rile cool, Jack was just the opposite. He went off like a powder charge at the first goading.

"Caulk up, you scurvy-ridden chicken-humper!" the old timer exploded. "Else old 'gramps' will feed your liver to your asshole."

The smart-ass kid was rocked back on his heels by this peppery retort. Obviously, Fargo realized, he was too green to know who he was dealing with. His grinning companions were watching, forcing him to save face.

"Well, dad! Guess that tongue of yours was pickled in brine."

"So was his heart," Fargo spoke up quickly, staying Jack's gun hand. "So it's best to ease off on old Yellowstone Jack here."

Hearing the notorious name, the troublemaker *did* ease off. Few men were eager to go toe to toe with "The White Devil of the Plains" as Jack had become known to the Indians up north in the Yellowstone drainage.

Fargo tossed back half of his whiskey, a belly-burning concoction with the kick of Taos Lightning. He noticed one of the men come in from the attached trading post and whisper something to Mike Winkler's man.

"Boys!" the spy suddenly shouted, though still avoiding Fargo's eyes. "Colonel Oglethorpe was the last hope for peace in this territory! And there's talk it was that snoot-nosed Cherokee bitch, Sarah Blackburn, that done for him. And we can thank the goddamn Indian lovers like Talcott Mumford for this whole mess."

"And the Indian lovers that work for him," another voice chimed in.

"Hold your powder," Fargo whispered to Jack, whose fuse was sizzling.

The hardcase continued to spew his hateful venom. Fargo glanced through an open doorway that led to a rickety jakes out back. The sun was slowly setting behind a flaming scarlet bank of clouds, leaving the night sky to a full moon and a wild explosion of stars.

"So much for the goldang soldiers bein' on our side," Jack grumped as he took down his second jolt of whiskey, listening to the mouthpiece at the bar. "This trash got your message before Mumford, I'd wager."

But Fargo never expected soldiers to seek the truth—that wasn't their job.

"We gotta get this 'uprising' business settled quick," he told Jack. "It's about to blow up like a gas pocket."

Darkness began to fill the chinks in the walls. The Kickapoo grabbed a handful of crumbled bark from a pail beside the hearth and dropped it on the hearthstones. It took only a few strikes with his flint and steel to set the bark ablaze. When he had a tiny flame, he lit a candle and used it to light several more along the bar.

"Them two white braves at the end of the bar don't need a candle, Chato," the hard case snarled out, well oiled with whiskey now. "They just rub sticks together, see, and that keeps their wig wam—get it?"

"Ease off," Fargo snapped to Jack, whose hand was stroking his pistol. "You go out front and get our supplies. I got to use the jakes."

Jack instantly grinned, recognizing Fargo's I-mean-business tone. He knew now why Fargo had been so patient.

Fargo ambled casually toward the back door, seemingly unaware that he was the subject of discussion. He made sure he passed close to the hard case, and sure enough, the fool rose to the bait by sticking out one foot, trying to trip Fargo.

There had been several close attempts on Fargo's life in less than a week, and he figured it was about damn time word got out: you'll pay dear for a piece of Skye Fargo's hide. So when this mouthy fool stuck out his foot, it was over in less than ten seconds and left the barroom speechless.

Fargo wasted no time with insults or threats. He set both heels hard, lowered his body mass, then punched with all his weight and muscle, a vicious uppercut that lifted the cur off his seat and sent several loosely anchored teeth flying in a spray of blood and saliva.

The man lay in a crumpled mess on the floor, his breath blowing and snorting like a played-out pack animal.

"Now me," Fargo said to the shocked room in a mild tone, "I'm particular who I drink with. That piece of shit on the floor ain't fit company for diseased hogs."

Fargo moved on to the leaning four-holer out back and, leaving his trousers tied up, sat down with his ears attuned for anyone approaching. When the long, nearby howl of a dog filled his ears, Fargo was slow at first to understand. Only after the animal fell silent did Fargo realize he'd been tricked—that hound was provoked into howling to cover the sound of approach.

A heel scraped the dirt just outside the door. Fargo had his Arkansas Toothpick only halfway out of its boot sheath when the door was violently kicked open. He glimpsed the ruined, enraged face of Winkler's spy, then the single, un-blinking eye of that big dragoon pistol.

Ka-voom!

A shattering roar of detonation, and a heartbeat later another one as the would-be murderer discharged his pistol, then collapsed like a sack of grain.

Fargo felt a nasty, white-hot line of bullet burn across the meat of his right shoulder. But he felt grateful to be alive—thanks to Yellowstone Jack, who had just blown the man to glory in time to throw off his aim.

"Christ on a mule, Skye, was you playin' with it in there?" Jack roweled him. "Hell, you shoulda knowed this lily-livered mangepot ain't got enough hard in him to kill a man in a fair fight!"

Fargo glanced around, as men poured out of the building into the moonlight, and realized he and Jack had no time to stand around reciting their coups. The next comment made clear why.

"Hey, hold your horses!" said the bartender, kneeling over the body. "This bullet hole's in the *back*."

Several of the men's mouths formed grim, straight lines of anger when they learned that their companion had been shot from behind. On the frontier, most men didn't raise much hell when they found a body with a bullet hole in the front. But a back-shooter was lower even than a barn burner or a horse thief.

A man slapped leather, but Fargo beat him to the draw. Jack, too, had his .38 at the ready.

"A man attempting murder," Fargo told them, "has got *no* rights in the matter—front, back, it's all one. Any one-man jury who tries to stop us from leaving here will get a belly full of lead for his trouble."

"And a dose of this," Jack added, busy urinating on the corpse.

Fargo bit his underlip to keep from laughing, but in fact this vulgar blasphemy was a wise move Jack had used for years—it helped create the reputation that he was a bit "tetched," and thus, a good man to let alone. No one made a move as the two men walked around front to their horses.

Fargo knew the "back shooting" just now had made them plenty of new enemies—and at a time when enough stone-cold killers were already trying to hurl them into eternity.

11

Baptiste Menard's hired murderers set to work around the same time that Fargo and Yellowstone Jack were fighting their way out of Clayton Station. Mike Winkler and his men were quick and merciless, and they left no survivors to tell the bloody truth.

Just across the border from the Indian Territory, near the Arkansas hamlet of Van Buren, an Overland stagecoach carrying three Methodist missionaries was savagely attacked. The driver and all three passengers were murdered and scalped, the coach burned to a pile of ashes.

Around the same time, in the Kansas-Osage Indian sector of The Nations, a lone mail-express rider was waylaid and literally beaten to a bloody pulp with a stone war club. He was also eviscerated, and most of his organs consumed by predators, before the next rider discovered the unspeakable remains.

Far to the east, near the confluence of Cache and Medicine Bluff creeks, bustling Fort Sill occupied a timber-rich plateau. A soldier on wood-cutting detail was sent to capture a spooked horse that had fled into the woods.

Because the broadleaf trees were still in foliage, and darkness was coming on, his vision had been dangerously blocked. Eventually he would be found beheaded, Cherokee fashion, much of his body mutilated.

Thus, like a howling wind whipping over the plains, the panic would soon spread like wildfire through the nervous whites: *Indian uprising!*

As soon as Fargo felt it was safe to take his eyes off their backtrail, he booted his Henry and reined in for a moment to get his bearings by the stars. Yellowstone Jack swung down, kneecaps popping loudly, and placed three fingertips against the trail.

"Them peckerwoods ain't followin' close," he announced. "But they're sure's hell a-followin'. Now, happens they was boner-fee-day vigilantes, out to arrest us, don't it seem likely they'd ride hell-bent for leather, a-puffin' and a-blowin'?"

"That's their usual style, all right," Fargo said, still gazing skyward. "They mean to kill us, that's why they're holding back. Plan to sneak up and snuff our wicks while we sleep. Hell, why not? We're 'Indian lovers,' ain't we?"

"*You* sure's hell are," Jack barbed. "First time I mounted a squaw, I figgered she musta shaved off her pussy hair. Then, after I topped a few more, I realized: Injins got damn little body hair."

"Oh, hell, you gotta write a book someday," Fargo replied, sarcasm etching his tone. "All the marvelous things you've seen out West."

Fargo located the polestar and swerved a few degrees east of the due-north path it indicated. That set them on a course tracking along the eastern shore of vast Lake Sardis. Despite their bone-weary exhaustion, they rode late and made camp by starlight.

"Leave a false camp?" Jack asked Fargo as both men spread their bedrolls.

Tired though he was, Fargo agreed. The false camp was an Indian trick, one of the most useful he had ever learned from them. Indians who were being pursued by enemies at night sometimes pitched a second, false camp close by on their backtrail—burning fires, sleeping "bodies" that were actually mounds of leaves, even a horse or two. Quite often, the gullible pursuers opened fire on it, alerting the real camp.

"Never did get our damn grub back in Clayton Station," Jack carped as they rode back down their trail to leave a false camp. "I'm so hungry my backbone is rubbing 'gainst my ribs."

"I'll make a rabbit snare before I turn in," Fargo said. "Too late for cooking tonight, but maybe we'll have some meat for tomorrow."

Fargo kept his eyes in motion, watching the dark wall of

forest on their left, the dazzling surface of the lake on their right, reflecting like a sea of fire-lit diamonds.

"Why do you keep watching the damn lake, John-a-dreams?" Jack demanded. "Them yellow-bellied night riders is somewhere straight ahead."

"Thought I saw something down on the water. Prob'ly just a reflection."

"Lookin' for your little Cheraw play-pretty, uh?" Jack roweled him. "Mebbe you two can play a little slap 'n' tickle?"

"When you visit those knotholes you're so partial to," Fargo retorted, "who picks out the splinters afterwards? Or does an old relic like you just keep time to the church bells?"

"Fargo, you're on the verge of hellacious death!"

Despite their levity, Fargo did wonder about Sarah and fervently hoped the headstrong beauty wasn't on a suicide mission. They found a good spot by the trail, quickly built a fire in a circle of rocks, then made the dirt-and-leaf mounds as decoy sleepers.

"No point in risking the horses," Fargo decided. "Won't need 'em here. That bunch at Clayton are gun-throwers, right enough. But gunmen are townies, they require sheets and barbers and cafes. Their trailcraft is piss-poor, and soon's they spot this camp, they'll open fire on us."

"Be damn," muttered Jack, feeling the ground again. "Christ, they ain't but twenty minutes off. Why'n't we just hunker down and give 'em a proper reception?"

Fargo liked that idea. "If we make it hot enough for this bunch, we could have a free trail behind."

They picketed their horses well back in the trees, then took up secure positions behind a fallen cottonwood. Fargo thumbed reloads into the Henry's tube magazine; then he laid his Colt ready to hand.

"Won't be long now," Jack said, his ear just above the ground.

Sure enough, a few minutes later Fargo heard the metallic clinking of bit rings. The sound stopped when the riders halted out on the trail. A few minutes later, low-crouching figures appeared in the moonlight.

Fargo stayed his friend's hand, wanting this to be attempted murder before they opened fire.

A moment later, it was. A red streak of muzzle flash, a whip-cracking sound of gunfire, and the lead figure had fired on the closest "sleeper."

"Put at 'em!" Fargo barked, and chaos and death suddenly seized the night.

Fargo couldn't be sure how many men he counted in range, how many more were out on the trail. But the sharp cries of pain and terror, as the ambushers were ambushed, proved their fire was effective.

At first, one or two of the gang were returning effective fire themselves. Fargo took a hard knock when a chunk of gnarled cottonwood bark flew into his forehead. But soon several men were down, the rest put to rout. The ones waiting on the trail hadn't even delayed for their friends, bolting at the first sign of trouble.

"Goddamn weak sisters," Yellowstone Jack crowed, reloading his magazine in the first lull of combat.

"This bunch ain't high caliber," Fargo agreed, reloading his Henry by feel in the darkness. "But we can expect rougher sledding from Mike Winkler and the gun-throwers he keeps as his personal gang."

"That shines. And Winkler is peaches and cream 'longside Wolf Sleeve and Iron Mountain."

Moving cautiously, they went out into the moonlit clearing. Three dead men, a fourth who was groaning piteously.

"Help me, old-timer," he begged Jack, clutching his ankle.

"All right," the veteran explorer said, immediately shooting him in the head. "Feels better, don't it?"

Fargo had no objection—once these ruthless, lawless savages had opened fire, they announced they were nothing but murdering scum. Extermination was the best defense against their kind.

"We'll sleep all right tonight," Fargo predicted as they rode back to their real camp. "With four men dead, they'll make no more fancy forays. But with Gabe gone now, and no law in his place, they'll be reporting their own version of that shooting back at Clayton."

"A-course, and likely claim we also murdered them maggots that're growing cold back yonder. But so what, these tinhorns ain't law."

Fargo said nothing, his thoughts roaming far afield. For

him and Jack, all this began five days ago with the poison-dart murder of Trooper Robinson. In less than one week, the ante had been upped to raw massacre in the Ouachitas.

He had seen the pattern before, and Fargo feared the worst savagery was yet to come—unless he and Yellowstone Jack could pull off a frontier miracle, and mighty damn quick.

"Ain't had no decent chuck in days," Jack groused. "*Now,* by the Lord Harry, I tie on the feed bag."

He made excited little grunting noises as he rolled fist-sized balls, made of cornmeal and water, that he'd mixed in one half of his bull's-eye canteen. Jack had saved some bacon to press into the batter. When they were ready, he tossed the balls directly into the ashes of their fire to bake.

"Tonight, turd, we eat good fixins," he gloated to Fargo.

"Speaking of that . . . we still got tomorrow to worry about."

Fargo was resting with his head on his saddle. He reached into a pannier and removed a one-yard length of twine. He found a good spot nearby and used a few green twigs to make a rabbit snare.

"This damn shoulder burns," Fargo told his companion, rubbing the raw bullet crease. "I'm going down to the lake to find some mud."

"Gonna diddle your little Cheraw princess?" Jack called out behind him. "Hey! Bring *me* a chaw off that stuff!"

"Just keep your nose to the wind, Methuselah," Fargo told him. "And try not to drool on my supper."

Fargo left his Henry in camp and threaded his way down a tree-covered slope to the grassy shore of the lake. He gathered soothing mud for a poultice. Packing it into a piece of thin cloth, he started tying it around his arm.

"Mud is good, Skye Fargo, but this is better."

Fargo had developed steady nerves over the years. How else could a man survive all the scrapes he'd been in? Sudden gunshots or rockslides, explosions, the *thwap* of a deadly arrow—these dangers and more he had taken in his long stride.

But the sudden sound of a melodic female voice, when he was sure he was alone in the wilderness, made it feel like a cold hand had squeezed his heart.

Sarah Blackburn, the "Beautiful Death Bringer," stepped out from a thicket into the luminous moonwash.

"This is what you need, Skye," she told him, looking away from him as was the Cherokee custom when speaking.

She removed a huge leaf from her parfleche. She had filled it earlier with a paste of gentian root, anticipating an injury while she was in the Ouachitas.

"I heard the shooting earlier," she told him. "I am happy this is your only wound."

Fargo already had his shirt off, the brisk night wind goose-pimpling his flesh. The moment she touched the soothing, cooling paste to his burning shoulder, relief washed over it.

"Feel good?" she asked, her hand still rubbing his arm.

"Damn good," he assured her, "and the good feeling is starting to spread."

Fargo felt a familiar stirring and was on the verge of inviting Sarah back behind the thicket. Then he got a closer look at her. Clearly, the beauty was worn to a frazzle and showed obvious signs of hard, fast travel.

"When's the last time you ate?" he asked her.

"When your God was a boy," she admitted, and they both laughed.

"C'mon, we got plenty," Fargo told her. He led her back toward the camp.

"Mind if I ask what you been up to?" Fargo asked. "You went up into the Ouachitas, right?"

She nodded. "I went to kill Baptiste Menard," she announced bluntly. "But the low-crawling spawn of a worm has hidden himself while his paid killers carry out his orders."

"That's his style," Fargo agreed.

"Yes. And he is unleashing the worst hurt in the world for us Cherokees."

"For *all* the tribes in the Indian Territory," Fargo corrected her. "And the whites, too, if this 'uprising' turns real."

Loud, off-key singing reached their ears.

"Is that the snowbeard?" Sarah asked, amazed. "In a *good* mood?"

"Ah, the old fart ain't had a solid bite in days," Fargo

said. "He's about to wrap his teeth around his favorite meal, corn dodgers with bacon. The man's in transports."

Just as Fargo and Sarah broke into the camp clearing, the cruel farce unfolded. Jack walked away from the campfire to gather a few sticks. Instantly, his sly ginger gelding, on a long tether nearby, seized the moment.

The ginger pranced over to the fire and quite deliberately began stomping on the corn dodgers and pawing the ground to crush them.

"God-in-whirlwinds! You spavined bucket of glue!" Yellowstone Jack roared out in passionate denunciation of all things four-legged. "You ugly, dish-faced, ricket-riddled, hell-born bastard! I'll cut you to wolf bait, you grass-grubbing whore!"

Despite their own exhaustion, and the loss of their supper too, Fargo and Sarah laughed so hard at the spectacle that they had to drop to the ground. Jack was still so sputtering mad he was shaking a fist at the ginger, which switched its tail in smug indifference.

"Simmer down, you old fool," Fargo called out a minute later. "I just checked and we already got a rabbit in the snare. We'll just scorch it quick."

"Scorch your ass," Jack snapped, still angry.

Fargo bled and rough-gutted the animal, then skinned it quick and stuck a green branch through it as a spit.

Yellowstone Jack had already changed his opinion of Sarah after watching her do battle on the Buffalo Trace. He had calmed down by now and was putting on a show of manners for the Cherokee royalty.

"Good evening, Your Purple," he greeted her, adding an awkward bow. "I hope you'll pardon my hot-jawing of that . . . durned horse a minute ago."

"I enjoyed it, truly," she assured him. "A woman can learn many new words from you. Mostly unrepeatable, but all colorful."

Fargo tore off a singed quarter of meat and served it to Sarah on a broad piece of bark.

"And you two?" she asked Fargo. "You also rode into the Ouachitas?"

His face going grim at the memory, Fargo nonetheless gave the increasingly horrified Sarah a brief but vivid account of the massacre they'd discovered earlier that day at Broken Bow Lake.

Sarah, her voice shaking from the news, said, "So *that's* what happened. I knew there was bad trouble. Coming out of the Ouachitas, I heard some tribe's danger drums—Chickasaw, I think. But I could not read the signal."

She lapsed into moody silence while the campfire snapped and sparked.

"Both of you," she said after a long pause, "are good men and did all you could. But you are white. These Creeks . . . they were simply put into the ground, without being prepared for the Great Journey. Now their spirits must hover on earth so long as the grass grows and the rivers run."

"No offense, pretty lady," Fargo said, "but it ain't the spiritual side of it you need to fret right now. I'm told the Creeks and the Cherokees get along like horses and bears. And, once again, there were Cherokee weapons planted."

Sarah nodded, taking his point. Fighting off yawns, she told Fargo and Jack everything she'd overheard up in the mountains, including the talk of simultaneous strikes.

"I do not believe," she concluded, "that the three of us can stop this thing now. Not unless we kill Menard, and he must be found first."

"Happens you got any ideas, Your Highness," Jack mumbled around a greasy mouthful of scorched rabbit, "toss it into the hotchpot. Time's a-wastin'."

"I have nothing, snowbeard," she admitted, her oval face framed in the firelight by a profusion of shiny black tresses. "All I know to do is keep looking for Menard."

"That's a plan," Fargo granted. "And it'll likely work *if* you find him—and then also manage to kill him. Many have tried, and gone under for their trouble. Menard may wear heavy perfume, but that man is six sorts of dangerous."

"You need not tell *me* about him," she replied, her pretty features suddenly so hard they looked chiseled.

Time was indeed pressing, and since the afternoon Fargo had been mulling a risky idea. An idea Talcott Mumford had inadvertently planted when he said: "Even a fool can put his own clothes on better than a wise man can do it for him."

"Out West," Fargo began, feeling weariness weigh at his

eyelids like coins, "a man—or a tribe—has got to paddle his own canoe. The U.S. government, even when it means well, can't be counted on to take the right action in time."

Sarah nodded, watching him intently. "True words. Are you talking about a Cherokee resistance?"

"Resist? Christ, he better not be," Yellowstone Jack snapped, no longer nodding off. "God's git-fiddle, Fargo! That's ig-*zac*ly the charge Menard is framin' 'em for."

Fargo ignored Jack, watching Sarah. "Menard is planting signs of the Keetoowah. But the Nighthawks are disbanded, right?"

"Completely," she assured him.

"But not," Fargo went on, watching her even closer, "the Man Killers, right again?"

"Oh, Jesus jumpin' Christ," Jack groaned. "The Man Killers? Fargo, do you *want* a massacre?"

Jack, too, had long seen various signs that this elite Cherokee warfare society was still organized, though not active. Those warriors designated Man Killers all wore the striped sashes of those who had scored kills in combat.

At first, Sarah avoided Fargo's question. Then she seemed to realize the wisdom of his proverb about paddling one's own canoe.

"A few dozen Man Killers could be mustered," she admitted. "All men, for I am the only active War Woman."

Sarah hesitated and seemed to debate something within. Then she added, "My older brother, Nacona, lives on Blue Feather Ridge. Like me he has taken the last name of our British father. But he . . . well, he *might* be useful to you in the future."

She yawned again, and Fargo realized all of them were done in. The night was crisp, so he unpacked his buffalo robe for Sarah. Knowing the Ovaro was an excellent sentry, Fargo tethered the stallion near his bedroll. Then he fell asleep before he could even unbuckle his gun belt.

Fargo rarely slept deeply on the trail, especially in times of danger, but exhaustion was a cruel master, and for several hours he was dead to the world.

A soft snort startled him awake, and Fargo sat up with his Colt to hand.

He judged it was a couple of hours until dawn. Both

horses were contentedly grazing on pine needles. Yellowstone Jack was rolled up tight in his blanket, snoring with a racket like a boar in rut.

Sarah's buffalo robe was empty.

Fargo stood up, leathered his Colt, and started down toward the lake. He didn't have far to look.

Princess Sarah Blackburn stood naked in thigh-deep water, wringing the moisture from her long hair. Moonlight burnished her ample charms. Fargo didn't have to gaze on her long before his buckskins were tented in front.

"Hello, Skye," she called up to him, teeth chattering. "I had to bathe. I hoped you would come down to the water. It is cold, but very bracing. Won't you join me?"

It was damn chilly, but Fargo was no fool. In moments he was naked, then gasping when he plunged into the lake. He swam toward her underwater, tasting her sweet breasts as he broke the surface again and popped up to join her. The size of his erection forced her to step back and make room.

"Yes, *just* like that," she urged while Fargo's hungry mouth teased the stiff but pliant nipples into hard, sweet points tasting vaguely of mint.

Her groping hand locked around his organ and started pumping while also giving quick squeezes. Fuel on fuel to the raging fire in Fargo's loins.

"I like a little warm-up, darlin'," he told her as he swept her up into his arms, water running off her in sleek rivulets. "But if I get any hotter, my beard will catch fire."

"Hot is good," she murmured, her tongue tickling his ear. "I will show you."

As soon as he set her down on shore, Sarah led him to a spot where she had cut spruce boughs and made a soft little bed.

"I made this hoping you would come down here," she told him, stretching out full length and pulling him down onto her. "Feel this?" she added, guiding his hand to the moist folds between her legs. "That is not from the lake. It—it—oh—*ahh!*"

They both gasped when the very tip of Fargo's manhood parted the soft portals of flesh and then probed deep into the delicious heat at the core of her need.

"Deeper . . . *harder!*" Sarah encouraged, locking her

ankles behind Fargo's back. "Oh . . . *oh* . . . Skye, it's so *big*, you're filling all of me, *all . . . annhh!*"

Her shrieking climax was only the first of many for both of them. Later, as they dozed off depleted but happy, limbs entwined, Sarah muttered, "Can we do it, Skye?"

"Do what?" he muttered back.

"Can we stop Menard?"

"Sure we can," he replied.

But Fargo was awfully glad she hadn't asked him *"Will we stop Menard?"* Because, as of right now, Fargo didn't much like their chances.

12

Seven sleeps after the death of Oglethorpe, Wolf Sleeve and his band had returned north to the Arkansas River country. Their orders now were to stop Fargo and Yellowstone Jack, and to capture the Cherokee she-bitch if they could find her.

Just past sunrise, Wolf Sleeve posted one of his best marksmen, Tangle Hair, on a timbered ridge overlooking the office of Talcott Mumford.

"Mirror flashes report Fargo and the old one are coming, probably this day," Wolf Sleeve told his man. "But this is a difficult shot with the bow, and do *not* attempt it unless you are sure of a hit."

Tangle Hair nodded, finding a good spot behind a tumble of rocks for himself and his osage-wood bow.

"Menard wants Fargo killed," Wolf Sleeve continued, "but why do it so quickly? I prefer a more fitting way to kill such a worthy enemy."

Wolf Sleeve reached down and slid the long, thin, cast-iron Russian knife from his knee-length moccasin. He ran a fingernail through one of the long blood gutters.

"The blue-eyed white devil is famous with firearms. But I also hear how he is terror unleashed with the knife in his boot. If you can kill him today, sobeit. But, if not, I am eager to pit my steel against his."

He glanced at the sky. "The sun may be a problem early on. If you cannot get a bead on Fargo, kill anyone," Wolf Sleeve ordered. "Menard tells me there will be an important bluecoat chief here today. A 'Cherokee' killing will help convince him there is a red rebellion."

Tangle Hair gave a scornful snort. "Rebellion? These

dirt-scratching reservation squaws? I, for one, am sick of this place and eager to return to Blanco Canyon."

"Soon, brother, soon," Wolf Sleeve promised him. "And with new repeating rifles and other riches from Menard. For now, be patient and seize the moment when it comes. From here on out let your thoughts be nothing but bloody."

Lieutenant Jimmy Briscoe stood at ramrod-straight attention.

"Sir, my unit has been on roving patrol since the death of Colonel Oglethorpe," he reported. "We have covered the territory from the Kansas line, up north, to the Red River down south. As ordered, we did not ride west of the Chickasaw reservation leaving that vast area to soldiers from Fort Adobe."

The sunburned, freckle-faced redhead fell silent, and Fargo watched Lieutenant Colonel Hiram Steele frown so deeply his silvered eyebrows touched. Steele had been sent to the Indian Territory from the War Department's field office at Fort Scott in nearby southern Kansas.

"Lieutenant," he snapped, "it is of no interest to anyone how much *riding* you've done. You were ordered to arrest any Indians who behaved as hostiles. How many have you detained?"

Fargo watched Jimmy flush to his very earlobes. "Well . . . none, sir."

Steele, a spit-and-polish man in an expensively tailored uniform, looked stunned. Fargo, Yellowstone Jack, and Talcott Mumford exchanged sympathetic glances.

"None?" Steele repeated. "Son, are you telling me you disobeyed your orders?"

"No, sir, of course not. But the only hostilities we've encountered have been a couple of ambushes by free-ranging Indians, not from any local tribes."

"Free-ranging? Lieutenant, are you an expert on American Indians?"

"No, sir."

"Then you are hardly experienced enough to make such judgments," Steele said pedantically.

"Jimmy's young, Colonel," Fargo inserted mildly, "but you'll notice how his boots are worn thin on the stirrup side."

"And mine aren't, is that it?"

Exactly my point, Fargo thought. Men behind desks seldom took the arrows. But he said nothing else. Steele, who had all the arrogance of a Boston Brahmin, had disliked the buckskin-clad Fargo from the outset of this meeting at the Indian Agency—and disliked Yellowstone Jack, who gave off a ripe odor, even more.

"Lieutenant Briscoe," Steele resumed in his officious manner, "the brutal torture-murder of Colonel Oglethorpe, by Cherokee criminals, has initiated a profound crisis in the War Department. We have determined that a Cherokee-led uprising *has* begun. Yet, you saw *no* hostile Cherokee behavior?"

Fargo hated to keep butting in, but Jimmy lacked the rank to defend himself without facing charges of insubordination.

"Colonel," he said, "that was a Comanche torture trick that killed Oglethorpe, not Cherokee."

"Bosh, Fargo! The evidence is overwhelming. Including simultaneous strikes, two days ago, with yet more evidence of Cherokee involvement."

"The evidence," Fargo insisted, "ain't worth a cup of cold piss. The obvious frame-up proves it's white men holding the reins—a typical landgrab pattern."

Fargo's lake-blue eyes cut to the sash window behind Mumford's desk. Earlier, when he and Yellowstone Jack had swung down to tie off their mounts, Fargo had gotten an uneasy feeling about that long ridge above the far bank of the river.

"As I understand it, Fargo," Steele's razor-edged voice sliced into his thoughts, "it was your idea to bury the colonel out in that godforsaken wasteland?"

"Actually, it's pretty country along the Sweetwater, Colonel."

"That's hardly the point. The condition of the body might have helped the investigators."

Jimmy started to speak up, taking responsibility for the burial order. Fargo beat him to it.

"I gave the order because it had to be done," he insisted. "The man's head was literally cooked. His aides were beheaded, their brains scooped out. Imagine the condition by the time they were shipped back east. Even lime wouldn't help."

"It appears to me, Fargo," Steele said, "that you seem very intent on deflecting blame from the Cherokees. Could you perhaps have a personal stake in helping them hide their crimes? I've heard reports you've been . . . *friendly* with Sarah Blackburn, the Keetoowah leader?"

Talcott Mumford, like Yellowstone Jack, had remained silent so far—Jack at Fargo's firm orders. But this last remark was too much.

"Colonel Steele," Mumford spoke up from behind his large oak desk, "there *is* no Cherokee Keetoowah or Nighthawk Society. It's long defunct."

"As I understand it, Mumford, you *are* an expert on Indians. Nonetheless, I'll thank you to stay out of this. Your obvious partiality toward the savages is the main reason you're about to be given marching orders."

Fargo felt anger coming to a slow boil, but he kept his tone civil.

"Colonel, a tribe in the middle of an 'uprising' ain't got time nor inclination to hoe beans and corn, to trap furs, to tend livestock. But the Cherokees are doing just that."

"Hell, Fargo, a few women can keep up the 'peaceful' show. The red aborigines have proven very cunning when it comes to murder."

Fargo said, "You spend plenty of time hot-jawin' the tribes. But, damnit, I'm telling you: the Indians doing the damage and killing around here are mostly outsiders. In fact, mostly Comanches and Kiowas from the Staked Plains area of the Texas Panhandle."

"Precisely," Mumford chimed in. "The Indian Territory has also become a haven for white outlaws because they can't be tried by Indians, and white lawmen steer wide of here. The superficial evidence may show it's Indians carrying out the raids. But it's white criminals pulling the strings and Indian outsiders doing the raiding."

"Talk is cheap. Can you prove that?" Steele demanded.

"Soon enough," Fargo promised. "And the man behind the trouble is Baptiste Menard."

At this intelligence, Steele looked startled, but he quickly recovered. First he dismissed Jimmy and sent him packing. Then, eyes narrowing, he turned to the Trailsman.

"All right, Mr. Fargo," he said, an ironic smile flitting across his lips. "Since you evidently have godlike knowledge of events, you tell me precisely what Baptiste Menard is up to."

"Well, he's trying to frame the Cherokees as ringleaders, but he wants the U.S. government to believe a full-bore Indian uprising is going on. Otherwise, he'd be making the Cherokees the *only* tribe in trouble."

"Why a 'full-bore' uprising?"

"Can't say for certain," Fargo admitted. "But I'd wager he hopes to cause a spate of fort building. Menard made a fortune, out in California, selling milled lumber during the gold strike in the Sierra."

"He did?" Steele said, momentarily losing his know-it-all manner. "First I've heard of it."

"And the Cherokee sector," Mumford added, his monocle hanging from a fine gold chain, "is tree rich, with plenty of water to transport cut trees to a sawmill."

For some time Steele remained silent, his neatly whiskered face troubled.

"Gentlemen," he finally said, "I was sent down here with orders to liaise with a knowledgeable local citizen and obtain a complete briefing on the situation. I did so. And that citizen's name is Baptiste Menard."

Yellowstone Jack came up from his chair, snarling, but Fargo slammed him back down. "Ease off," Fargo muttered.

"And you believe his briefing?" Mumford asked Steele.

"It makes more sense than the swamp gas I've heard this morning," the officer replied. "Especially your defense of Sarah Blackburn—in light of the evidence."

"Evidence?" Fargo repeated.

Steele glanced at Mumford, whose bookish face suddenly looked miserable. He unlocked the top drawer of his desk and handed Fargo a harmonica pistol, a rare type of firearm Fargo hadn't seen in years.

"It's a presentation gun," Steele explained. "Read the inscription."

Fargo did. The Royal Society of London had presented it to Princess Sarah Blackburn.

"That pistol," Steele said smugly, "was found lying near a dead and scalped female after an attack on a stagecoach two nights ago in Van Buren. It remains in Mr. Mumford's possession because, technically, it's Indian Bureau property.

114

But it is also potential evidence, and the Provost Marshal at Fort Gibson has charged Mumford with holding it for possible use in court."

"Colonel Steele," Fargo said, "would *you* ever fire a solid silver, presentation weapon like this? It's worth a small fortune. And even if you did, would you leave it behind afterward? Especially with your name on it?"

"No." The prompt and frank answer surprised Fargo. "I have considered that it might have been stolen and then planted, Mr. Fargo. Sarah Blackburn, after all, has some college in her background and is an accomplished young woman. But she is also a veteran War Woman with kills to her credit. Will *you* admit she has been seen lately, fully armed for battle?"

Fargo nodded. "Sure, she's a woman who takes the bit between the teeth. Especially when her people are being framed like they are now."

The old Osage squaw who worked in the office was bustling around, preparing the stove to make coffee. She kept catching Fargo's eyes and shamelessly flirting with him.

"Mr. Fargo," Steele said brusquely, "Sarah Blackburn will get her day in court like any other accused person. But right now I need to know where she is."

So that's the way of it, Fargo realized. As an investigator from the War Department, Steele's job was to find a "ringleader" to execute for the murder of Oglethorpe. With the blame now officially fixed on the Cherokees, Sarah was the prime candidate.

Fargo knew right where she was—searching for Baptiste Menard in the Winding Stair Mountains down south, where the man was reputed to have a hideout.

"I don't work for the army right now," Fargo replied. "I'm under contract to the Indian Bureau."

"So you won't tell me where she is?"

"Nope."

Steele slammed the desk so hard a quill pen leaped from its holder. "*Why,* man?"

"Because there's one helluva difference between real crimes and hatched-up charges."

Steele fumed in silence. Fargo watched the old squaw head outside to gather a few stove lengths from a pile under a tarp. Again, his eyes lifted to that distant ridge, but before he could examine his uneasy feeling more closely, Steele spoke up again.

"All right, Mr. Fargo, remember this was your call. I gave you a chance to surrender Sarah Blackburn to us peaceably. You chose not to cooperate."

Steele turned his angry eyes toward the beleaguered agent.

"Mumford, my report will be filed within a few days. I am to decide whether or not there should be a sweep, in force, of the reservation by combat troops."

"There is no uprising now, Colonel Steele," Mumford said. "But if soldiers sweep the rez, there will be."

"Don't threaten me, Mumford! Frankly, after all I've seen around here, and heard this morning from you and Fargo, I have no alternative. Things are out of control, and I seriously doubt"—Steele glanced dubiously at Fargo and Yellowstone Jack—"that you are going to secure this out-of-control reservation. Especially with a pair of chawbacons who look like savages themselves—and have just been accused of a back-shooting down at Clayton Station."

Jack had somehow restrained himself until now. Steele's remark tore it, and this time Fargo let him go. He figured Steele deserved to meet a true "savage" face-to-face.

"H'ar now, you high-toned mouthpiece!" Jack fulminated. "Insult me wunst more, and we *will* commence to huggin'!"

"What did you call me?" Steele demanded.

"Any damn thing I want to, Soldier Blue. I ain't in no goddamn army, and that fancy yellow pipin' down your leg ain't worth a jackstraw to me—*yellow* meanin' what it does."

"Now, see here—"

"And I don't need no colored ribbons pinned over my tit to tell me I got a set o' stones, neither. How's it that the soldiers with the littlest pizzles always strut the most?"

Steele made the mistake of scraping back his chair. In an instant Jack sprang to his feet, handing his pistol to Fargo to hold for him.

"Let's step outside and get thrashing, you fancy featherbed soldier!" Jack shouted almost gleefully, adding a Cheyenne war whoop. "I'll whip you till that perfumed hair falls out!"

Steele, realizing the folly of tangling with such a rough frontier specimen, hesitated, looking awkward.

Fargo placed a restraining hand on Jack's arm. "Come down off your hind legs, you blockhead," Fargo whispered. "We want to smooth his feathers, not ruffle 'em."

"Why the hell for?" Jack retorted. "Christ, Steele and Menard was talkin' chummy! Hell, we can't trust him any further 'n we can throw a bull."

"He's not bent, just arrogant," Fargo whispered back. "And totally ignorant of Indian ways. But that news about Menard's past *did* make an impression on him."

"So will my fist when—"

Jack paused when the door opened. The Osage squaw, her arms filled with wood, stood framed in the doorway, morning sunshine slanting in past her. She sent Fargo a toothy smile, fluttering her eyelids.

A heartbeat later, a thick rope of blood spurted out when the entire front of her throat was ripped out by an arrow!

The wood clattered to the floor, and the squaw took two shambling steps, choking loudly on her own blood. She was dead before she hit the floor.

That ridge . . . that damn ridge, Fargo fumed. It had bothered him, being so conveniently located for just this type of strike.

He and Yellowstone Jack, old hands at sudden, violent death, had reacted quickly. Jack sprang to the fallen woman while Fargo, fearing that doorway was still covered, literally dove through the front window in a spray of glass. He dashed out front and took cover behind a cottonwood tree, studying the wooded ridge across the river.

He spotted no one, either in force or a lone rider.

Back inside the office, Mumford and Steele were slower to recover from the shock. But, as Fargo examined the arrow, Steele proved he had learned something about Indians.

"Quartz-tipped," he announced, his voice charged with I-told-you-so triumph. "And even from here I recognize the clan marking of a Cherokee."

"Looks that way," Fargo said with weary sarcasm, watching a white-faced Mumford cover his dead assistant with a blanket. "But it was *meant* to look that way."

However, Steele was not seeking subtle, complex truths; rather, he was looking to justify violent action by the army. He ignored Fargo and stared at Talcott Mumford.

"Mumford, I am recommending your immediate removal from this reservation—*forced* removal, if necessary. As for you, Mr. Fargo, and your insubordinate friend . . . I am not surprised that you two have been charged with murder at Clayton Station. Perhaps, before too long, you'll share a cell with your murdering Cherokee 'princess'."

Steele left in a huff.

"There goes trouble," Fargo fretted. "Once he files that damned two-bit report of his, the War of the Plains *will* start. Treaties allow small patrols like Jimmy's in The Nations. But a full-fledged military campaign is an act of war."

"Maybe I *should* be cashiered," Mumford mused with downcast eyes, staring at the blanket-covered body. "I've bollixed up everything."

Yellowstone Jack, who'd never had a kind word for "schoolman Mumford," surprised Fargo by speaking up.

"Bullshit," the old salt told the agent. "You're a good man doin' a hard job. One a you is worth a dozen Steeles."

"Thanks. But you heard Steele—the fat's in the fire now. It's too late to stop what's coming. It's happened before, and it will again. The Cherokees will be rounded up, shipped off somewhere. They'll lose everything they've worked for."

"Not necessarily," Fargo said, recalling his recent conversation with Sarah.

Mumford glanced at him, holding his monocle in place. "How's that?"

"Remember that time you let the Indians hunt rather than starve waiting for rations?"

Mumford nodded.

"Same thing here," Fargo insisted. "I'm thinking it's best if *Cherokees* handle these criminals on their rez, not outsiders."

Mumford goggled. "Cherokee warriors, you mean?"

Fargo grinned. "I wouldn't leave it to the papooses."

"But then that phony army report about an Indian uprising becomes true," the agent objected.

"No, it's self-defense, not an uprising. They'd be fighting

118

only criminals, not the U.S. Army. And think about the alternative, Talcott—a bloodbath if they *don't* act."

Mumford nodded, his face troubled. "You're right, Skye. But *are* there any Cherokee warriors left, besides Sarah?"

"It's best," Fargo said as he and Jack headed toward the door, "that you not know too much, case this winds up in a court somewhere. You just hang on a bit, and we'll get word to you somehow."

"You bein' a pacifist and all," Yellowstone Jack added, "one word of advice?"

"Surely."

"Get you a gun," Jack advised bluntly, nodding toward the corpse. "Lotta that goin' around."

13

On the day following the meeting in Talcott Mumford's office, Sarah Blackburn was still in the Winding Stair Mountains, "sleeping rough" and searching for Baptiste Menard and his rumored hideout.

The Winding Stair, just north of the Ouachita Mountains, were a small range, but thickly forested. Sarah had already spent one full day scouring these twisting, winding mountains without success.

Then, toward late morning, she ran into incredible luck: Baptiste Menard himself, riding a fine and rare *grullo* stallion with dark blue tints to its coat.

Sarah, on foot, leaped behind a tree and watched him pass well below her position. She dared not move closer. Menard, who was obsessed with evading surprise capture, always had a good hunting dog trotting along beside him. Before Sarah could get close enough to risk a shot, that hound would catch her scent. Menard, despite his paper collars and heavy perfume, was a longtime frontier survivor—and a deadly shot with that Volcanic lever-action repeater resting across his thighs.

He was riding at a slow trot, his eyes constantly scanning the terrain. Keeping plenty of trees between herself and him, Sarah fell in behind him, at times running to keep the gap closed. She was glad now that she'd left her musketoon and cumbersome bow and quiver hidden with her bateau.

She soon realized he was leaving the mountains, exiting from the north. If he was headed back up north to the Cherokee range, she fretted, she'd never catch him.

But just before actually leaving the front slopes, Menard turned up into a small, almost hidden gulch. At the upper end of the gulch, partially hidden by a screen of vines and foliage, was a cave entrance where waited a dusty sorrel, still saddled.

She recognized the horse of Mike Winkler, leader of the white outlaws in the Indian Territory.

Once Menard had arrived and hobbled his horse, he let the hound go bounding after birds and squirrels. Despite her avid desire to kill Menard, Sarah was loathe to enter that dangerous cave. She might indeed manage to kill her nemesis, but her scent-bottle pistol held only one charge, and Winkler would surely kill her then.

But she *must* go in. Even now the canvas-covered bone shakers of the white men were crawling across the desolate buffalo plains, through the dangerous mountain passes, crowding and displacing the red man. If full-scale war broke out in The Nations, the resulting conflagration could not only destroy her people—it would consume the West.

"According to my sources, Mike," Baptiste Menard said in his good, but heavily accented, English, "it will soon be official, if it's not already: the Cherokees *will* be blamed for the uprising. Their removal won't be long in coming."

Menard and Winkler occupied a cavern the size of a large double parlor. The place had long been used by outlaws. It was too well known to serve as Menard's secret hideout in the Winding Stair, but he trusted it for quick meetings like this.

Golden-yellow light slanting through the entrance showed a fire pit for heat and cooking, and a few crude shakedowns with shuck mattresses. A shoulder of bacon, wrapped in cheesecloth, hung from a tree limb just outside the entrance.

"I'll bet the Cherokees will soon be on their way to some desert hellhole," Winkler agreed. His scarred visage was ugly in the stingy light. "And now Skye Fargo and that old mountain-man relic with him are roving targets for every vigilante in the territory."

Menard, seated on an old packing crate, smiled at that thought. "That's good news, indeed, out of Clayton Station. We all know how deplorable a back-shooter is, *non*?"

"But the woman, Sarah what's-her-name, has dropped out of sight, boss. That bitch is trickier than a redheaded woman."

Menard's eyes flicked to the cave entrance. He could hear his dog barking farther up the slope.

"Yes," Menard said, "dropped out of sight. But she'll turn up, I think. Like Fargo, she's a crusader. Just remember, Mike, and remind your men: the woman is *not* to be killed, only captured."

Among the men on Menard's payroll was a headquarters company clerk at Fort Gibson, located in the eastern Indian Territory. He reported that the harmonica pistol, planted near a murdered woman by Winkler's men, was indeed being held as potential evidence against Sarah. Menard's intent was to make the beauty a fugitive from a murder warrant—then offer her the only protection she could hope to find.

Inch by slow inch, hugging the ground like a snake, Sarah slowly moved close enough to kill Baptiste Menard.

Her plan was highly risky. Since she had only one shot in her pistol, she'd have to get close enough to the Frenchman to guarantee a kill with one ball. Then, before Winkler could clear leather, she meant to bury a war hatchet between the outlaw's eyes.

If only that cursed dog did not return too soon.

The shoulder of bacon, dangling above the cave entrance, reminded Sarah how hungry she was—but no hunger matched her great need to kill the odious murderer, thief, and rapist, Baptiste Menard.

Sarah decided to slither through the entrance toward the right-hand side of the cave mouth, where a profusion of hawthorn bushes partially blocked the view. She could hear their voices now, even catch snippets of the conversation.

"But we've plowed all this ground before," Mike Winkler told Menard. "Why'd you *really* have me ride down here, boss? Is Mumford causing trouble?"

"Mumford?" A brief, scornful twist of his mouth showed Menard's contempt. "Hardly. That poncy-man would let Apaches top his wife if an Indian treaty required it. No, I want you and your men to conduct another simultaneous-strikes raid."

"When?"

"As soon as you return north. We'll go with only two strikes this time, no point in overdoing it. Half of you will attack a train of muleteers out of De Queen, Arkansas. One leaves daily, right after sunup. The other half will terrorize farmers and set hayracks ablaze up in Kansas. Two typical evil deeds of redskins."

Menard's pale-agate eyes kept watching the cave entrance. When he judged the time was about right, he loosed a sharp, piercing whistle. Outside, the well-trained hound responded with rapid barks that grew louder as it raced back to the cave.

"This new strike sounds like money for old rope," Winkler said, standing up to leave. "I'll get on it quick."

He looked surprised when Menard drew his Colt Navy. The Frenchman sent Winkler a high sigh, nodding toward the bushes. Winkler, too, filled his hand.

"All right then, Mike," Menard called out as if nothing were happening. "So long and *bon chance*."

For Sarah, the desperate hour had arrived.

She had made it to just inside the cavern entrance, where bushes and shadows gave her precarious cover. But Menard, as if anticipating trouble, stayed close to the back wall—a long shot for her cap-and-ball pistol.

The hound was only moments away, and she saw that both men had drawn their pistols. If she wasn't already discovered, she soon would be. Sarah knew she must seize this last moment of opportunity, and pray her aim was true.

Being taken alive, she reminded herself, was not an option. Not among rapists. She had imbibed the Black Drink, and now it was victory or death, no third way.

She aimed her scent-bottle gun at Menard's lights and squeezed the trigger. As usual the primer cap popped. Then, her heart sinking, she heard a sickening fizzle like spit simmering in the stem of a pipe—the fizzle of damp, useless powder! It must have clumped during the night— she had forgotten to check it.

"Take her alive!" Menard exclaimed.

"Oh, *hell* yes," Winkler replied. "That stuff is better warm."

Fargo and Yellowstone Jack heard plenty of drum activity as they patrolled the Cherokee sector on the eighth day following the shocking massacre at Sweetwater Creek.

"Read 'em?" Fargo asked Jack.

The grizzled old campaigner shook his head. "Nah. I can read Sioux and Cheyenne drums, a little Arapaho. This here's naught but gibberish, to me."

"Same here."

Each tribe was loathe to let outsiders learn their drum language, and deliberately kept the code complex to discourage learning it.

"Whatever the word," Fargo added, "it's heap big doin's. The message comes from south of us."

"Where Her Purple headed," Jack observed.

Fargo nodded, his lips a grim line surrounded by a thick, short beard. Both men rode a narrow and overgrown trail that crisscrossed the extensive Arkansas River bottomland. Fargo felt hemmed in and vulnerable.

"That gal has really stepped into it," Fargo said. "When Steele got going on the harmonica pistol yesterday, I realized they mean to make her the scapegoat for Oglethorpe *and* this jackboot 'uprising'."

"Sure, on account Menard has bamboozled 'em with planting that pistol and the rest of his dirty tricks. She's up agin' Menard, Winkler, and them thievin' barn rats in Winkler's gang. Turd, *them* boys ain't Bible raised. Matter fact, they require killing."

"We'll have our chance," Fargo said, studying everything around them. "They've been turned loose on us, too."

The two men had spent the best part of the morning scouting the up-country of the Arkansas. The action proved advisable since there was plenty of fresh sign that the Staked Plains renegades had returned to the area. Fargo needed to know what they were up to.

"Be damn," Jack muttered as a shadow fell over the landscape. "Lookit that sun."

Fargo did look. He watched a dramatically dark and boiling cloud bank spread across the lower part of the sun like an ink stain. Then, rising like thick smoke, it obliterated the sun entirely.

"Tarnal hell!" Jack swore. "Now *that's* a—"

"Another damn omen, I know," Fargo finished for him. "I can't keep a head count on all these funerals the sky and wind are foretelling."

"You mock, boy. But a wise man don't ignore the signs."

Actually, Fargo suddenly realized, Jack might have a point. Both of the earlier omens Fargo had seen had been immediately followed by death. But he didn't need omens to remind him he was up against it. In fact, the *real* signs showed that the renegades were watching Fargo and Jack—watching and waiting. Fargo had also spotted prints made by iron-shod hooves, and though hard to believe, sometimes they were mingled in *with* the renegades.

"God's long-handles, Fargo!" Jack suddenly complained. "You never told me this job would be teetotal. A man needs to wash his teeth now and then."

But Fargo ignored his friend's bitter complaints, for since yesterday's meeting he was filled with time urgency.

"Jack," he said, "that damn Colonel Steele won't let any grass grow under his feet. Not after seeing that Cherokee arrow kill the squaw yesterday. Once his report's filed, an army sweep will follow and the Cherokees will get the boot."

"Reckon that rings right. Happens you got some brainy plan, trot it out. Otherwise . . . me and you ain't doin' shit, just washing bricks."

Jack reined in his sly gelding. "This here's the area where I set out snares this morning," he said. "Le'me go check 'em."

Jack reined his ginger off the trail, heading back through a thick forest of silver spruces and pines. Fargo swung down and watered the Ovaro from his hat. The grateful stallion nudged his velvet muzzle into Fargo's neck.

"My turn, boy," Fargo said, pouring a hatful of cooling water over his own head. Nights were cooling off, but the days still produced oven heat.

Fargo, eyes closed, was still sputtering and shaking water from his head when the Ovaro nickered a warning.

Fargo slapped for his Colt, but his vision was still completely water-blurred. He reached up a hand to swipe at his eyes, but a crushing blow to the head made a bright orange starburst explode inside his skull.

Fargo staggered, then his knees came unhinged and he crashed to the forest floor, still conscious but only barely. He felt his holster lighten as his assailants took his sidearm. His Arkansas Toothpick, too, was jerked from his boot.

"We *got* him, Lorenzo!" gloated a tobacco-roughened

voice. "The *great* Trailsman! Don't look like such a much now, does he?"

"Unh!" Fargo gave a hissing grunt when one of the men sent the toe of a boot crashing into his ribs. More blows rained down, vicious kicks and more strikes with some kind of club. Warm blood ran into his eyes, and he could see little.

"You're *dead,* Injin lover," gloated a second voice, and Fargo tensed when he heard the metallic *snick* of a gun being cocked.

"Hang on, Seth," said the voice of Lorenzo. "You still got that running iron we used down in Texas?"

"Say, *that's* the ticket, all right! Even better than killing him, we'll put his goddamn eyes out like we done that Ranger down in Laredo. Fargo won't do no tracking for the Indian Bureau then, will he?"

Fargo vaguely recognized the names Lorenzo and Seth—two of Mike Winkler's lick-spittles. He could see well enough now to make out the running iron Seth took from a pannier—a small branding iron used by rustlers to quickly alter existing brands on stolen cattle.

While Lorenzo held the muzzle of his six-gun to Fargo's temple, Seth pulled all the makings for a fire from his other pannier. Within just minutes flames were crackling, and the business end of the running iron was heating up to a red-orange glow.

Lorenzo abruptly stunned Fargo with a blow from his handgun, then quickly bound his wrists and ankles.

"Funny how they like to fight at the last moment," he said, adding a chuckle. "Specially when they first smell their own eyeballs starting to cook. Hell, if you don't know what it is, the smell could make you hungry."

Fargo, like most frontiersmen, had come to terms with the reality of violent death. But to savagely blind a man, then leave him in an agony of indescribable pain followed by lifelong helplessness—such monstrous evil came straight from hell itself.

"Maybe we'll fry his oysters, too," Seth japed. "We got *plenty* of hot iron. Well, she's glowing like an express-train coal box. Let's get cooking."

As the gunman stalked closer, holding out the glowing iron, Fargo felt his pulse exploding like hoofbeats in his ears. The copper taste of fear coated his tongue, but even now he refused to surrender to black panic. His moment would come, and he must not miss it.

"You'll hear a frying noise, Fargo," the owlhoot named Lorenzo tormented him. "Like bacon sizzling in hot grease. And the smell of seared meat. But o'course, the *pain* is all you'll notice for the first few hours—days, actually."

"That," Seth chimed in, "and the darkness. Dark as the inside of a boot. For the rest of your miserable, helpless, pathetic life. Here it comes, big man! *Enjoy!*"

Fargo could indeed feel the heat as Seth thrust the red-hot iron closer and closer to his face. He shut his eyes, but Lorenzo trapped his head so he couldn't turn away.

That sudden, acrid smell, Fargo realized, was his eyebrows starting to singe. His ankles were tied, but not the rest of his legs. He lifted them up and back, planted both feet on Seth's chest, and launched him on a tumbling somersault into the bushes.

A hideous scream, the stink of cooking flesh, and Fargo realized Seth had fallen right onto the hot running iron.

"All right, big man," Lorenzo muttered, "so you die right now instead. It's your call, and either way you're blind, ain'tcha?"

He stood up, leveling his Smith and Wesson at Fargo's head. The Trailsman gathered his strength for a hard roll to the right, but just then Lorenzo's brains blew out one side of his head in a bloody spray.

"You skin that varmint, Fargo!" Yellowstone Jack shouted in his rusty bray, still some distance away. "Whilst I kill the other one!"

Seth had just climbed to his feet, still screaming. Despite the god-awful burn to his abdomen, he was goaded into action by the sight of his companion's violent death. He clearly wanted to toss a bullet into Fargo, but Jack's deadly hail of lead forced him to leap onto his horse and escape.

"God's linen!" Jack exclaimed when he arrived and found a badly battered Fargo tied up next to a dead man. He gaped like a skull-struck fool, then untied his friend.

Fargo, feeling like a fortunate greenhorn, admitted that the two thugs had gotten the jump on him. Jack looked fit to be tied when he learned about the running iron.

"Skye, might could be you and me oughta think about

backtrailing ourselfs from this Indian Bureau job," he suggested. " 'Pears to me there ain't nothin' we can do, anyhow, 'cept get kilt for a lost cause."

Fargo, his head and chest sore from blows, shook his head. "It's a dirty business, all right, and will get dirtier. But there ain't no way we can wangle out of it."

Fargo had learned, long ago, that life on the frontier meant being a soldier—always. Any man who demanded to live free must also expect to fight for the right to do so. And not just once but over and over, for the enemies of freedom were legion.

"Ahh, you're right," Jack said, staring at the man he had killed. "We started it, we'll finish it. We always do."

He rolled his head over one shoulder, indicating the dead man's horse. "Turn it loose?"

"No, let's send our dead friend back to the nest. His horse will go to the oats. Should have a nice little effect on the rest of the rodents."

With Jack doing most of the work, they lifted the dead outlaw onto his horse, then tied his ankles to the girth strap, his wrists to the horn with rawhide lariat. Fargo swatted the horse's rump, and it was gone.

Fargo gauged the time by the fall of the sun: early afternoon. His time urgency was back, in spades.

"C'mon," he told Jack, wincing at the pain as he swung up into leather. "Let's go take a ride over to Blue Feather Ridge."

"The princess's brother, huh?"

Fargo nodded.

"Is that such a bright idea?" Jack wondered. "Stirrin' up the Cheraws?"

"We got no choice," Fargo said flatly. "A man's got to match his gait to the horse he's riding, right? Either the Cherokees paint for war, or they lose every damn thing they've worked for. And some will end up in prison—or at the end of a gallows limb."

14

Blue Feather Ridge was located north of the Arkansas River, in the heart of some of the best land in the Cherokee sector—indeed, some of the best land in all of the Indian Territory.

"Lookit all that prime timber," Yellowstone Jack remarked. "That's what's got Menard slavering."

The two men had crossed the river on a shallow, rocky ford. With the earlier ambush of Fargo very much in mind, they were doubly vigilant. Renegades were watching them constantly now.

"Those damn drums won't let up," Fargo said. "The news from the south country is big."

"Hate to say it," Jack suggested, "but it 'pears likely Sarah was either kilt or took captive. She's a game little lass, one hell'va warrior. But goin' into them mountains by herself was just plumb stupid, and naught else."

Fargo nodded agreement. "Stupid, but also brave. Well, we don't know for a fact she's—*haw*!"

Fargo suddenly reined in the Ovaro. He and Jack were climbing the face of a steep hill. Fargo pointed down toward the flat tableland behind them.

"Looks like we got company," he told Jack.

About a dozen renegades, Kiowas and Comanches, had deliberately shown themselves. They sat staring up at the two white men.

"That's Wolf Sleeve wearing the scalp cape," Fargo said. "And that big Kiowa with the copper brassards on his upper arms is Iron Mountain."

"Goddamn stinking fleabags," Jack grumped. "Anyhow they ain't fixen to charge."

"No," Fargo agreed. "We've got the high ground. They're just trying to make us sweat. And warning us not to push this thing."

"They can *push* their lips agin' my lily-white backside," Jack fumed. "That Injin trash and Winkler's white trash, too. Tryin' to put a man's eyes out, killin' babies in their sleep . . . even snake shit ain't *that* low."

Fargo pointed ahead toward the divide, the high point between the two valleys surrounding them. "Bunch of houses clustered there. Let's see if Nacona lives there."

As the two white men crested Blue Feather Ridge, they met a typical, silent reception. A few Cherokee children smiled shyly, and work slowed down in the fields. The adult faces were closed, but not hostile.

"Look," Fargo said without pointing. "That house on the knoll is bigger than the others. And that tattered flag flying in the yard is a Union Jack."

"Got to be the brother," Jack said. "Or Lord Nelson's frontier hideaway."

They rode closer and dismounted before the large, split-log house.

"Glom that doorway," Jack muttered. Bright pictographs, painted on the door frame, depicted Cherokees in battle. "Peculiar sorta artwork, hey, for a dirt farmer?"

The two visitors were still hobbling their horses when a tall, well-dressed Cherokee in his early thirties stepped out into the yard. He wore a hand axe in a belt sheath. A well-equipped "farmer," Fargo noted with approval.

"May I help you gentlemen?" he asked with cool politeness. His English, like Sarah's, was excellent—*far better than mine,* Fargo admitted to himself.

"Nacona?" Fargo asked. "Nacona Blackburn?"

The Cherokee nodded.

"I'm Skye Fargo, and this old wagon wreck beside me is Yellowstone Jack. Just stay upwind of him and you'll be fine."

"Mind your pints and quarts, Fargo," Jack warned in a mutter.

"I know of both of you," Nacona said. "My sister has mentioned you to me." He hesitated a moment, then added, "Favorably."

"How is your sister?" Fargo asked.

Nacona's sternly handsome features hardened even more. "She has been taken prisoner by Baptiste Menard in the Winding Stair. Senecas saw Menard moving her from one spot to another, her head bloody."

"Damn," Fargo said softly. "I knew the drums spelled bad trouble."

He looked at Nacona. "Sarah and me are both working on the same side here. She sent me to you for help."

"Words are cheap," Nacona replied, "traded freely by old women."

"H'ar, now," Jack protested, but he fell silent when Fargo looked a warning at him.

"I don't blame you for your . . . secrecy," Fargo told the Cherokee. "But let's lay our cards on the table, Nacona. This entire area is about to go up like dry tinder. And your sister is the captive of one of the most despicable sons of bitches ever hatched from a reptile's egg. This ain't the time to play it proud. We need to join forces or we'll all—white *and* red—sink separately."

Nacona mulled all this, looking at both visitors. "Please come inside," he finally said. "My family are visiting neighbors. I have something to show you."

Inside the well-constructed, solidly furnished house, Fargo and Jack gaped in astonishment at the polished timber floors and furniture covered in costly fabrics. Even more astounding, Fargo glimpsed through the open rear door and saw a flagstoned courtyard out back!

But Nacona hadn't invited them inside to ogle his fine house. He led them to a fireplace in the center of the house and stooped down to trip a lever. The stone hearth slid back to reveal a ladder. Nacona leading with a lantern, all three men climbed down into a secret cellar.

"This is our armory," he explained, holding up the lantern. "Modern weapons are both forbidden and hard for us to come by. But we have quite a collection of older weapons, all in good repair."

The oily yellow light revealed almost three walls covered with weapons: ancient flintlock muskets; German muskets with sawed-off barrels, musketoons like Sarah's; even old British fowling pieces.

"You say 'our' and 'we,' " Fargo remarked, fishing for more information.

Nacona nodded, pride shaping his features. "I am the leader of the last Cherokee Man Killers. There are about thirty of us. Warrior societies are outlawed by treaty, but *some* warriors must remain, as events currently prove. The news today, about my sister's capture, is the final straw. We Man Killers intend to strike the war trail, consequences be damned."

"That's the gait," Fargo approved with a nod. "But I thought Cherokees are river warriors? I notice your people don't have many saddle horses."

"Let's take a walk," Nacona said, leading them back upstairs and then out the backdoor of the house.

He took them down toward the river by a secluded path. Rambling dog roses crowded the banks. Nacona led them to a well-hidden spot, then lifted a cleverly designed vine net.

"God's gonads!" Yellowstone Jack exclaimed.

Fargo, too, marveled. Three brightly painted Cherokee war canoes, in excellent repair, were secreted within the bushes. Their high, narrow prows had hideous death masks carved into them.

"Water surrounds this place," Nacona said. "Each canoe holds up to a dozen men. We Cherokees know every foot of every waterway. We can take the fight anywhere, and quickly."

Neither white man bothered asking why so much cane and dry brush were stuffed into the canoes—it was for immediately burning any captives at the stake. Like most Indians, the Cherokees had no culture of the "prisoner of war."

"How soon," Fargo asked, "after the hail goes out could the Man Killers be mustered for battle?"

Nacona looked proudly confident. Before answering, he loosed a piercing whistle.

"It will take only as long," he replied, "as it takes them to converge on this spot."

Only minutes later, in response to Nacona's whistle, an athletic Cherokee youth, perhaps fifteen years old, showed up.

"This is Battle Road, my cousin," Nacona said. "He is my runner and word-bringer. He has the best ears of any Indian in this sector. When it is time, Fargo, fire two rapid shots, then two slow shots. He will summon the Man Killers."

Nacona paused, watching Fargo's face. "Or . . . is it *already* time?"

Fargo shook his head. "Close, but not quite yet. I'll be making a quick ride to the Winding Stair first."

Fargo didn't mention Sarah, nor did Nacona. But the Cherokee understood that Fargo intended to rescue his sister, and relief washed over his face.

"As you say," Nacona said politely. "Now I know the time is near, and I trust you to see when it has arrived. I will have each Man Killer carefully check his weapons and equipment."

"So the Cheraws're goin' to war," Jack said in a low tone to Fargo. There was evident awe in his voice as the two men rode down from Blue Feather Ridge. "Just hope you know what you're unleashin', turd. One time back east, I seen this buncha Cheraws torturin' the hell out of a helpless little baby while some young warriors just stood there and watched. Turned out it was all just so's them warriors could learn to witness hard sufferin' and ugly sights without going puny. They're a hard tribe wunst they grease for war."

"Good," Fargo said, recalling the appalling massacre at Broken Bow Lake. "That means hard justice, doesn't it?"

Fargo and Jack, weapons to hand at all times now, finished the ride back down the face of Blue Feather Ridge, then forded the Arkansas.

The afternoon air was hot and still, the hum of cicadas and the chuckle of the river current the only sounds. But there was something else in the air, something Fargo had felt too many times in his full, violent life—the sense of impending doom.

"H'ar now," Yellowstone Jack growled, drawing rein. "Here's fresh sign of our feathered friends."

"As usual," Fargo said, without dismounting, "they're riding single file so they can't be counted. But they're close by, all right. Prob'ly watching us right now."

"When we headin' south to the Winding Stair?" Jack demanded.

"We? Hell, old man, you pitched a fit about our first ride, into the Ouachitas. I figured to leave you up here, sucking your gums."

"Figure a cat's tail," Jack snapped. "When Yellowstone Jack signs on for a job, by Godfrey, he pulls his freight. You're just wantin' me to stay here so's you can diddle your little princess."

Fargo grinned, shaking his head. "You crusty old bastard. Well, hell won't have you, but I will. We'll ride out as soon as we rendezvous with Jimmy. His unit is camped here along the river somewhere."

Both men fell silent and studied the wall of trees on their right, the high grass of the riverbank on their left. They edged around a bend, then reined in to watch a group of Cherokee children play near the water.

"Why, hell, them little tads is catchin' polliwogs in a jar," Jack said, chuckling. "Done that myself when I was in short britches."

Fargo's smile melted away, however, as the sight of these kids forced him to recall yet again the slaughter of Creek Indians, including children, at Broken Bow Lake. It was children, he told himself, who were the real victims of treachery and violence out West. Adults made stupid decisions the kids had no say in.

Earlier, having been within seconds of losing his eyes, Fargo found himself wondering what the hell he was getting into here in The Nations, but watching these innocent kids at play answered that question for him.

"As the twig is bent," he muttered, "so the tree shall grow."

Even grizzled old Jack was touched by the innocent sight. "Cute little buttons, ain't they? Cheraws are a handsome people."

His resolve thus bolstered, Fargo led them another mile downriver until they discovered Jimmy Briscoe's unit camped on a grassy bench overlooking the river.

A sentry at a picket outpost waved them past without challenging. Fargo noticed that every trooper carried his carbine, and the horses had been hobbled in camp instead of being sent out to graze.

Fargo swung his leg over the cantle and dismounted, landing light as a cat.

"What happened, Mr. Fargo?" the young lieutenant asked, staring at Fargo's bruised face and singed eyebrows.

"Oh, thanks to Yellowstone Jack there's a fresh soul in hell," Fargo said dismissively. "What's the news, Jimmy? I take it you're spotting plenty of renegades?"

"Everywhere, but technically not hostiles—yet. They still haven't attacked us."

"They won't, by daylight. It'll be too obvious it's not Cherokees. But they're planning a big strike, all right."

The kid nodded. "That's what the Osage scouts told me, too. In fact, Ten Bears and Standing Feather quit. They've returned to their reservation up north, after warning me we're all going to be slaughtered."

"Slaughtered? That's calamity howling," Fargo gainsaid. "But the lid *is* about to blow off. And you, as an officer and a gentleman, have got a hard decision to make."

"Sir?"

"Here's the way of it," Fargo said. "The right to self-defense is permitted to any man or group by the U.S. Constitution, wouldn't you agree?"

The kid nodded. "I took an oath to that constitution."

"Jimmy," Fargo said, "the Cherokees are not a danger to you and your men, you can see that, right?"

"Sure. Command thinks otherwise, but it's renegades from outside The Nations we need to watch for."

"And white gun-throwers," Fargo cautioned. "So, if you notice Cherokees going to war, remember your belief in self-defense. Because that's all it is."

"Besides," Yellowstone Jack added, "you're cavalry, son. Anything you see on the *water*, now that's navy business, am I right?"

"Navy!" The kid looked confused. "But there's no navy out here."

Jack grinned. "Damn, ain't that a shame?"

"You be extra careful from here on out, son," Fargo advised. "It's coming down to the nut-cuttin'. By day, keep your men in skirmishers formation. By night, double your picket guard. Try to lure some stray dogs into your camp and let 'em sleep there—excellent sentries."

"Trouble's coming, all right," Jimmy replied. "I'm not supposed to divulge this information, Mr. Fargo. But you and Jack have taught me more soldiering, in just a few weeks, than I learned in four years at The Point."

"What information?" Fargo pressed.

"Three-hundred fresh troops have been sent from Kansas and Texas. Experienced Indian-fighting troops, with artillery pieces. They're staging out of Fort Gibson in the next few days."

Fargo and Jack exchanged a troubled glance. Time was going to be tight, especially with a trip south to the Winding Stair ahead of them.

"We figured it was coming," Fargo said. "Jimmy, you just be damn careful if you engage those renegades. And whatever you do, if you hear a so-called 'war cry' go up, retreat at once. That's *not* a war cry, it's a death song. It means a brave has given his soul to the Everywhere Spirit. He has accepted death and *he fears nothing.*"

With the last of the day's copper-colored sun balanced on the horizon, Fargo and Jack pointed their bridles south.

"The crusading fools headed south a few hours ago," Mike Winkler reported to his minions. "No doubt to make a big rescue of the Cherokee skirt. Menard's got her now."

"Bully for Menard, the frog son of a bitch," complained Seth Lofley bitterly. "I got a burn welt the size of Texas covering my belly, and Lorenzo's dead, his brains spread all over a tree. Meantime, Menard is down south gettin' high-grade pussy."

Stone Jeffries and Tom Trumble, the other remaining members of Winkler's gang, chimed in, supporting Seth. It was well after dark now, and Winkler had ridden practically nonstop to make it back in one day from the Winding Stair. He had immediately called this meeting at a moonlit clearing beside the river. Nights were turning cooler, and Winkler wore a warm sheepskin jacket.

"Lorenzo was stupid," Winkler said bluntly. "You don't goddamn play games with a hard twist like Fargo. *Blind* him . . . Jesus! Seth, you two shoulda plugged the bastard the second you had the drop on him."

"Sure, Mike, but that partner of his—"

"Save it for your memoirs," Winkler cut him off. "Face it, boys, sometimes men get killed in our line of work. Hell, we all gotta go sometime, anh? The point is, we're *done* dying. Now it's the other side's turn to bleed and bleed hard. Starting with Skye Fargo."

Winkler paused, listening to drums throb. He couldn't interpret them, nor even identify the tribe, but the beat was urgent. A smile spread across his scarred visage.

"These brand-new strikes Menard ordered won't even be necessary, boys," he said. "Word leaked out today that the army will be occupying the rez. Troops have been moved in. And they'll be puttin' the collar on the Cherokees."

"Yeah," said Trumble, a rangy Texan, "but the frog needs them relocated, not just 'pacified.' Have there been enough killings pinned on them to guarantee they get the boot?"

Winkler chuckled. "Menard may be an insufferable barber's clerk, boys, but he ain't one to do something by halves. Just before those soldier boys come hoo-rawin' onto the rez, there's gonna be a long, bloody night of terror. Wolf Sleeve, Iron Mountain, and those stinkin' gut-eaters of theirs are going to create a 'Cherokee' massacre even worse than they done to them Creeks down in the 'chitas. For the Cherokees, it's gonna be a prison camp for sure."

He looked at Seth. "And Skye Fargo is yours."

It was too dark to see how Seth's face paled. "No thanks," he said quietly. "I'd rather tangle with a smallpox blanket. I'd have a better chance."

15

Throughout the long and dangerous night, Skye Fargo and Yellowstone Jack pushed their mounts hard while keeping their red-rimmed eyes to all sides.

Fargo considered it a rescue mission, but given the nature of the enemy, he wasn't sure there would be enough of Sarah Blackburn to save.

They rested only long enough to water their horses, occasionally feeding them crushed barley from their hats. By dawn, Fargo's saddle-sore tailbone throbbed like a Tewa tombé, and both eyes were swollen and water-galled from grit. His belly burned, trying to digest food that wasn't there.

"*Thank* you, Jesus, for another glorious day!" Jack roared out sarcastically as the sun broke over the eastern flats. The Winding Stair Mountains were closer than the Ouachitas, and now loomed big on the southern horizon.

Fargo shared his friend's rough mood. Last night's hard ride, the constant danger, the hunger and exhaustion and aching joints—these were the details the hero-hungry newspapers and nickel novels never included.

"Renegades been watchin' us like cats on rats," Jack reported.

Fargo nodded. Both men were jumpy and nerve-frazzled. At one point last night a screech owl had suddenly let loose nearby while they were spelling the horses. Fargo had nearly jumped out of his boots.

During the night he had wondered if he would ever see another sunrise. Now he had one before him, and even this early, dust hazed the lowland plain lying between them and the mountains.

"Renegades?" he repeated. "Yeah, but just a handful.

Likely, they'll try to kill us when we move farther out of the trees. Right now, though, we best find water or they won't *need* to kill us."

The best way to locate water was to watch where the birds flew just after sunrise. Fargo followed the flying crowd east to a clump of sandbar willows beside a large creek hidden by the hip-high buffalo grass.

"Hell, that's Antlers Creek," Jack said. "I forgot it was here."

Fargo drew rein and swung down. "Our friends didn't forget. They plan to tank up here themselves soon as we clear out."

Fargo nodded toward their backtrail. At least four braves were waiting where the trees ended and the grass plain began.

"Sons of bitches," Jack grumped as he threw the bridle so his ginger could drink. "I only count four. Let's put at 'em—we got repeaters, they ain't."

"A bow and arrow counts for a repeater," Fargo assured his friend. "Anyhow, we'll be huggin' with 'em soon enough. But this isn't the right time. Our horses are near played out, and so are we. And I don't cotton to entering a fight with my belly empty. Right now they're biding their time, waiting. Let 'em."

Jack grunted, agreeing with his friend's logic.

"This latest hatch of flies is murder on the horses," Jack remarked, for both the ginger and Fargo's black-and-white stallion were snorting and stamping at the pesky deerflies.

With a solid *whap,* Yellowstone Jack's gelding swung his tail hard into Jack's face, so hard the old campaigner swallowed his cud of chewing tobacco. When he finished retching up tobacco juice, Jack loosed a stream of creative cursing at his horse.

Grinning despite his weariness, Fargo plunged his head into the chilly creek. The morning air was nippy, and he shivered in his buckskins.

"Happens Baptiste Menard pulls this landgrab off," Jack remarked as they stepped up into leather, "he could take the whole damn she-bang for hisself. The entire Cherokee Nation in one land deed, damn greedy-guts. Ain't right, all these 'empires' bein' formed in the West. Use to, a feller could fill his hand with a barking iron and fight for what he owned, bury the losers afterward. Now it's all these Philadelphia lawyers stealin' it with crooked laws writ in Latin—and Greek to me."

"Amen, brother," Fargo agreed, looking back over his shoulder. "Our trail companions are edging closer."

Jack, still all wroth over those damned worthless, pettifogging lawyers, ignored his friend's remark.

"I been a-thinkin' on it," he said. "Been many moons since the Cheraws seen a battle. What if they get chicken guts when it comes time to fight or show yellow? You 'n' me will be left with our asses hangin' in the wind. Agin' renegades tough as bore bristles."

Fargo pulled down his hat against the swirling dust. "You frettin' these renegades, dad? Watch this."

Fargo had perfected a defensive move that literally allowed him to instantly turn the tables on a pursuer, his own version of the border shift. Without interrupting the Ovaro's forward progress, he dropped the reins and braced one hand on the pommel, the other on the cantle of his saddle. He lifted himself straight up out of the saddle, spun around, and in an eyeblink he was facing the renegades and backward in the saddle.

The unexpected move caught their pursuers by surprise. Fargo speared his Henry from its saddle boot, levered a round into the chamber, and dropped a bead on the lead rider, a Comanche riding a claybank.

"It's live and let live, with me," Fargo muttered. "Until it's kill or be killed."

The Henry bucked into his shoulder, a red plume of blood exploded from the warrior's bare chest, and he crumpled dead to the ground. Yipping in surprise, the other three wheeled their mounts and retreated another hundred yards or so.

Yellowstone Jack whooped. "*That* kissed the mistress, Mr. Trailsman! You know how superstitious Injins are about sudden death. That oughter shake 'em off our tail."

With this bunch, Fargo wasn't so sure. Most Indians, unlike these lawless Staked Plains renegades, held life to be sacred, not cheap. It was respect for life, not an act of cowardice, that made most Indian war parties retreat after losing only two or three respected warriors. Normal rules didn't apply to these outlaw braves.

"They're still behind us," Fargo said. "But *farther* behind us. C'mon, let's raise dust."

The morning sun was well up when both men began to notice a familiar rumbling noise out ahead where a huge brown cloud of dust hovered over the grass. The ground beneath them vibrated, spooking the horses.

"Great day in the morning!" Jack exclaimed when they caught their first sight of the massive herd of buffalo thundering across the Plains. "Boy, them shaggies must stretch back to the Big Muddy. We might as well homestead right here till they pass."

Fargo knew Jack was stretching it, but not by much. The "great die-up" of the buffalo had not yet begun in full force, and many herds were still so huge they staggered the greenhorn imagination. Once, in east Texas, Fargo barely made it onto a rock pinnacle before a herd swept by—it was a full twelve hours later before the beasts passed and he could climb down.

This herd was easily as big as that one. But Fargo noticed how a stiff wind pressed the grass flat.

"We ain't waiting," he told Jack, licking his finger and sticking it into the breeze. "C'mon, turn your horse into the wind."

Whooping to embolden their nervous mounts, both men charged the herd. No sense was more acute, in the buffalo, than the sense of smell. Fargo watched the big sentinels of the herd lift their huge, shaggy, bearded heads to sample the air. The human smell moved through the herd like wildfire on the wind, turning them southeast.

"A buffler is a stupid damn critter," Jack said on a hoarse chuckle. "But the warm liver is good fixens. Wish we had time to kill one. I'm so hungry I could eat a raw skunk without salt."

"Oh, we got time to *kill* a buff," Fargo said. "But not to skin the damn thing. Quit beatin' your gums about food, wouldja? I'm trying not to think about it. Especially with our friends still dogging us."

Another uneasy hour passed, and the Winding Stair range was now close enough to make out details such as gulches and erosion gullies, but they were still at least two hours off.

"Lookit there," said eagle-eyed Yellowstone Jack, nodding to the right. "Pronghorn buck."

Fargo saw the white rump flashing in the sun as the pronghorn fled from the now turned herd. The Trailsman's stomach clenched like a fist, closing on nothing.

"Antelope meat's a little tough," Jack hinted. "But it's better'n jackrabbit stew."

Fargo glanced behind them. The renegades still kept a respectful distance.

"Ahh, t'hell with this," he said, sliding his brass-framed Henry from its boot. "Our bellies are crying out for fresh meat."

It wasn't a simple matter of hunger. Despite his time urgency, Fargo also knew it was fatal to go into a hard fight feeling hunger weakness. Warriors needed meat, and plenty of it.

With Jack keeping a watchful eye on the renegades, Fargo shot and quickly dressed out the small pronghorn. They scorched a few bits of the best meat. It tasted delicious to the famished men. They had no time to dry and jerk the rest, so they simply cut out some choice parts and wrapped them in wet cloth.

Jack belched loudly, then yawned. "Hell . . . had me some poon and forty winks, wouldn't be a bad day a-tall."

Fargo, too, yawned—sating their hunger inevitably left them sleepy. Especially given their dearth of sleep in the past eight or nine days.

"Poon, I can't help you with," Fargo told his friend. "Doesn't travel well in saddlebags. But the forty winks you mentioned might be advisable before we ride into those mountains."

"That shines. What about the blanket asses?"

Fargo studied them. They had halted when the white men halted, and now were simply watching. They were at least three-hundred yards away, staying out of easy rifle range.

"You sleep first," Fargo decided, "while I stand watch. Then we'll switch off. But it's gotta be a short nap, old son, thirty minutes at most."

Jack was snoring the moment he laid his head on his saddle bow. Fargo, knowing the Henry had kept the renegades respectful earlier, made sure they saw plenty of it now. The Indians, too, needed sleep and seemed content, for the moment, to keep only one guard awake.

But that'll change soon now, Fargo told himself. The renegades' quarry was now crossing the last open flats before the Winding Stair. They would make their move anytime now.

Fargo kicked Jack's boot. "Christ, Methuselah, you snore like a grizzly with a head cold. Up and on the line, it's my turn."

Cursing all creation, especially Fargo's corner of it, Jack took the Henry from his friend. The Trailsman had no idea how long he'd been asleep before Jack's hoarse shout jolted him awake.

"Roust out, boy! We got us a dustup a-comin'!"

Fargo couldn't get his first words out until his tongue had scraped away the nasty film on the roof of his mouth. He came to his feet just in time to see the trio of renegades rushing them. A bullet hummed past Fargo's head.

Jack was making things lively with the rapid-firing Henry, and his bullets turned them away.

"I see *these* boys're feelin' sparky! Dig in or ride?" Jack asked tersely.

"If we dig in," Fargo replied, "we might get pinned down in a long siege. But we have to get back up north before the army sweep. I prefer a running battle—at least we'll be moving."

While the braves were regrouping, Fargo and Jack quickly rigged their horses. By the time the two men vaulted into their saddles, the whooping and yipping renegades were thundering toward them again.

"*Thank* you, Jesus, for the noble red man!" Jack shouted even as an arrow, buzzing like a blowfly, streaked past his hoary head.

Both horses laid their ears back flat as they galloped across the waving, blue-green sea of grass. A few bullets, and an astonishing number of arrows, blurred the air all around Fargo. By habit, he spun sideways to reduce the target he offered his enemies.

Jack, who had sided Fargo in many a scrape, knew what was coming. Skye Fargo had survived, all these years, by seldom doing the predictable. Surprise, confound, and confuse your enemy, that was his way.

"Now?" Jack shouted over to him above the throbbing drumbeat of hooves.

"Now!" Fargo affirmed, suddenly tugging rein to wheel the Ovaro hard right.

In a matter of moments, both men were suddenly charging their astounded pursuers.

Fargo had already thumbed reloads into the Henry's tube magazine. He had sixteen rounds at his disposal, and he kept the lever in constant motion. The well-engineered ejector mechanism clicked smoothly and repeatedly, and hot shell casings spewed everywhere, glittering in the sunlight. Jack added to the din with the solid cracks of his magazine pistol.

However, Fargo had pulled this once before, and these were not cowards in this trio. Instead of veering off, they thundered forward, sending a flurry of arrows before them. One caught the heel of Fargo's left boot with such force it tore his foot from the stirrup. Another just missed the Ovaro's head and glanced off a saddle fender.

Fargo's Henry, hard used lately, was heating up dangerously. Just before he snatched his Colt from the holster, he scored a hit with the rifle. A Kiowa on a fourteen-hand pinto threw both arms out when a neat hole suddenly opened in the center of his forehead. The lifeless body hit the ground and bounced a few times like a bundle of rags.

Jack, forced to larger targets by his pistol's limited range, sent a second brave tumbling ass-over-applecart when he dropped the renegade's stallion.

" 'She has freckles on her . . . butt I love her!' " he sang in a raucous bray.

The Henry's magazine was empty, gun oil sizzling inside the hot barrel. Fargo saw their gambit had worked. The only remaining mounted renegade stopped long enough to pick up his stranded companion, then, riding double, they escaped to the north.

"They won't be back," Fargo predicted. "They've lost half their men."

Yellowstone Jack whooped, thumping his chest. Despite the trouble they still faced, down here *and* up north, Fargo indulged his friend now in a few moments of bragging. On the frontier, every victory was hard-fought. A man bragged when he fought well, for bravery was the hardest thing, and always had to be celebrated.

But the celebration passed, leaving those oddly shaped,

twisting mountains just ahead. The two riders reined their mounts in that direction.

"Damn you, devil nag," Jack growled, for his feisty ginger was fighting the bit. "I'll learn you to muck with your betters."

Fargo, barely suppressing a laugh, watched the old flint grab his pommel and lean far forward in the stirrups. He took the gelding's tender left ear into his mouth and champed down hard.

"Bastard! They's more where that come—*Tender Virgin!*"

Like an indifferent catapult, the ginger simply pitched the old man forward out of the saddle. Jack landed hard in a cursing heap, on the verge of pulling out his pistol and shooting the rebellious horse.

Fargo laughed until tears streaked the dust coating his face. "You damn fool. You took your butt clear out of the saddle."

"So you could kiss it, Fargo. Damn that horse! Son of a bitch is cunning."

"That's what you get, gramps, for riding a horse that's as ornery as you are."

The mirth bled from Fargo's face as he stared at those dark, mysterious mountains.

"Get horsed," he ordered Jack. "Assuming she ain't dead yet, we got a princess to rescue."

The grass grew so high on the lower slopes of the Winding Stair Mountains that it shined their boots as Fargo and Yellowstone Jack rode through it. As they ascended higher into the mountains, they were forced to follow an old, dried-up creek bed. It made for easier riding than did the thickly forested upper slopes.

"Been riders through here lately," Jack said, reading the dry bed. "Mostly white men."

Fargo nodded. "The most recent track is leading out. One rider with a dog trotting along."

"That would be Menard," Jack said.

"No doubt. Let's just hope it means Sarah is still here—and alive."

There was fog on the mountains even this late in the morning, a shifting saddle of pure white cotton the sun couldn't yet reach. Now and then Fargo felt it clammy on his face, like sticky cobwebs.

"Let's leave the bed and turn right," he told Jack, pointing. "Past this point, no more tracks in the creek. Besides, that's an unstable landslide slope above us. So I'd guess we're near a hideout."

Fargo's hunch panned out. Both men swung down and led their mounts through the thick pines and silver spruces, weapons at the ready.

"There," eagle-eyed Jack said, pointing with his chin.

Wind-twisted jack pines almost concealed a small but solid cabin of notched logs. Both men hobbled their horses out of sight and continued forward, leapfrogging from tree to tree.

When they were only a stone's throw away, Fargo spotted a calico gelding of sixteen hands tied beside the cabin. Its flank was spur scarred, its ribs protruding like barrel staves.

"That is one sore-used horse," he said with disgust. "*Got* to be an outlaw's mount."

"Ain't Menard's," Jack said. "He rides him a fine-lookin' *grullo*."

"Yeah, but I'll bet *my* horse this is one of his hideouts," Fargo said. "How many mountain cabins got freshly oiled paper for window panes? That's his style—plenty of comfort, even when he's back of beyond. Watch for my signal."

Colt in hand, Fargo dashed forward and crouched under the window. Slowly, he raised his eyes over the sill.

One corner of an oiled paper pane had torn out, allowing him a clearer look into the single room. It was dark here under the dense canopy of trees, but a blazing coal-oil lamp hung on a nail from the rafters. It showed a solid, raw-lumber floor, a hearth and fireplace. In a horsehair-stuffed chair, cleaning his fingernails with a horseshoe nail, slumped a doltish-looking, slope-shouldered, long-jawed man in worn-out range clothes.

"Well, what if I just *take* it, sugar britches?" the man suddenly said, making Fargo flinch at the unexpected sound of his voice.

The Trailsman remained confused until he spotted Sarah in the rear corner, tied to a narrow but comfortable-looking bed. It took him a moment to recognize her. Evidently, Menard had tossed her own clothing and forced her into a pinch-waisted Parisian gown of emerald green with a ruffled flounce. Her black hair was in two thick plaits.

Fargo waved Jack forward even as the man in the chair raised his voice. "How 'bout that, Princess? I just *take* it, anh? Menard won't miss a slice off a cut loaf."

"Recognize that peckerwood?" Jack said quietly. "That's one of the cockchafers that was loafing at Clayton Station. Does jobs for Winkler."

Fargo nodded. "Menard musta left him to guard Sarah. Well, let's get this over with. You cover the window, I'll kick open the door."

Fargo did just that, his strong right leg a well-muscled battering ram. The door crashed open, and he leveled his blue-steeled Colt on the thug.

"Make any quick moves," Fargo warned, "and I'll shoot an airshaft through you. Jack, grab that hogleg off his belt and keep him covered."

"Skye!" Sarah exclaimed. "Am I ever glad to see you!"

"You're easy to look at yourself," Fargo assured her with a grin.

"You're makin' one helluva mistake, Fargo," the hard case warned, mustering bravado as Fargo untied Sarah. "This'll cost you dear. That little piece now belongs to Baptiste Menard."

"Mister, case you ain't noticed," Jack fumed, "you ain't got no friends here. That mouth will bury you."

"Skye Fargo ain't no murderer," the tough said with smug confidence. "*He* plays by the rules. Got him a 'code'."

"Well, I ain't," Jack warned. "And I don't like your lip."

By now Sarah was up and taking short steps to restore her circulation while she volleyed questions at Fargo. Jack loosed an appreciative whistle at her altered appearance.

"God's gutta-percha! Your Purple, you look pretty as four aces. How's 'at corset feel?" Jack teased, eyeing the hourglass waist.

"What corset?" Sarah responded.

Jack stared closer. "Well, by the Lord Harry! She ain't wearin' one!"

Fargo kept his eyes on the man in the chair while he asked Sarah, "How'd Menard snare you?"

She flushed, for she had taken a vow not to be taken alive by Menard. She explained how her pistol had misfired in the cave, how Menard's well-trained hound had pinned her down long enough for Menard and Winkler to knock her out and tie her up.

"Luckily," she said, "he did not have time to take his filthy pleasure of me. By the time he got me here, he had received a message from *this* pig's afterbirth"—she nodded toward the chair—"telling him to ride north immediately."

Fargo and Yellowstone Jack exchanged a worried look. Briefly, Fargo told her about their visit with Nacona, and the quick plans they'd made for battle.

"We gotta head north ourselves," Fargo said. "It's about to go up like a steam boiler."

"What about the mouthpiece here?" Jack said, wagging his pistol at the captive. "How's 'bout I send him to the Land of Nod—permanent like?"

"Nah, we'll just take his horse," Fargo decided, though his voice was reluctant. "That way he can't warn Menard from a telegraph station. I know he prob'ly deserves killing ten times over, but we got no proof."

"Kill him," Jack insisted. "He's a cowardly back-shooter, it's writ all over his ugly map."

At the mention of taking his horse, the cocky look left the outlaw's doltish face. This was no country in which to be left afoot, waiting for Menard to return and kill him for losing the woman. What happened next caught everyone by surprise.

Brasher of London, gunsmiths, manufactured a two-shot, .38-caliber "muff gun" that was popular with gamblers, prostitutes, and others who employed small hideout guns. The owlhoot in the chair pulled a Brasher out of his shirt pocket and aimed it straight at Fargo's lights.

Fargo had holstered his Colt, in order to untie Sarah, and had no time now to clear leather. He grabbed Sarah and dove to one side even as Jack kicked at the outlaw's gun hand.

The two-shot flew across the room, but not before one of the over-and-under barrels discharged with an impressive roar.

Followed by a second roar, of human pain, as the slug chewed into Jack's stout thigh.

"Mister," Jack hissed to the outlaw, teeth clenched in pain as he crumpled to one knee, "you're a gone-up case."

Sarah cried out in concern for the brave snowbeard, leaping down to look at his wound. The man in the chair, face sweating now, stared down the Colt's barrel. He decided to try bravado again.

"Well, Fargo," he said, chuckling, "looks like your clover is deep today, my friend."

Fargo glanced down at the faithful old friend who had already saved his life—and his eyes—when those two owlhoots tried to blind him. Now Jack had literally taken a bullet for him. Fargo saw, from the old salt's trembling lips, that he was slipping into shock.

"Let's get the facts clear, mister," Fargo said, his right fist filled with steel. "You are a known criminal who was taken as our prisoner. You knew we were about to let you go. Yet, just now you pulled a hideout gun and tried to kill me, wounding my friend instead. Is that about right?"

"Reckon so, but you mean to take my horse. And like I said, don't matter that I shot at you, on account your clover was deep—"

"*Yours* ain't, you low-crawling, murdering son of a bitch," Yellowstone Jack cut him off, momentarily rallying and shooting the miscreant straight through the heart.

Fargo felt nothing. The man had lost any rights in the matter when he stupidly shucked out that hideout gun.

"How's it look?" he asked Sarah, who was busy examining Jack's wounded thigh.

"Bad," she said bluntly. "It was very close range. The bullet is lodged deep in muscle. Infection will set in soon. And the bleeding is heavy. He is a strong old man, Skye, but blood loss will kill even the strongest."

Fargo knew it was indeed bad when a delirious Yellowstone Jack muttered, "Oh, Moses on the mountain! It was some strange and terrible, mother. Naked savages tryin' to skin your little boy alive."

"Let me guess," Sarah said to Fargo. "That's the first time you've ever heard him mention his mother?"

Fargo nodded. "Claimed he never had one, that a bird shit on a rock and he hatched from the sun."

He thought a few moments more. "All right," he decided. "They don't come much tougher than that old strip of leather. Nor much braver. I don't care if it makes us late, Sarah—before we join any battle up north, you and me got surgery to perform."

149

16

"Surgery?" Yellowstone Jack repeated, shocked back to awareness. "H'ar now! Fargo, you must be the joker in this deck. I can still cut the bacon," he insisted, managing to sit up. "Happens that wound don't mortify, I'll live. A poultice might fetch it."

Fargo shook his head. "It *will* mortify, the bullet's in too deep. We'll have to cut it out, old son. The worst'll pass quick—"

"Don't coddle me, goddamnit," Jack snapped, wincing at the pain. "Ain't no need to cut a-tall, that bullet's a long way from my heart."

Fargo and Sarah ignored the old scutter's protests, hauling him over to the bed. Sarah found a bottle of Kentucky bourbon in a cupboard above the old Franklin stove. Jack, gurgling like a happy baby, took the level in the bottle down at least four inches.

"He's as ready as he'll ever be," Fargo decided, working Jack's trousers down over his hips to expose the ugly, red-puckered flesh surrounding the wound. "Let's work quick while Old Churnbrain has him."

Sarah lifted the chimney off the lamp so Fargo could heat the blade of his Arkansas Toothpick. Though plenty drunk, Jack sucked in a hissing breath when Sarah wiped the bloody wound with a wet cloth.

"Pour some whiskey right in the wound," Fargo told her. "That's it, slop it in there good."

She did, Jack flinching as it seeped deeper into the hole, burning.

"Knife's glowing," Fargo muttered to Sarah. Then, to himself: "Do it once, Fargo, do it fast, do it right . . ."

Fargo's first move was to probe for the bullet.

"Christ on a cracker!" Jack bellowed drunkenly. "You two ain't carvin' jade. Cut the son of a bitch out. Just . . . oh, *Christ,* that hurts!"

Fargo had felt the tip of his knife make contact with the slug. Wasting no time, for blood was blossoming up now, he cut straight down to it. Jack was awash on a sea of pain now, and Sarah slipped his leather belt between his teeth.

"There," a relieved Fargo finally announced, holding a flattened slug out between thumb and forefinger.

But now comes the fun part, Fargo thought. If that wound wasn't cauterized, it would pus up within a day—turn to gangrene in two.

Sarah helped a delirious Jack down a few more jolts of whiskey. When Fargo's knife blade glowed red-orange again, he quickly laid it against Jack's wound, searing the ragged edges together. There was a sound like bacon sizzling, and Fargo almost gagged at the stench of scorched flesh.

"All the devils in hell!" Jack roared out, his body bending like a drawn bow before he passed out.

"It's gonna hurt like the dickens when that whiskey wears off," Fargo told Sarah quietly. "We had to cut deep."

"With that wound he will not be able to ride," Sarah fretted. "And obviously we cannot leave him here for killers to find. But the way Menard hurried out of here to go north, I fear the final crisis has arrived. We are needed up north, and immediately."

There was despair in her melodic voice, and Fargo understood why. But no matter how bleak things looked, Fargo never succumbed to pessimism. Once a man mated with despair, he was worthless.

"We won't leave him," Fargo replied, "nor will he need to ride. We'll make a travois."

Sarah beamed. "Of course! Not being from a Plains tribe, I didn't think of it. But I hear they are easier to pull than a cart."

Fargo nodded. "It's easy on a horse, way it's designed. A wheeled conveyance shakes and bounces like hell at every rut. The travois is lots easier on the injured, too. And quick to make."

Fargo went outside and carefully checked for unwelcome visitors. Then he cut willow poles, using them to fashion the travois. When it was ready, and lashed tight with raw-hide thongs, he examined the sore-used calico.

"Bad temper," he muttered when the gelding repeatedly tried to bite him. "Outlaw's horses are bad medicine, been too abused. Best leave him."

Jack's gelding, too, was ill-tempered, but only with Jack. So Fargo decided to hitch the travois to Jack's horse and let Sarah ride the ginger.

When Fargo finally checked on his Ovaro, guilt lanced into him. The stallion's mane was still matted with sweat from the ride down, and the breeze was chilly.

"Sorry, old warhorse," Fargo said. "You been pushed hard lately, and there's more to come."

The pinto snorted, as if to say *no complaints*. Fargo stripped off the saddle and let the stallion shake out the trail kinks with a minute of serious bucking. Then the Trailsman tacked the horse again and retied his bedroll and slicker under the cantle straps.

He checked the slant of the sun: midafternoon. Sarah was right. Time was a bird, and the bird was on the wing.

He and Sarah lashed a woozy Yellowstone Jack to the travois. Fargo helped Sarah into her saddle, then stirruped and swung aboard himself.

"Shoulda asked sooner," he said, "but do you know how to ride?"

She nodded. "My brother taught me. He keeps a saddle horse."

"Goddamnit," Jack fumed as they headed down the creek bed, "I feel like some pregnant squaw."

"Pipe down, you jay," Fargo snapped at him. "You're lucky I don't shoot you and leave you for wolf bait."

Sarah was more sympathetic. "Does it hurt, snowbeard?"

"Hurts somethin' fierce," Jack admitted through clenched teeth. "Your Regalness," he added.

Fargo wished they could slow down, make this a leisurely trip for Jack's sake. But, well out ahead, message drums were throbbing. Sand was slipping through the glass, and all too soon, for the Cherokees and many others, time would run out.

Baptiste Menard thumb-snapped a lucifer to flaring life, then slid back the cover of his watch to check the time: just past midnight.

"I knew the time for bloody business must be coming soon," said the stern voice of Wolf Sleeve, who sat his fine golden buckskin beside Menard's prized *grullo*. "But I expected more delay. One or two more sleeps, time for my men to paint and dance for battle. You want us to attack this very night?"

"For *battle*?" Menard's laughter was a single, harsh bark that made Wolf Sleeve scowl. "Buck, in a fight you stand behind no man, and that blade in your moccasin is death unleashed. But this tonight will be no battle. It will be like the raid at Broken Bow Lake. You start with the Choctaws and simply work your way over the ridges, killing, pillaging, burning crops. You create a full-blown 'Cherokee' massacre."

Wolf Sleeve looked unhappy in the luminous moonlight. Not dance for courage? Impossible!

"But why now, this very night?" he complained. "I have four good men still away, watching Fargo."

"You bend with the breeze or you break," Menard replied. "I *had* to ride up here and change the plan. There is a bluecoat eagle chief named Hiram Steele. He was about to accept my story about events here in the Indian Territory. But Fargo said some things that made Steele look into my past. A bloody strike tonight, by 'Cherokees,' will discredit Fargo, Steele, and Talcott Mumford."

All these details bored Wolf Sleeve. His right hand slid down to touch the cool, hard haft of the knife tucked into his moccasin.

"I have longed to feel the vital heat rush from Fargo's body when my knife opens him from his neck to his manhood," the Comanche said. "Now, that time may not arrive. For you have said we renegades must leave right after the massacre."

"Naturally. We can't blame it on Cherokees," Menard explained, "if your band are still trespassing in The Nations."

"Must it be so soon?"

"Yes, for several reasons. Including the fact that the leaves will be falling soon, your braves won't be able to find cover for camps."

Menard paused for dramatic emphasis.

"As for gutting Fargo," he added, "don't worry, you may

well get your chance. He has a knack for showing up at the first whiff of powder smoke, and soon enough there'll be plenty."

A spur jingled in the nearby darkness, alerting Lieutenant Jimmy Briscoe. He unsnapped his flap holster and filled his fist with one of the heavy-framed Smith and Wesson revolvers issued to army officers.

"Who goes there?" he challenged, trying to listen beyond the surf-crashing roar of his own pulse in his ears.

No response. Just the ghostly soughing of wind in the trees, the steady chuckle of the nearby Arkansas River. But Jimmy, who had left the main camp to inspect the picket outposts, had definitely heard a spur.

"Some of Menard's mercenaries are definitely out there," he reported to Talcott Mumford when he returned to camp. "They've been watching us all day. I wonder where Skye and Jack are."

"So do I," Mumford admitted. "After all, Menard was counting on Judge Moneybags to hand him an empire, and Fargo is the chief obstacle to his dream."

It was long past midnight, and both men planned to be up all night. Mumford, whose home had been torched the night before, had joined Jimmy's unit for his own safety.

"Something big is planned soon—perhaps this very night," Mumford said, his tone heavy with worry. "There's too much activity out there to simply be Winkler and his small bunch of hard tails. Wolf Sleeve's renegade band are also preparing to strike—at somebody."

"Yeah," Jimmy said with bitter frustration. "And with legal charges being filed left and right, I'm under strict orders to take no action except in immediate self-defense. Command fears that any U.S. Army action might ruin their case."

"I know it's frustrating," Menard agreed. "Especially now that we know Menard, Winkler, and the renegades are all feeding at the same trough."

"Well, if anyone attacks *us*," Jimmy said boldly, "we're ready. Still . . ."

The young officer's gaze shifted beyond the glow of the campfires to the dark ring of trees. "I sure-god hope Skye and Yellowstone Jack get here soon."

With false dawn glowing on the horizon, Fargo, Sarah, and Jack reached the tableland south of the Arkansas River. The last sign of human life Fargo had seen was the short-line stage that ran between Red Oak and Fort Smith.

But "human life" was everywhere in the form of Wolf Sleeve's hidden spies. All the owl hoots and coyote barks didn't fool Fargo.

"I'm so hungry I could boil my hat," he remarked to Sarah as he swung down, near Eagle Creek, to look for sign in the bright moonlight.

Jack, who'd been drifting in and out of consciousness, heard his friend's remark.

"River-water soup for everybody!" he brayed. "Air pudding for dessert! Nothin' but good eats when you side Skye 'Grim Reaper' Fargo!"

"Pipe down," Fargo snapped at him. "Sound travels at night."

He dropped onto one knee. When he found plenty of fresh tracks made by animals, Fargo relaxed somewhat. Men hadn't been here recently or animals would have stayed away.

"If they're waiting for us in ambush," Fargo said as he led the Ovaro forward to drink, "the trap's not around here."

"The route you picked was a smart one," Sarah praised Fargo. "It missed all their usual trails."

"Horse apples!" Jack called out. "He coulda found a nigher route. Damn my eyes! This country needs a few thirst parlors!"

"Calm down, snowbeard," the Cherokee princess soothed him, kneeling to examine his wound.

Fargo watched over her shoulder as she unwrapped the injury. Caked blood covered it. He asked no questions when she quickly scraped the dried blood away with a piece of bark until the wound was bleeding fresh. That old blood was dirty and had to go.

Jack let out a howl of curses.

"*I'm* the one should cuss," Fargo said as he bent down to hoist up his stout friend. "At least this is the last creek I'll have to lug your fat ass across."

From the north bank of Eagle Creek it was a short, easy

ride to the Arkansas and the heart of the Indian Territory. They had been riding only about twenty minutes, holding an easy trot, when Fargo heard distant voices and drew rein.

Heads almost touching, he and Sarah strained their ears.

"It's Indian singing," Fargo said. "But I can't tell the tribe or the occasion, can you?"

She shook her head in the moonlight. "It is not an Eastern tribe, I would know the singing. This is a Plains tribe."

"Best not to ignore it," Fargo decided, swinging down and pulling his Henry from its boot. "Wait here, and keep Jack's gun to hand."

Hating the delay, but considering it prudent, Fargo headed on a plumbline straight toward the sound. As he drew nearer, threading his way through a maze of trees and bushes, he also began to hear the rhythmic drumming of sticks against hollow logs. Sawing flames showed ahead.

By now Fargo knew, stomach sinking, that the singers were Kiowas and Comanches, the drumbeat that of a war dance. Sure enough, when he pushed a branch aside he spotted a large, grassy clearing in the forest—filled with renegades dancing themselves into a glassy-eyed battle trance around the fire.

The Cherokee-style arrows stuffed into their fox- and coyote-skin quivers convinced Fargo that the mother of all "Cherokee atrocities" was about to be staged. When he saw an Indian boy leading mustangs forward, already rigged for the trail, he knew the attack was imminent.

"Let's make tracks," he told Sarah the moment he returned. "Damn it, it's later than we thought. The moment we get far enough away from here, I'm sending up the signal for the Man Killers to muster. But from what I just saw, these renegades are ready to hit the warpath now. It's a damn long chance, but the Cherokees *might* be able to muster in time."

"The Cherokees will muster, and in time," Sarah assured him proudly. "My brother has kept them battle ready."

"Maybe," Fargo said, watching the surrounding pall of darkness closely. "Your brother seems like a good man. But even if they muster, then we still got to figure out how warriors in dugouts can close with and destroy mounted warriors on land. Jesus, pile on the agony. Well . . . this should be far enough past those dancing renegades."

The Trailsman knew it was sure defeat to wait any longer. Figuring they were safely beyond reach of the braves, he aimed his Henry at the sky and levered and fired four times—the signal he and Nacona had agreed upon: two closely spaced shots followed by two widely spaced.

Fargo had just fired his fourth shot, when at least two repeating rifles began to spit flame and lead at them from a dangerously close position. Winkler's cockroaches . . .

The ominous whine of rifle slugs filled their ears, so many whiffing projectiles that the wind from them fanned their hair and clothing. Still, Sarah did not panic nor even delay. Exhibiting the cool courage of a trained War Woman, she directed fire from Jack's magazine pistol accurately toward the muzzle flashes, as did Fargo.

"C'mon, Princess!" he shouted when the rifles momentarily fell silent. "Let's get out of the weather! Gee up, boy!"

They heeled their mounts forward even as the next deadly volley of lead swarmed over them.

17

Despite the signs of scattered riders during the night, Lieutenant Jimmy Briscoe wisely had not split his force. Though champing at the bit to investigate, he had held off, remembering his latest orders from Fort Gibson: only in self-defense, or if white civilians were attacked, could his troops use force.

Now, with just enough predawn light to show the yellow cavalry cord on his campaign hat, Jimmy and Indian Agent Talcott Mumford rode out from the Arkansas River camp. They could hear an ominous sound from the direction of Blue Feather Ridge north of the river.

They forded the Arkansas at one of its many gravel bars, noticing how the sound increased as they neared a stagnant deadwater behind the river. Although inexperienced on the frontier, Jimmy's heart raced as he swung down and ground-hitched his sorrel. He knew what the sound must be, all right, even without the help of Mumford, an Indian expert.

"*Ho*-ly moly!" he whispered after peeking around a fat cottonwood. "Cherokees! Only, I've never seen them look like this."

"Thank your lucky stars for that, son," Mumford whispered back. "You're gazing at some of the fiercest warriors in the New World. At one time they were the Vikings of America's rivers."

Even now they danced, kicking high and sending up a rhythmic rattling noise from the tortoise shells, filled with pebbles, tied to their legs. Jimmy thrilled at the glimpses of red everywhere in the glaring firelight, the color of valor—from their brightly dyed plume feathers to their vermilion-streaked faces and the scarlet strouding draped around them.

"That especially tall one with the painted shield," Mumford explained, "is Nacona Blackburn, Sarah's older brother. And those two who look especially gruesome are the Adawehis, or conjurers. They wear those bird and animal masks to ward off evil spirits."

"But what are the Cherokees up to, painted like this and dancing?"

Mumford knew, at least in part, what was going on— Fargo had told him the main details. These elite Cherokee Man Killers (their striped sashes gave them away) expected trouble at any moment, and were almost surely dancing now in preparation for the signal from Skye Fargo.

"Jimmy," he replied, "best if you don't know all the details—you know how it is, Indian Bureau versus the military. Just know this, my brave young friend: Fargo is making the plans now, not the War Department."

Jimmy nodded, still staring in fascination at the whirling circle of red-painted, red-clad warriors.

"If it's Skye holding the reins," the kid replied, "I'm with him till the hubs fall off. Even if it means a court-martial. Besides, who wants to fight *them*?"

The very moment Jimmy fell silent, four gunshots rang out from the south of the river. There was a shouted command from Nacona, a whooping cheer from his men, and the Cherokees began heading toward the bluff behind them.

"Was that Skye's signal?" Jimmy wondered aloud.

Mumford, his monocle reflecting red-orange flames, could just make out the kid's face in the gathering light of day. It was *the* signal, all right, and Mumford of all people knew just how crucial the upcoming battle would be. Not just the fate of the Cherokees was involved—if the dreaded, widespread War of the Plains broke out, *everyone* in this vast region, white, red, or purple, would be in a world of hurt thanks to Baptiste Menard.

"Never mind who sent the signal," Mumford replied. "The less you know, the better. But do believe this: the Cherokees are not just fighting for their own survival, but for the peaceful future of The Nations. Jimmy, most men go to war for land, riches, or slaves. These Cherokees, and Skye Fargo, are fighting so that men might be free."

Well out ahead, a hideous female scream rent the dawn silence, and Fargo knew the renegades had begun their campaign of terror.

"We're officially up against it," he announced to Sarah and Yellowstone Jack. "Get set for a fight to the death."

The sun had still not risen, but the sky was already showing pockets of pale blue. Fargo's sleepy but vigilant eyes constantly scanned as he rode.

"Even if your people did muster," Fargo fretted aloud to Sarah, "we got us one humdinger of a strategy problem. Namely, how to get those renegades down off the ridges and near the water, where the Man Killers will be."

"You are now talking to the best lure in the world," she reminded him. "Me. Menard is up here somewhere, overseeing his mayhem. If he sees me, he will send his killers down immediately. To him, it means the world to own me."

Fargo nodded, liking the idea. True, Sarah had just escaped capture by Menard, but she was already in grave danger, anyway. Besides, Fargo wouldn't insult any War Woman by worrying aloud about her safety. She did not fear death, only dishonor.

But it had to be tried quickly. The marauding renegades had swept onto Choctaw Ridge, and a racket of gunfire and whoops, of terrified screams, foreshadowed the long massacre to come if they couldn't be drawn off. Before long they would be out of sight of the river.

Fargo intently studied the Arkansas as they rode closer.

"There," he said triumphantly, pointing upriver to a good-sized river island covered with cottonwoods. "It's perfect for our plan. See how a thick marsh has formed back of the river? Cuts out any rapid escape. So do the steep bluffs on the other side of the river. Wolf Sleeve's band would be sitting ducks on that island."

"But Cheraws attackin' from the river ain't got much pertection," Yellowstone Jack pointed out, straining to see everything from his travois. "And the renegades got them cottonwoods, the double-poxed hounds."

Fargo nodded grim agreement. So far there was still no sign of the Cherokees. He couldn't even be sure they had mustered. All he could do was hope—and trust in their distinguished martial history.

"Yeah, those renegades . . . I'm hoping to bait 'em out," he said. "But *who's* the real bait? We'll just have to chance it."

Sarah, still quite fetching despite the rigors of the trail, nodded agreement. She had split the skirt of her gown in order to ride, and Fargo got tantalizing views of creamy inner thighs. The three friends were almost directly across from the long, narrow island.

"They have already seen me," Sarah remarked without staring obviously toward the bluff. "A white man with binoculars, hiding behind a hogback atop the ridge."

"Mike Winkler," hawkeyed Jack supplied. "I seen his scar."

"If Menard's up there," Fargo said, "we just *might* pull off this little bait and switch. I'm assuming the Cherokees will show up in time to put paid to it. Otherwise, we're gonna have a hornet's nest on our hands."

Fargo knew this trap, if it worked, was a rare opportunity to prevent the renegades from their favorite escape tactic: constantly subdividing as they fled, forcing pursuers to take many trails. This trap would force them into a white-man style battle in a fixed position.

"I can see how we might lure them down," Sarah said as she and Fargo dismounted. "But how do we force them onto the island?"

Without pointing, Fargo said, "See the only path down the bluff? Narrow and steep, and there's places where there's room for only one rider at a time. Me 'n' Jack will take up positions in the trees just below it. Once they ride down, I cover the path behind them with my Henry, make it hot to ride back up. Jack peppers them down on the open bank where you are. Plains Indians do *not* stay in the open and keep taking casualties. If I can keep them off that escape path, they'll have to fort up on the island—the river's shallow there, they can ride out to it quick."

"Sounds jake to me," said an ashen-faced Jack. "Long as we don't get the Princess kilt. But where's 'em dang Cheraws? Happens they don't show up in time, we'll be aroastin' over hot coals like them red Arabs done to Colonel Oglethorpe."

"My people are out there," Sarah said confidently. "They are waiting, with lookouts posted, for Skye to draw the final battle map."

The marauding sweep, up on Choctaw Ridge, now produced a steady din of whoops, shots, screams.

"Stay here," Fargo told Sarah as he transferred the travois to his own stallion. "Look at one of the ginger's hooves like maybe it's come up lame. Don't pay any attention to the bluff."

Fargo, staying behind tree cover to fool the sentry above, quickly secreted Jack's travois, and the Ovaro, in a hidden copse. With Jack propped up behind a big log, he had an excellent line of fire on the narrow north bank of the river.

Fargo, whose Henry held sixteen rounds in its magazine, needed to get closer than Jack if he hoped to shut the back door on the enemy—dangerously close, in fact, or he could not guarantee there'd be no escapes up the path.

"Hell's a-poppin'!" Jack roared out from behind Fargo. "Menard musta give the order to grab Her Highness. Let's go, Brother Ball!"

Fargo, with only deep grass to hide in, watched the renegades—and at least two white riders—come boiling over the lip of the bluff, their mounts plunging down the steep trail. Fargo gave a quick puff to clear blow sand from the Henry's mechanism.

"One bullet, one enemy," he whispered, quoting the battle-hardened Sioux. Right now it *all* came down to B. Tyler Henry's excellent workmanship—and Skye Fargo's courage to stay frosty and shoot plumb while a horde of hard, tough killers swarmed him.

Sarah made no attempt to escape, pulling out her scent-bottle pistol as if to make a last stand.

"Shit, there's that ugly Wolf Sleeve," Jack grumped. "That's a good man to let alone."

Fargo spotted the fierce Comanche battle chief, riding a light fawn mustang known as a golden buckskin. Equally fierce was the big Kiowa riding beside him, protected by a bone breastplate, with copper brassards around his arms—the aptly named Iron Mountain.

The light was good now, but thick yellow plumes of dust

rose as the renegades charged the river. Fargo lost track of Mike Winkler in the confusion, a fact that bothered him. But right now, Sarah was about to be descended upon.

"Bust caps, Jack!" he ordered. "Drive 'em back toward the path. I'll take the reins from there."

"It's a corker!" the old salt called out gleefully as his magazine pistol began its explosive chatter.

At first, Fargo's plan went reasonably well. Jack's deadly accurate fire turned the exposed Indians, now along the grassy bank, back toward the path. At which point Fargo's pitiless Henry took over, wiping rider after rider off his horse. Eventually, a dying mount partially blocked the narrow path.

Jack was well hidden in the trees and took no return fire. Fargo, in contrast, was forced to show himself each time he fired, and soon the livid renegades had a fix on his position.

A flock of deadly arrows *zwipped* through the blowing grass, some so close the fletching cut or burned his skin; a bullet thumped into his black, low-crowned hat and sent it cartwheeling; only hair-trigger reflexes saved him from decapitation when a throwing axe spun in with frightening accuracy. Fargo continued to lever and fire, methodical, taking his time, going for accuracy, not volume of fire.

Frightened and confused, unable to return topside, the braves gave up on Sarah and took to the river as Fargo had hoped—but not toward the island.

"Bleedin' Holy Ghost!" Jack groaned. "They got 'em a gravel ford! They're a-headed for the south bank!"

Fargo cursed himself for a fool. In his hurry to cobble together a plan, he hadn't checked for fords. Though a marsh blocked their escape to the south, the renegades could still flee along the river bank, either to east or west.

Fargo turned to redirect his fire toward the escaping braves. Suddenly the thunder of charging hoofs, then yipping kill cries, rose above the larger din.

"Skye!" Sarah warned.

Fargo tucked and rolled, just in time to avoid Wolf Sleeve and Iron Mountain. Their ponies bore down on him, for they had peeled away from the rest to kill this overrated white devil.

Fargo dropped his Henry during the mad roll to save his life. He came rocking up onto his heels, Colt to hand. Iron

Mountain, Wolf Sleeve's longtime companion in war and crime, raised his bow and notched an arrow.

The Colt leaped in Fargo's fist, spitting orange flame. Iron Mountain's head snapped back, spuming gouts of blood, and he slid sideways off his horse, dead instantly.

Wolf Sleeve cried out in rage and grief at the killing. He flung an axe that damn near parted Fargo's hair. The deadly Indian's eyes were smoky with murderous wrath.

"Fargo, my next bow will be strung with your gut!" he roared out before he, too, reined his golden buckskin around to escape with his men.

Fargo, ears ringing from his gunshots, felt his heart sinking like a stone. True, a good number of the enemy had been killed or wounded just now. But once the remaining renegades regrouped, the Cherokee water warriors would never get the chance to engage them in battle. They would continue their rampage on land.

However, not one marauding Indian had yet left the river—nor, evidently, were any going to, just yet. Fargo's jaw dropped in astonishment when Jimmy Briscoe's cavalry troop, rifles sheathed, flying no swallow-tailed battle guidon, and blowing no bugle calls, pounded along the south bank in a wedge formation to cut off the escape.

"Well, I'm plumb knocked out!" Jack shouted from the trees. "No shootin' means no hostilities, right? The saucy pup's followin' orders."

The renegades may have noticed the charging bluecoats were firing no weapons, but big, seventeen-hand cavalry horses charging full bore made for an imposing obstacle to escape. Both reluctant and enraged, Wolf Sleeve blew his shrill eagle-bone whistle, ordering his men out toward the only option—the river island.

As if guessing what Fargo was up to, Jimmy immediately wheeled his men into a fallback position along the bank, well out of the way, yet preventing any escape. For the moment, at least, Wolf Sleeve's band was trapped. The same band of demented cutthroats, Fargo reminded himself, that had massacred the peaceful Indians at Broken Bow Lake and tortured Oglethorpe's party at Sweetwater Creek. The same band helping Menard destroy the lives of the innocent, long-suffering Cherokees.

Jack whooped as Sarah, her brave task completed, hurried down the north bank to join Fargo.

"*Now* we're whistlin'!" Jack shouted from his hidden position. " 'Bout time to show these goddamn, murderin' renegades what happens when you wake up the Cheraw Nation! They'll wish they'd gone to hell instead."

Fargo, busy searching the terrain with slitted eyes, felt far less elated than did Jack. For one thing, there was still no sign of the Cherokee war dugouts. If Nacona and his Man Killers delayed much longer, the rattled renegades on the island would form a plan to escape.

Just as bothersome . . . again Fargo's lake-blue eyes scoured the river country in the first rays of new sun. Two white men came down that slope, one of them the gutsy and resourceful Mike Winkler. Fargo had wounded the other man, who still lay in plain view, but Winkler disappeared somewhere—and he certainly wasn't out on that island with the renegades.

So where the hell *was* he?

18

With the wounded Yellowstone Jack still hidden in trees along the north bank, Fargo quickly reloaded his Henry and ran a wiping patch down the sizzling-hot barrel. Then he and Sarah crept to the river's edge and watched the island from the partial cover of deep grass.

"I was afraid of this," Fargo said. "Jesus, where are the Man Killers? Look—the renegades're planning a breakout toward the north bank. If Jimmy has to stop them again, it'll mean fireworks and casualties—and prob'ly the end of the kid's military career. Besides, half the tenderfoots in his unit couldn't hit a tent from the inside."

"Never mind that," Sarah's triumphant voice said. She pointed upriver. "*You* look. See now why my people waited?"

Even as Fargo turned his head, the sun finally broke in its full glory, revealing a staggering spectacle floating on the river. The carved, narrow prows of three large war dugouts glided smoothly through the dark water—ghostly dream images in the morning light. Each was manned by a crew of twelve fiercely painted warriors, closing for the kill. Their well-synchronized paddles of tautly stretched beaver skin dipped into the river with an eerie whisper.

The Cherokees, like most Indians, firmly believed that bravery emanated from the east, where the sun was born every day. So the first full-scale attack they'd mounted in decades was launched just past dawn from the direction of the sun's birthplace.

"Son of a bitch," Fargo breathed in a whisper. Cherokees in war dugouts versus southern Plains horse warriors—a battle Fargo never expected to see.

He chuckled. "Look at Wolf Sleeve. I didn't know a pure-quill Comanche could turn that white."

Clearly in awe at what approached, the renegades stared in paralyzed stupefaction at these red-plumed Cherokee warriors in full battle dress. Indians were easily unnerved by evil magic—and the high, narrow prows of the war dugouts were topped by hideous death masks carved into the wood.

"There is my brother!" Sarah said proudly. "The first warrior in the first dugout—naturally, for a true warrior leads from the front."

Fargo shared her pride in these gutsy men who had secretly maintained their warrior skills, but the renegades were overcoming their surprise and starting to fight. One after another, they took up exposed positions at the eastern tip of the island, opening fire on the approaching Cherokees. When they shot holes in the dugouts below the waterline, the Cherokees simply used gourd dippers to bail them out.

"Attacking an occupied island is one of the toughest jobs in warfare," Fargo told her. "These next few minutes could end the fight."

"Just wait," Sarah said confidently.

A moment later, in a well-practiced paddling movement, Nacona's lead dugout suddenly shifted until it was broadside to the island. A dozen men with powerful long bows opened fire, mowing down several renegades and driving the rest deeper into cover.

"Your brother knows his oats," Fargo praised. "They could use him at West Point. But here's bad trouble coming."

The renegades, hidden deeper behind the big cottonwoods, were rolling onto their backs with arrows notched in their bows, preparing to shoot into the sky and rain arrows on the Cherokees. Fargo had faced it himself nine days ago. And at the moment, the Cherokees couldn't see it.

The battle din was steady and loud, but Fargo caught Nacona's attention by deliberately shooting at his rawhide shield. When the Cherokee glanced across the river at him, Fargo mimicked a man shooting an arrow into the sky.

Nacona nodded and shouted a crisp command to his

braves. Just in time, with arrows already hurtling into position above them, the Man Killers expertly overlapped their shields in a strong phalanx. Fargo and Sarah cheered when the arrows thumped harmlessly into toughened rawhide.

By now the lead canoe was about to scrape bottom on the island, and the fight was fierce. Shouting Cherokees were racing ashore, several already dead or dying in the water. Fargo, like Sarah, intended to act as a roving skirmisher, moving around the edges of the battle and pitching in only if necessary.

Fargo stayed alive by never ignoring hunches. Right now he had a strong suspicion that gun tough Mike Winkler was still on his side of the river. He rode down with the others, but Fargo doubted he had forded. Nor was Baptiste Menard accounted for.

Reluctantly, for the other dugouts had landed and the battle was nearing fever pitch, Fargo tore his eyes away. He glanced behind his and Sarah's position toward the dense patch of trees where Jack was hidden.

"Jack!" he shouted. "How's by you, old son?"

But the battle din was too great—even if Jack heard him, Fargo hadn't heard the old explorer's reply.

"Be right back," he told Sarah. "Don't get too caught up in the fight. Winkler is around here somewhere."

"So is Menard," she replied, and the deadly set of her pretty features made it clear she hoped to meet up with him.

It's just the old man, Winkler finally realized, anger making his blood race. All this time spent creeping up silently on this spot, and no sign of the Cherokee woman. Just the ginger she'd been riding and this drooling old fool, snoring with a racket like a bull in rut.

But because Fargo was somewhere nearby, Winkler stayed cautious. He left his shooter leathered, planning to use the bone-handled knife in his belt to kill Yellowstone Jack in his sleep. It was Sarah Blackburn who Winkler truly hoped to capture—Menard might lose everything else after today, but he'd still give a purty to own the Cherokee beauty.

The old man lay behind a log, which he used as a pillow. Winkler stopped beside him, slid the knife from his belt, knelt to line the blade up with the old man's exposed throat. Be like slicing into a cheese . . .

Jack's eyes snapped open, twinkling with devilish humor. "H'ar now! Walk your chalk, you white-livered shirker."

He'd been hiding his magazine pistol beneath him while he faked sleep. When Winkler saw it, he turned white as river foam.

"Jesus! Say, I'm sorry, sir! Can you forgive me? See, I mistook you for—"

"Forgive ya? Hell, I *always* forgive my enemies," Jack assured him, "after I kill 'em."

His pistol barked, a slug tore into Winkler's intestines, and instantly a deep, fiery pain straight from the furnace of hell sent the outlaw crumpling to the ground, shrieking like a banshee.

Jack dug at a tick in his beard, letting the low-life sage dog suffer a few moments. Then, tired of the screams, he tossed a finishing shot into the man's skull.

"Musta made your mama proud," he said sarcastically.

Fargo had heard both shots as he approached, recognizing Jack's pistol. "Don't shoot, Methuselah," he called out before he entered the trees.

Fargo stared at the body, instantly recognizing the ugly facial scar.

"So far," he remarked, "that's Iron Mountain and Mike Winkler feeding worms. Leaves Wolf Sleeve and Menard."

Behind him, the sounds of battle were heating up. Fargo started to return to the river, but just then a comic scene arrested him.

Sarah had left the ginger tethered near Yellowstone Jack. Now the gelding's rump blocked Fargo's path.

"Gangway, you damn son of Satan!" Jack snapped at his horse. "You got the manners of a rented mule. Leave the man get by!"

Big mistake, Fargo told himself, already grinning.

Promptly, the offended horse swung its rump over Jack and dumped a steaming load of horse apples on the cursing, ducking man.

Despite the six sorts of deadly trouble surrounding them, Fargo laughed so hard he had to drop to one knee.

"You contrary old fool," he sputtered. "*Now* I'm ready to die, I've seen it all."

A moment later, however, Jack's contrary nature was forgotten, and Fargo was sprinting toward the river.

The *true* medicine, Wolf Sleeve told himself, belongs to Skye Fargo. A Comanche brave enough to kill him and eat his warm liver would then possess Fargo's power and magic.

Wolf Sleeve had no intention of dying without glory on that island. Not when a worthier foe—and immeasurable glory—was so close by. Taking advantage of the confusion when the Cherokees first attacked, he had swum underwater back across the river—just in time to see Fargo disappear in those trees.

Wolf Sleeve was waiting when Fargo, intent on returning to the river, hurried out of the trees. The Trailsman cursed his own carelessness when the Comanche stepped from behind a chokecherry bush. A .38 caliber flintlock pistol with over-and-under barrels was aimed at Fargo's lights.

"I shoulda known," Fargo remarked, "that you wouldn't be honorable enough to die with your men."

"Honor is for weak men afraid to sin. Your insults mean nothing, hair face," Wolf Sleeve snarled from a weather-seamed face. "This day, you will join those in the Land of Ghosts. Once I have freed your soul, I will skin your face, tan it, and sew it proudly to my shield. The greatest medicine bundle of them all."

"Then just pull the trigger," Fargo said. "I prefer death to the stench blowing off you."

A lupine grin spread across the Comanche's oval, homely face. "No triggers. Place your rifle and gun belt on the ground. Keep your knife and go over there."

The outlaw Comanche pointed to a broad, flat, grassy expanse between the trees and the bluff—well secluded from observation. At least, Fargo thought as he eased the Arkansas Toothpick from its sheath, he was getting a fighting chance. Then again, everyone knew Wolf Sleeve was death-to-the-devil in a knife fight. He had never lost one.

"Now, whiteskin 'legend,' " Wolf Sleeve taunted when they had both squared off, "soon you will taste *this*."

His long knife with its deep blood gutters in the blade was already in hand. He waved it back and forth as he closed on his man.

"I will make a parfleche from your manhood and give it to an old grandmother."

"The bigger the blade, the littler the man," Fargo taunted him right back.

Fargo expected a fast, hard thrust, but Wolf Sleeve rarely did the expected. Instead, the small but wiry brave leaped at Fargo, intent on knocking him down first.

Wolf Sleeve had learned early on that each move in a knife fight should do double duty. So as his weight slammed into a startled Fargo, he also brought his left forearm up into the frontiersman's neck, while his knife hand made a fast, direct thrust toward Fargo's vulnerable torso—all this in one well-coordinated movement.

"*Now* you cross over, whiteskin devil!" the Comanche shouted triumphantly.

Fargo, overwhelmed and staggering backward, ignored all the dangers except the one that mattered—that deadly blade. He caught Wolf Sleeve's right wrist *just* in the nick of time. He yanked the Comanche into the direction of their momentum, then relaxed his muscles for the hard impact when they hit the ground. Even before he whammed into the grass, Wolf Sleeve began fighting.

He was like the very wendigo himself, Fargo thought with stunned amazement. The tough renegade writhed, kicked, bit, all the time cursing and howling like a madman—when his teeth weren't actually gnashing Fargo's flesh.

To Fargo, trapped beneath this whirling red dervish and trying to get his breath back, it felt like five men were on him. He suddenly winced as white-hot pain licked at his chest—Wolf Sleeve's blade had just pricked flesh.

"Do you feel it, beef-eater?" Wolf Sleeve tormented him. "Do you feel where my blade is? Poised between the fourth and fifth ribs. From there, it is a straight, easy thrust into the warm and beating heart."

"Then push the son of a bitch home and shut up," Fargo grunted in reply. He arched his back quick and hard, throwing the Comanche clear.

Both men leaped to their feet, again circling, knives outthrust. The renegade slashed at Fargo rapidly and repeatedly, as relentless in his advance as a swarm of wasps. His method was brutal and direct: overwhelm his opponent, wait until he was rattled and dropped his guard, then make the kill thrust.

"I will not waste one part of the great legend after I carve him up!" a confident Wolf Sleeve goaded.

While the Comanche taunted and twirled, Fargo instinctively stuck to a cold, calm, lethal patience, waiting for the moment that he knew would come.

Soon enough, it did. Wolf Sleeve made a needlessly fancy feint to his left, but carelessly placed his propelling foot on a loose, flat rock. One leg flew out from under him, and he went down hard. Unleashing his own savage kill cry, Fargo leaped straight up, bent his legs in midair, and came down knees-first, hard, on Wolf Sleeve's spine, snapping it.

To make sure, Fargo yanked his opponent's head back by the chin, and with one powerful cut sliced his throat open deep from ear to ear.

Leaves only Menard, Fargo thought as he stood catching his breath, grateful to be alive. Then he wiped off his bloody blade on the dead Comanche's leg and hurried to gather up his weapons.

Back on the river, the battle had reached a dangerous stalemate that must quickly favor the renegades. The enemy had retreated to the full cover of cottonwoods and bushes and were now dug in deeper than ticks on a hound. Fargo watched a long line of courageous, advancing Cherokee warriors, red plumes dazzling in the morning sun, forced to retreat under withering fire.

"My people are dying fast now!" Sarah despaired, the warrior in her knowing the issue was in serious doubt. "I must run fire bundles up to the tree line. It is our only chance."

Fargo feared she was right. Flaming arrows alone were of little use—they went out too quickly to burn anything. But the arrows in combination with Cherokee fire bundles were effective in smoking an enemy out of hiding. They were simply quickly made bundles of cloth and dry tinder, such as crumbled bark, easily flammable. Once placed against a combustible object, they could be ignited with well-aimed flaming arrows.

Sarah hadn't wasted her time while Fargo was gone. Four fire bundles lay in the grass, and her gown was torn. She was barefoot and her shapely legs unencumbered.

Fargo wanted to offer to do the deadly errand himself,

but these were Sarah's people in battle, and she was an elite warrior. He would insult her if he offered. This was an Indian-on-Indian battle, and Fargo hoped to keep it that way.

He jacked a round into the chamber of his Henry.

"All right, Beautiful Death Bringer," he told her. "I'll cover you. Run like a scalded dog, hear? *Go!*"

Fargo had never seen a woman run so strong and fast, nor many men. Using the gravel ford, elbows and knees pumping, she sprinted across the river and right past her surprised Cherokee comrades. At the first sign she'd been spotted by the dug-in enemy, Fargo went to work with a vengeance, laying down covering fire.

Powder smoke soon hazed his position, and Fargo's rapid volley drew enemy attention to him, as he'd hoped. A rifle ball thumped into the bank near his left knee, so close he actually shifted as the dirt moved underneath it.

He'd succeeded—a cheer rose up from the Cherokees when Sarah escaped the island, all four bundles in place. Flaming arrows streaked in, and in only minutes flames crackled and black smoke began to blanket the long, narrow island. The pitiless Cherokee warriors slaughtered every renegade as he broke cover and fled, tossing many of them right back into the flames.

Fargo watched it with a heart hardened by the horror of Broken Bow Lake. Old Testament justice . . .

"As usual," he remarked to Sarah, "Baptiste Menard is the only fly in the ointment. Looks like he escaped to do it all over again."

Sarah, smiling mysteriously, led him down the bank about fifty feet. Menard, his face blue-black and hideously swollen, lay dead in the lush grass, a Cherokee poison dart protruding from his neck.

"But you left your blowgun with your canoe down south," Fargo pointed out.

"True, but my brother has his. From the river, Nacona saw Menard sneaking toward me. I wish *I* could have done it. But at least the revenge stays within my family, as it should."

It was a simple meal of bean soup and cornbread, but to Fargo it was a feast fit for kings—or at least a princess.

"One of Winkler's surviving men was arrested, and he's already talking," Talcott Mumford said. "All about the frame-up of Sarah with her harmonica pistol, the so-called Cherokee raids, all of it. Even without his confession, the special court in Fort Smith has thrown out the murder charge against Skye and Yellowstone Jack. Nor am I to be cashiered."

Mumford, Fargo, Jack, Sarah, and Lieutenant Jimmy Briscoe all shared Mumford's office in the agency building, enjoying the meal prepared by Mumford's new cook and housekeeper, a Choctaw widow. It had been four days since the already famous battle on the Arkansas River.

"Murder charge," Jack repeated hotly as he dipped a soda biscuit in the pot liquor. "Pee doodles! All we done was step on a roach."

"As for you, young man," Mumford said to Jimmy.

The kid paled beneath his freckled sunburn. "No need to explain why you sent for me, sir. I'm being recalled to Fort Gibson pending disciplinary action against me, right?"

Mumford laughed as he tucked his silver snuffbox inside the folds of a ruffled sleeve. "Yes, you're being recalled. But only long enough to receive a medal for superior leadership."

Fargo watched the kid's lower jaw drop like a cowcatcher.

"Apparently," Mumford added, "local commanders are quite impressed by your tactic of charging with weapons booted—showed great presence of mind in one so young."

Fargo was glad Mumford left one key fact out: it was Skye Fargo who'd recommended the shavetail for a medal. The kid deserved it, that was all Fargo cared about. Jimmy's quick action had saved the battle—and the Cherokee lands.

His face beaming at the bombshell news, Jimmy said his farewells and left to rejoin his cavalry troop. Later, after saying good-bye to Mumford, Fargo lingered out front to say his good-byes to Sarah and Yellowstone Jack.

"Well, it's time to cut loose from these here diggin's," Jack opined as he checked his cinches. "Mebbe I'll dust my hocks out toward Santa Fe. Mumford says the army needs scouts in the Navajo country."

"And you, Skye?" Sarah asked. "Are you riding on, too?"

Fargo nodded. For him, it wasn't just curiosity and the "tormentin' itch" to move on. It was also a determined defiance that kept pushing him past the next ridge. A defiance of anyone, or any damn government, that tried to keep a free man from yondering on God's green earth.

"Think I might head out to the Front Range of the Rockies," he replied. "Gold-strike camps are paying good money to hunters."

"Turd, it's the Stony Mountains," Jack corrected him as he heaved himself into the saddle. He believed in using the old names.

"Careful, Methuselah," Fargo called out as Jack started to ride out. "See that sky?"

Fargo pointed up, and Jack reined in to follow his finger. "See that skinny cloud slashing across the sun? That's an omen, hoss."

Superstitious Jack stared, suddenly nervous. "Straight-arrow now, it's an omen? The hell's it mean?"

"Means you're so full of shit, granddad, your feet are sliding in the stirrups."

Fargo and Sarah broke up laughing at the dark scowl on the old salt's walnut-wrinkled face. Then Jack, too, shook with mirth.

"Fargo, I'll knock you into next Sunday! Godspeed, Princess!"

With a final bow to Sarah, Yellowstone Jack and his ginger-from-hell rode out.

"And you, Skye?" Sarah asked, a flirtatious smile playing on her ripe-berry lips. "Can nothing convince you to delay another day—or so? My home is not so fine as my brother's. But it is comfortable and private . . . and I have a feather mattress."

Fargo glanced at the remarkable Cherokee beauty. She had combed her long hair smooth and close, then plaited it. Her eyes were big and almond shaped, her lips full, her nose long and aristocratic, befitting royalty. She wore a dyed buckskin skirt and a short jacket secured with silver broaches, revealing a few inches of bare midriff.

"Saw an omen just last night, too," Fargo replied, grinning with his eyes. "An owl flew across the face of the moon."

"Meaning? . . ."

"Meaning there's a *feather* mattress in my future. The Rockies ain't going nowhere—let's head to your house, Princess."

LOOKING FORWARD!
The following is the opening
section of the next novel in the exciting
Trailsman series from Signet:

THE TRAILSMAN #290

MOUNTAIN MAVERICKS

*The Montana high country, 1860—
where the most dangerous beasts
go on two legs instead of four.*

The young woman burst out into the clearing, running hard,
her dark braids trailing out behind her head, her breasts
heaving under the buckskin dress.

The big man, who was also dressed in buckskins, was
ready for her. He stepped from behind a tree, thrust out
an arm, and caught her around the waist. The impact as he
pulled her to a halt staggered him a step, despite the
strength in his muscular body.

She didn't gasp or scream. She just fought in silence,
flailing at him with small, hard fists as she tried desperately
to squirm out of his grip. But he was too strong for her.
He got both arms around her, picked her up, and swung
her around so that her back was pressed against the tree
behind which he had been hidden.

Skye Fargo's lake-blue eyes peered intently into the young woman's dark brown ones. He loosened his grip with one hand, lifted it, and held his forefinger to his lips in the universal sign for quiet.

He stood close to her so that her breasts touched his chest. Fargo was aware of that contact and under other circumstances would have found it quite pleasurable.

Right now, however, he had other things on his mind—like the crashing sounds in the brush that allowed him to track the progress of the young woman's pursuers as they came closer.

She had stopped trying to fight him and was staring at him in confusion instead. Fargo wasn't sure yet what tribe she was from, so he used sign language to tell her that he was a friend. She relaxed slightly, but he could tell that her body was still poised for flight.

Fargo dropped his right hand to the walnut grips of the Colt revolver holstered on his hip. He eased her farther around the tree with his left hand and stepped back, hoping that she wouldn't run.

She didn't. She stayed where she was, her back against the tree, and watched him. Every few seconds her eyes cut nervously toward the sounds of the approaching riders.

"Damn it, I know good and well she came this way. I saw her run into the woods."

It was a man's voice, rough and husky, about twenty yards away. A second man asked, "You sure you didn't just imagine it because you been so long without a woman, Devlin?"

"No, blast it, I saw her! If you think I'm lyin', you can go to hell!"

"Take it easy. If she's in here, we'll find her."

They would find more than they bargained for, thought Fargo.

The hour was late afternoon. He had made camp in the clearing not far from the Yellowstone River. The thickly wooded slopes of Crazy Peak rose a short distance to the north. A narrow, fast-flowing creek ran through the woods only a short distance from the clearing before merging with the Yellowstone. Fargo had hooked a couple of nice trout in the creek and had been about to start cleaning them for his supper with the Arkansas Toothpick when he'd heard someone running through the trees toward his camp.

Fargo hadn't lived as long as he had on the frontier without learning a few things, like how to be careful. He had warned the big black-and-white Ovaro stallion to be quiet, then stepped behind the tree to see what was going to happen.

He didn't know what to expect. His mind was open. But he had been a little surprised anyway when he saw the young, pretty Indian woman run into his camp.

Now the voices he'd heard explained a great deal by their mere presence. A couple of white men chasing an Indian girl through the woods . . . They could have only one thing in mind.

All across the frontier, a decent woman was sacrosanct. Not even the most bloody-handed reiver would molest a woman.

But for most men, that applied only to white women. Indian squaws were different, fair game for a man who hadn't been with a gal for a while.

Anger burned in Fargo's belly. He didn't believe in taking a woman—any woman—by force. A man who would do that was lower than a snake and deserved whatever he got. He found himself almost hoping that the two riders in the woods would find the camp.

But it would be better for the young woman behind him if they didn't. You never knew what might happen in a fight. Random violence was no respecter of persons. If it came down to shooting, she might be hit by a stray bullet. Fargo was reasonably confident he could handle any threat the two men represented, but it was impossible to guarantee that.

So he hoped they would just ride on without discovering him and the young woman. It was possible. He hadn't started a fire yet, so they wouldn't smell any smoke. And the woods were thick. The men might pass within fifty feet of the camp and never see it.

Fargo glanced over at the stallion. The Ovaro's head was up, his ears cocked. He knew there were other horses around, and his instinct was to call out to them. Fargo had asked for quiet, though, and the stallion was well trained enough to follow that command, even though it was hard.

The other horses suddenly nickered. They had scented the Ovaro. Fargo's jaw tightened under the close-cropped dark beard. The reaction of their mounts was liable to make the men more suspicious.

Sure enough, one of them said, "The horses are actin' like there's something over there."

"Let's take a look."

The hoofbeats and the crackling of brush came even closer. The men were almost on top of the camp.

Fargo held his left hand out toward the young woman, motioning for her to stay where she was. He moved farther out into the clearing, so that he would be clearly visible to the two men. He wanted their attention focused on him.

They reined in sharply as they rode out of the woods and saw the broad-shouldered man in buckskins and a brown hat waiting for them. Fargo stood there casually, his left hand at his belt, his right hanging beside the butt of the Colt.

"Howdy, boys," he said.

There were only two of them, for which Fargo was grateful. Though he had heard only two voices, it had been possible that there were one or more other men who had simply remained silent.

The one on Fargo's right was burly to start with and made even more so by the thick, buffalo-hide coat he wore. He had a short brown beard on a pugnacious jaw, and a battered old hat with a round crown and a narrow brim was pushed down on a thatch of tangled brown hair. He glared at Fargo.

The second man was slender and clean shaven, with sandy hair down to his shoulders. He wore a cowhide vest over a gray wool shirt and had a black hat cocked back on his head. His expression was more surprised than angry.

Both men were heavily armed, wearing holstered revolvers and sheathed knives. Rifle butts stuck up from saddle scabbards. Clearly, they were tough hombres.

But there were only two of them, Fargo reminded himself, and neither of them had a gun drawn.

"Who the hell are you?" the one in the buffalo coat demanded.

Normally Fargo would have been a little offended at being addressed in such an arrogant tone. Now he just kept a faint smile on his face as he said, "Just a fella who's camping here for the night."

The smaller man drawled, "Did you see a squaw come runnin' through here a few minutes ago?"

The tree behind which the young woman stood had a thick trunk. The men couldn't see her from where they were. Fargo didn't even glance in her direction as he said, "You boys are the first folks I've seen all day."

That wasn't true, of course, and Fargo didn't like to lie. He thought this one was justified, though. He might still be able to turn the pursuers away without a fight. That would be the safest in the long run for the woman.

"You hear anything, maybe somebody runnin' through the woods?"

Fargo shook his head and said, "Nope. Just your horses. That's all I heard."

The one in the buffalo coat sniffed, drawing in a big breath of air. He glowered at Fargo and said to his companion, "He's lyin'. I can *smell* that Injun gal."

The second man smiled thinly. "Well, now," he said without taking his eyes off Fargo, "If there's one thing Devlin here knows how to do, it's sniff out Injuns. You want to reconsider your answer, amigo?"

Fargo shook his head. "Nope."

"He's hidin' her!" the burly man accused. "He wants her for hisself! I say we kill him and then hunt that bitch down!" His hand moved toward the butt of the gun at his waist.

The other man put out a hand to stop him. "Take it easy, Devlin," he ordered in a tone of easy command. To Fargo, he said, "Look, be reasonable, amigo. A squaw ain't worth dyin' over. Just tell us which way she went, and we'll let you live." An ugly grin quirked his mouth. "Hell, you help us find her, and we might even share her with you."

"You better turn and ride away while you still can," Fargo said.

The grin disappeared from the man's face. "If that's the way you want it—"

His hand stabbed toward his gun.

Fargo figured the slender man was the faster of the two. That meant he had to be dealt with first. With blinding speed, Fargo palmed out his Colt and fired from the hip.

Even as fast as Fargo was, the man managed to get his gun out and squeeze off a shot. The two blasts blended into one. Fargo's bullet was a hair swifter, however, fast enough to throw off the man's aim as it slammed into his shoulder and slewed him sideways in the saddle. His lead gouged into the ground just to the right of Fargo's booted feet.

Another gun roared, hard on the heels of the first two shots. The burly man was slower on the draw, all right, but still plenty fast enough to be dangerous. Fargo felt as much as heard the wind-rip of the bullet beside his ear as he pivoted smoothly toward his second antagonist and fired again.

He had hoped to wound Devlin as he had the other man, but just as Fargo pulled the trigger Devlin's horse spooked at the gunfire and jerked to one side. The slug from Fargo's gun drove deeply into Devlin's chest instead of shattering his shoulder. Devlin rocked back in the saddle, his eyes going wide with pain and shock.

Devlin's gun hand drooped. He struggled mightily to bring it up again, but he was too weak. He swayed from side to side. His thumb looped over the revolver's hammer and slowly pulled it back.

Then as he hunched over from a fresh burst of agony, his finger clenched on the trigger and fired the gun again. The bullet hammered into the ground beside his horse. The animal reared up in fear and threw Devlin off. The man landed on the ground with a heavy thud and didn't move again.

That had taken only a handful of heartbeats. Fargo turned toward the other man again, but he was gone. A rataplan of hoofbeats echoing through the trees told Fargo that the man was fleeing. He had been hit hard, hard enough so that he was out of the fight. Now he was just trying to save his life.

A grim expression was etched onto Fargo's face as he stalked across the clearing and checked the man in the buffalo coat. Devlin was dead, staring sightlessly up at the canopy of pine branches above him. Even in the fading light, Fargo could see that life had departed from the man's piggish eyes.

He swung around sharply and holstered the Colt. As he did so, the young woman stepped out from behind the tree where she had been hiding. She paused, trembling a little like a deer about to bolt, and Fargo knew she was thinking about running again, running away from him this time.

But he didn't know if Devlin and the other man had had any friends with them. The woman might be safer staying with him, at least for a while.

"Take it easy," Fargo said, knowing she probably didn't speak English but hoping the calm sound of his voice would steady her nerves. "We'll get out of here, just in case that son of a bitch tries to double back on us."

"Son of a bitch," the Indian woman repeated.

Fargo had to smile. She knew what he meant by that, anyway. He nodded as he picked up his saddle blanket and tossed it on the Ovaro's back.

It only took a few minutes for Fargo to get the stallion saddled and ready to ride. The woman stood there watching him while he picked up the two fish he had caught and looped the stringer they were attached to around the saddle horn. That was all the packing he had to do. He swung up onto the Ovaro and walked the horse across the clearing. When he reached the young woman he held out a hand to her.

She hesitated only a second, then grasped his hand. They locked wrists, and Fargo pulled her up easily behind him. She straddled the Ovaro and slipped her arms around Fargo's waist to hang on.

He rode out of the trees, followed the creek down to the river about a quarter of a mile away, and then turned west along the Yellowstone, heeling the stallion into a ground-eating trot.

No other series has this much historical action!

THE TRAILSMAN

Available wherever books are sold or at
penguin.com